A LONG GAME

The third in the DI Kate Medlar series

Lin Bird

Tim Saunders Publications

TS

Copyright © 2024 Lin Bird

All rights reserved

The characters and events portrayed in this book are fictitious. Any similarity to real persons, living or dead, is coincidental and not intended by the author.

No part of this book may be reproduced, or stored in a retrieval system, or transmitted in any form or by any means, electronic, mechanical, photocopying, recording, or otherwise, without express written permission of the publisher.

Cover design: Tim Saunders Publications

PROLOGUE

The quiet of the workshop was broken by the stormy arrival of a man in a temper. Using the momentum of his anger, he strode across the room to where a young couple swung their legs from the counter top. Not stopping, the man delivered a head rocking back-hand slap to the young man, saying, "you've been told before, you're not welcome here."

The young man sat up and slid onto his feet, shaking his head. "And I told you, I don't listen to bullies."

The angry man lowered his head and peered straight into the face of the young man. "And I told you I don't want snivelling little shits hanging around here. So get out." The last was said with an accompanying shove that sent the young man sprawling onto and then across the floor. His head received a glancing blow on another work counter and then he lay motionless.

The young woman and the angry man stared at the motionless body. The girl put a hand to her mouth. "Oh my God. What have you done now?" She slid off the counter and ran across to the prone figure. She knelt down and tried to remember any first aid. She sought for a pulse in his neck. Then she looked up, her already pale face now a ghastly grey. "I can't feel a pulse." She looked down again and tapped the young man's face. There was no response.

Now the angry man's temper left him and he too knelt next to the body. His fingers also sought for a pulse. He couldn't find one but he said to the girl, "of course he has a pulse. Right, you get off and I don't want you seeing him again. Do you understand me?"

The girl nodded as she rose to her feet. With a backward glance she left the workshop.

The man tried again to find a pulse but his inexperienced fingers made the slight flutter impossible to detect.

CHAPTER 1

Detective Inspector Kate Medlar stretched to ease the cramp in her neck and the stiffness in her shoulders. Her short red gold hair was standing up in places; victim of Kate's frustration with her present task. She called across the room to Detective Constable Colm Hunter. His tall, broad figure looking overly large at the desk he occupied.

"Any luck, Colm? Please tell me *yes*."

Colm shook his head. "Sorry boss. Nothing."

"So, despite the fact that all the flats above the shops in Peace Way are occupied and that the thieves must have used something like a bull dozer, no-one heard or saw anything?"

"Not credible, is it? I reckon they're all frightened of the consequences. Whoever is behind this cash machine job has some major clout in the lower strata of Eashire."

"Thank goodness the machine was almost empty. The ATM firm confirmed that they'd not been able to restock it over the weekend so it had less than five thousand in it."

"Serves the thieving scum right!"

"Has Mike come up with anything from the traffic camera or CCTV?"

Colm clicked on his computer and said, "I'll send across his report but the gist is that the camera on the corner of Peace Way was put out of action by a masked figure at approximately one-forty-five that morning. No other traffic cameras pick up any large vehicles."

"So does that mean they have it stowed somewhere and will move it later?"

Colm ran his hands through his hair. "Could be. Shall I get uniform to do a walk round looking for suitable plots?"

Any answer was prevented by the arrival of Detective Chief Inspector Bartholomew. "Morning Kate. Colm. You need to get yourselves over to the Play House. Uniform have reported the possibility of a dead body."

Already reaching for her jacket and notebook, Kate queried, "Possibility?"

"Apparently, they think there is a dead body because of what the workman says but they can't see it!"

The mysterious message was soon made clear when Kate arrived at the Play House. The building was a product of Eashire's heyday in the Victorian era. Once a grand theatre, now it doubled as an Arts Centre but retained its Victorian auditorium. But this grandeur was not the scene of the crime. A uniformed officer led them through to the warren that consisted of the back stage area.

In a low-ceilinged workshop Kate found another uniformed officer and a grey-haired older man wearing a leather apron. The room itself was full of work surfaces, which in turn were covered with unexpected objects; the plaster head of a young woman, an ancient looking sword, a tray of cups and glasses. Kate caught a glimpse of a group of headless statues gathered together but unable to converse without their heads, as she surveyed the room. The centre of everyone's attention was a coffin-like box to one side of the space, which had been cordoned off with official police tape.

Approaching the officer, Kate raised a querying eyebrow. "Okay Len, what have we got?"

"Morning Boss. Mr Wheelan here," indicating the man with the leather apron, "believes that there is a body in that box."

"And is there?"

Mr Wheelan coughed and Kate turned to him. "The box is a moulding cabinet," he went on to explain as Kate and Colm looked at him blankly. "They're doing a production of 'Turned to Stone' and so need stone statues."

Kate was still none the wiser. "I'm really sorry, Mr Wheelan, but I still don't understand why you think that box," she corrected herself, "moulding cabinet, contains a body."

As though explaining to a four-year-old, Mr Wheelan elaborated. "The play requires some of the actors to be turned to stone and then remain on stage. So, we have made statues of them, using that cabinet. Normally, we just do the body and the head separate. The actor lies in the box and I pour in silicone, which sets around them. When it's set, I cut them out and then using the resulting mould, cast a plaster of Paris version."

"So, that box is full of silicone at the moment?" Kate inquired.

"Yes, and I didn't put it there."

"And no-one else could have done it?"

"Well, obviously someone else has done it because that's not how I left it last night."

"But what makes you think there's a body in it?" Colm asked.

"Because of the amount of silicone mix that is missing. It's not enough to fill the cabinet, unless something is in there. And, although the silicone is more opaque than clear, you can see the shadow of something that looks like a body."

"And you think a human body? Why not a box or a mannequin?" Kate continued, still a little bemused.

"Because the amount missing from the silicone is similar to the amount I would use with a person," he paused for effect. "I knew if I opened the mould I could ruin any forensics there might be so I can't say definitely but I think there is someone in there."

Kate had to admire his good sense. She turned to the officer. "Did you call for forensics when you rang this in, Len?"

Len Goodfellow nodded his affirmation and added, "they should be with us any second now."

Kate turned back to the moulding cabinet. She shivered a little and wasn't sure she would fancy lying in a coffin while it was being filled with gloop!

CHAPTER 2

Miles Edwards, Chief Forensic Scientist for the force arrived with his team. White-suited bodies began to set up lights and Mike took a closer look at the box before coming across to talk with Kate. "Morning, this looks interesting. A body?"

Kate moved Mike out of earshot of Mr Wheelan. "To be honest I'm not sure but the chap who operates this contraption is convinced there is someone in there."

Mike nodded his understanding. "Okay, we'll take this slow. We'll start with the floor around the box and work inwards." Giving Kate a knowing look, he continued, "it will be some time before we're ready to open everything up so I'll call you when we're ready."

She nodded her understanding. Mike didn't want to be rushed by an impatient detective hovering at his shoulder.

Kate turned to Colm as Mike went and detailed his staff to their tasks and the order he wanted things done in. "Right, Colm. I'll go and find whoever is in charge here and get a room set up for us. We'll start with a more detailed conversation with Mr Wheelan."

Julia Montgomery was the manager of the Play House and Arts Centre. Kate tracked her down to her office. She had been unaware of the police presence or the possibility of a body in the workshop.

"Oh for goodness' sake!" was her initial response when Kate explained that there was a possibility of a body in the Play House workshop but she retrieved the situation. "How awful! What do you need from me?"

"Is there somewhere private my colleague and I can interview your staff? And would you check if any of your staff are missing this morning or if anyone knows of anyone missing?"

"Of course. I'll show you the Falstaff Bar. It's a private bar area for our VIPs," Montgomery said, moving from her desk and round to the door. "If you'd like to follow me." She led the way to the first floor and to the back of the boxes on the left-hand side. There, a gold-lettered sign on dark wood announced they were approaching the Falstaff Bar.

Opening the door and standing back she said, "Will this be all right for you?"

Kate entered. The interior was red: red carpet, red comfortable seating and a red flock wall paper. All was relieved by dark wood tables, a bar and a drinks shelf that circumnavigated the room. Gold wall lamps and the gold and glass behind the bar reflected glints of light between themselves.

"This will be fine, thank you," Kate replied, thinking that a pair of sunglasses might be in order after a few hours in the red room.

"Good. I'll check and see who's here today and track down anyone who isn't."

Kate rang Colm. "We're going to be set up in the Falstaff Bar, on the first floor. Bring Wheelan with you. We'll have a more detailed story from him."

Before she could return her phone to her jacket pocket, it rang and Kate answered. "Medlar. Hi Mike, what have you got?" There was a pause as she listened intently. "So you're pretty sure that there is a body in there." Another pause. "Fine. When you're at the point of opening the silicone, call me." She was about to end the call when she remembered something. "Mike, has Gus been notified? Good."

Gus Lipstein was Eashire county's pathologist and despite Eashire not being in the forefront of scientific endeavour, he was an internationally respected professional. He would want to see the body in situ and would then carry out the post-mortem.

Left to her own devices, Kate checked the room. The door onto the corridor was the only entry point. At least they would not be overheard or interrupted.

CHAPTER 3

A few minutes later, Colm strode into the room with Mr Wheelan in tow. He gave a low whistle. "A bit posher than we normally get, boss!"

Mr Wheelan muttered, "As my old mum would say, 'all fur coat and nay knickers!'"

Kate smiled at the aptness of the saying. It was something her mum would also have come out with and it was true, wasn't it? Theatre was all about show and façade.

"Take a seat, Mr Wheelan. I'd like you to talk us through what happened yesterday and this morning."

Wheelan dropped heavily into a fireside chair whilst Colm and Kate sat opposite in padded dining chairs.

"What do you want to know?"

"Who normally works in the workshop and who was there yesterday, specifically in the afternoon?"

Wheelan scratched his head. "Well, mainly it was just me yesterday afternoon. I was working on Abigail Jennings' plaster head. You get the face and the head shape nicely with the silicone but you have to sculpt the hair."

"No-one else was with you?"

"Not to say 'with me'. People popped in and out all afternoon. They were putting the finishing touches to the scenery and props ready for the actors to start using the proper entries and props. So, if anything had been forgotten they'd pop back for it."

Kate nodded her understanding. She'd come back to him if she needed a more detailed recollection. "So what time did you finish?"

"It was just before five so I could catch the six minutes past, number 67 bus outside."

"And how did you leave the workshop?"

Wheelan looked at her blankly, before understanding the question. "Well pretty much as you saw it this morning, apart from the moulding cabinet."

"So, how did you know the cabinet had been in use when you arrived this morning?"

Another scratch of his head. "The cabinet lid was closed and I normally leave it open. There was a mess of droplets around it. I never leave it like that. I mean it's not even ours!"

"What do you mean, it's not yours?"

"We borrowed it from a university. The director's a friend of some scientist chap. It's got to go back tomorrow. That's why I did all the full body statues first. Miranda's is the first head I've done. It worked quite well."

Colm looked confused and quickly re-read his notes. "Jeff, I thought you said it was Abigail Jennings' head you were working on?"

"Sorry, the actress is Abigail and her character is Miranda."

"Got you. Thanks." Colm went back to his notebook.

Kate came in with the bad news, "I'm sorry, Mr Wheelan, but you're going to need to contact the university and tell them that they won't be getting their cabinet back tomorrow."

Another scratch of the head. "Oh, bloody hell! They're not going to like that."

"Well, if you need me to put in a word, in my official capacity, let me know. Explain to them that their cabinet is now crucial evidence in my murder case."

Wheelan savoured the word 'murder'. "I suppose it has to be murder doesn't it?"

"I'm afraid so, Mr Wheelan. Our forensic people agree with you that there is a body in there and I didn't see any breathing holes, did you?"

He shook his head solemnly. "No. That's why I didn't want to do whole bodies, heads as well, in one go. Too many risks. When I do the heads I can just concentrate on one thing."

Kate went for the million dollar question. "Any idea who could be in there, Mr Wheelan?"

He shook his head. "I could tell you who it wouldn't be, like Gary, the electrician. He's got a beer gut on him that the cabinet couldn't have coped with."

"So, whoever's in there would need to be quite slim, do you mean?"

"Yeh! And not too tall either. The cabinet is

only six foot long and the inside is a bit smaller than that."

"But no-one springs to mind?"

Another shake of the head.

"You lock the workshop at the end of the day?"

"No. It's open access because so much is stored in there."

"Were there still people around backstage when you left last night?"

"Yes. Some of the sparks were still working on the lighting rig and some of the actors were around. You'd need to check with Stan to find out exactly who was here."

"Stan?"

"He's stage door security. You can't get past his booth without signing in or out. He can tell you exactly who was around."

"Thank you for your help, Mr Wheelan. We may need to come back to you for more details and you will be asked to make a formal statement down at the station."

"Right you are." Wheelan heaved himself out of the chair and headed for the door. Before he left, he turned back. "It won't have been a nice way to go."

Kate and Colm nodded their agreement and as the door closed behind Wheelan, Colm said, "I hope the poor bugger was dead before he went in that cabinet."

CHAPTER 4

Julia Montgomery must have been waiting outside the door because seconds after Mr Wheelan left, she tapped on the bar's door and entered. She held a letter size sheet of paper in her hand. "I've checked the work schedule alongside Stan's signing in book and everyone is accounted for." She handed the sheet across to Kate. "This is a list of everyone who was in yesterday and again today."

Kate took the outstretched paper. "Thank you. Could we talk to Stan and see his book, please?"

Montgomery hesitated. "Could you interview him in his booth, do you think? It's just that he's our security and there's no-one else."

Kate nodded her agreement and she and Colm stood and followed Montgomery out of Falstaff's bar. "Do you need me to take you down or can you find your own way?"

"I think we should be fine. Thank you," said Colm, giving one of his winning smiles.

It had its usual impact and Montgomery offered, "Well, anything else you need, just let me know. I'll do my best."

Leaving Montgomery on the first-floor landing, Kate led Colm back through the auditorium. Smiling over her shoulder, she said, "do you have the same effect on Jenna?"

Colm was glad that the blush that spread across his face was hidden in the darkness of the theatre. "No, she's known me as her best friend's big brother, she knows all my foibles."

Once backstage, Kate was not so sure of her direction but there were plenty of people to ask and they were soon peering into a small booth by the stage door. There was a wide window with a purpose-built shelf holding a large ledger, and behind it sat Stan. Kate was not good at guessing ages but she thought he might be knocking seventy. How good was he at security? Before she had time to open her mouth, Stan stood up and squared his shoulders. "You'll be the police?"

Kate and Colm hunted in their pockets for their warrant cards and held them out for Stan to inspect. And inspect them he did before handing them back and nodding. "I heard they think there's a body in the workshop. You'll be wanting to know who was here late last night and since Julia can't find anyone missing, whether we had any strangers. Yes?"

Kate smiled. He may be seventy but he was on the ball, and then some. "Yes, please, Mr..?"

"Call me Stan. I've looked back through the book," he said, indicating the ledger in front of them. We had two strangers in last night," he pointed to two separate lines a few spaces apart, "him and him."

Kate peered at where he was pointing and

Colm got out his mobile to take a photo.

One signature was clear, Joseph Mallory to see Clare West. He signed in at five-forty and out at seven-ten. The other was T Lennon, signed in at six and out again at seven-fifteen.

Kate pointed to each name. "Do you know these people, Stan?"

"Mallory, no but Lennon, that would be Terry, he's the carpenter they got in to sort out the trap door."

"Did you see them sign out?" Colm asked, looking intently at the entries.

Stan coughed in embarrassment. "Err, no! One of the girls started screaming about a spider in the wash basin, so I went to sort it. I was only away for five minutes, but I did miss those two going."

"Could someone have entered in those five minutes?"

Stan looked even more uncomfortable. "Possible but unlikely. I'd have met someone coming in as I was coming back."

"Right. Thanks Stan."

As Kate walked away, a thought struck her and she turned back. "Did you catch the spider?"

Stan chuckled. "No. All that screaming - the poor thing had done a runner."

Kate waved her thanks and moved off. Out of a smooth-sided sink? Interesting!

CHAPTER 5

Kate and Colm headed back to the workshop. Again the myriad of runs backstage defeated them and they asked for directions. A small group had formed around the door of the workshop. Men in overalls or jeans and t-shirts and young women in dance shoes and tights.

Calmly but persistently, Kate made her way through the bodies. She could have sent Colm first to clear the way but she was determined to be acknowledged. These were the people she needed to interview and they needed to know that she was no push over.

Once inside the workshop, Kate spied Gus deep in conversation with Jeff Wheelan, examining the headless statues. Gus raised a hand in acknowledgement that he'd seen Kate and finished his conversation with Wheelan. Making his way to Kate and Colm, he said, "Fascinating idea. If you look closely you can see every wrinkle of the real person." Looking towards the cabinet where Mike had just lifted the lid to reveal an opaque white oblong shape, he continued, "You do get some interesting cases DI Medlar!"

Kate had to agree, she did. A heart attack that was a poisoning and suffocation. A missing person that became a younger murder than the evidence indicated. And now a body in a silicone mould. Yes, interesting cases. Kate's musings were interrupted by the arrival of Mike.

"Right! We're ready to open the mould. Jeff has shown us the inner ledge that marks the half-way line and has given us this tool for cutting." He held up a large knife with a very rounded end, almost like a palette knife but Kate could see both edges were sharp except at the rounded part.

Donning forensic gloves and shoes, Kate and Colm followed Gus and Mike to the cabinet. Mike was saying, "No finger prints on the outside but we do have this," he indicated a hole in the silicone top about two thirds of the way down the length. "At this stage I can only hazard a guess but I wonder if someone had to push some part of the body down and has left a void."

"Could we get a mould of that?" Colm asked.

Mike shook his head. "Doubtful. If the silicone was still malleable, I'm thinking it would have filled any void deeper but I'll give it a try once we're back at the lab."

Taking the special knife in his right hand and feeling for the inner ledge with his left, Mike gently inserted the blade and then began to slowly move down the length of the object. It took him ten minutes to complete a full circle of the shape. He stood straight and said, "Right, here we go."

Before he could move, Jeff Wheelan interrupted. "If you close the lid back down and insert these beggars," he held up two large paddles. They reminded Kate of the things they used to place pizzas in proper pizza ovens. Mike crossed to Wheelan and took the paddles and did as instructed. With the paddles being gently levered, Kate heard a squelch that reminded her of a spoon entering very set jelly. This time when the lid was lifted, half the mould stayed in it and the body was revealed.

All four officials peered in and stared at the figure. It was a young man. Quite slightly built, may be even a little emaciated. A stubble beard covered his cheeks and a thin moustache lined his upper lip. He wore the ubiquitous ripped jeans, a t-shirt and a black puffer-type jacket. There was no obvious sign of the cause of death. The four of them stepped back and allowed the photographer to do her job and then Gus approached the corpse again.

From a distance, Kate watched as Gus examined the body in situ. A couple of times he beckoned the photographer forward to take close-ups of some areas. He began to palpate the skull and then moved down the body. Before coming away, he examined the victim's pockets and brought over to Kate a wallet.

"I won't know for sure until I have him in my theatre but there are signs of a slap or punch on his face and his left temple feels soft; that may be the cause of death."

Handing the wallet over he went back to the victim and began to instruct his people on how he wanted the body moved.

Kate opened the synthetic leather wallet. It was worn and frayed at some of the seams. There was no driving licence but there was a bank card. Kate read out the name. "Joseph Mallory. Our victim has a name. We'll check him on the system for a photo ID and then we'll have to track down the next of kin."

Kate handed the wallet to Colm, who had an evidence bag ready.

"Okay, back to the station and I'll update Bart."

CHAPTER 6

Whilst Kate updated Detective Chief Inspector Bartholomew, Colm tracked down information on Joseph Mallory. He didn't look very happy when Kate returned.

"I think we may have a problem, boss."

Raising a quizzical eyebrow, she wandered over to Colm's desk.

"Problem?"

Colm nodded. "There's a drugs marker on Mallory's file. We're supposed to inform Detective Chief Inspector Wakeford from the drugs unit."

Kate experienced a sinking feeling. Don't say this is going to be a territorial matter. As far as they knew, at the moment, this had nothing to do with drugs. It was a murder and so her case.

"Okay, I'm assuming he was one of their informers. I'll go and tell Bart. He can ring Wakeford and see what happens."

Thirty minutes later, Kate was summoned to Bart's office. He looked far from pleased.

"Right, Kate. This is going to be a complex case but I think I've managed to convince Wakeford that it would look peculiar if one of his team began to investigate a murder, so the case is yours."

Before Kate could thank him, he held a hand

up and continued, "you will need to liaise with Terry Gilbert and keep them in the loop. I believe both you and Colm know Gilbert?"

Kate nodded her head. "Yes, he gave us some info on the Blaiseford case. I got on well with both him and DCI Wakeford."

"Good. I've told Wakeford that you and DC Hunter will go over to Prince Street station straight away. Terry Gilbert will meet you there and give you the background to Joseph Mallory and why he was in the Play House."

"So, was he one of their informers, sir?"

Bart shook his head sadly. "No, Kate. He was one of us: an undercover cop."

Terry Gilbert was waiting in Prince's Street car park. The front desk had been closed some years earlier at Prince Street but the drugs team worked out of the back offices. Gilbert hadn't changed much since their last encounter; still sporting the designer ripped jeans and the muscle- hugging t-shirt. He hurried across to them and with no preamble asked, "You're sure it's Mallory?"

Colm held up a morgue photograph for Gilbert to inspect. He took it and peered intently at it before sighing and answering himself, "Yes."

Once again they followed Gilbert down the institutional green corridor but rather than leading them to the main area he took them into a small, windowless office. Papers were already strewn across the table and Gilbert directed them to the far side of it.

As they all sat, Gilbert picked up a photograph of a young officer in dress uniform, "Detective Constable Simon Bradley."

Kate took a moment to study the face in the picture. He looked impossibly young. He also looked healthier and fitter than he had in real life, or death. Terry retrieved the photo from Kate's hands. "Bradley came to us for an undercover operation eighteen months ago. His task was to insinuate himself into Gary Phipps' dealings. And to that end he has been very successful."

"You were after Phipps' contacts?" Kate asked.

Gilbert nodded. "About a month ago we got intel from the Dutch police, via the Met, saying that they thought the Court Travelling Theatre Company was being used as a cover by drugs couriers. They didn't know who in the company or how but they were sure that the company was involved. Since the company was due here and we already had someone in position, it became our operation."

"When was the last time you had communication with Mallory, Bradley?"

"Just under a fortnight ago. I was his probation officer and we met fortnightly in a local café."

"And Mallory didn't think at your last meeting that he had been rumbled?" Colm queried.

Gilbert shook his head, "No. Phipps was excited and told his gang that there was some big money to be made soon but gave no details."

"And when did the theatre company arrive in Eashire?"

"A few days ago."

"So you don't know whether Mallory had contact with the company since its arrival?" Kate hazarded a guess.

Gilbert shook his head again. "He'd got himself in tight with Phipps so we think he probably was told something about the company. I mean, why else was he there otherwise?"

"Okay, what about next of kin?"

"Already sorted. Just his parents and they're in Huddersfield. Wakeford got the local force to send someone round."

"And you're convinced his death has something to do with drugs rather than his personal life?"

Gilbert gave a sardonic chuckle, "What personal life? He was under cover."

Kate persisted, "But wouldn't it have looked odd if he hadn't got a girlfriend hanging around? Wouldn't Phipps have found that suspicious?"

Gilbert conceded the point. "Oh, he made a

thing of having a fling with a few girls but he played it easy come, easy go. Nothing serious."

"So, you've no idea why Mallory was at the Play House or who he was supposed to be seeing? And you don't know who's involved with the drugs?"

"No, but we can assume that if his cover was blown his death would have been their only course of action."

"Or he pissed someone off he shouldn't have," Colm suggested.

Gilbert shrugged his shoulders. "That's your job. Find out who and why and don't queer our pitch with the drugs. We want to make an arrest and turn them to try and track the train back to their suppliers."

"Understood. For the time being we're going to treat this like any other murder. No second guessing about drugs."

"You'll need this," Gilbert handed over a thick manila folder. "That's all my reports from meeting with Bradley. And this one," passing a much thinner file is the intel from the Dutch."

Loaded with their information, Colm and Kate sat in their car. "It's got to be drug related, hasn't it boss? Too much of a coincidence otherwise."

Kate shook her head. "I don't want us to be narrowly focused. If we do, we'll make the evidence fit the theory."

Colm nodded slowly. "Okay. Where next?"

"Back to the Play House. Time to start interviewing people, especially Clare West."

CHAPTER 7

The route Colm took gave Kate a view of the smash and grab cash machine heist on Peace Way. The boarded area stared accusingly at her. Where had the vehicle gone that had been used? If the traffic cameras lost it, surely it must still be in the area. Colm drove down the side of the Play House to scrubland at the rear. On the far side was a site cabin and a digger. Kate shook her head. Could they really be that lucky? Close behind the Play House Mike's forensic vans were still there.

Kate used her phone, "Mike, how's it going? Before you leave, could you send a small team to give the digger in the car park a once over? I know it's a long shot but it could be our cash machine vehicle. Thanks, Mike."

"You don't really think we've just stumbled across our large machinery, do you, boss?"

"I'm not sure but it's nice and close to Peace Way and would account for why we couldn't chase it after the smash and grab. I'll check it out with the manager. Whilst I'm doing that, can you go to Stan and pick up his ledger as evidence? I want to see who else was still in the theatre at the same time as Joseph Mallory. And can you find Clare West? We'll meet up in the Falstaff Bar."

They entered through the stage door and

Kate left Colm working out how Stan could transfer today's information from the ledger before he seized it for evidence. Kate felt quite pleased with herself that she negotiated the backstage area and found her way to Julia Montgomery's office. She knocked and waited. Montgomery's voice carried clearly. "Enter."

Montgomery was staring intently at a large computer screen to one side of her desk. "Two secs. I just need to save this."

Kate waited patiently as Montgomery clicked her way across the screen. A final tap and she sat back and looked at Kate. "I understand you found the body of a young man? Not someone from the theatre?"

"No. The man was called Joseph Mallory and he was visiting one of the theatre company, we believe."

"So, how can I help you?"

"The list you gave us. Was that all the theatre people, including the visiting theatre company?" Kate drew the sheet out of the file she was carrying.

Montgomery leant across the desk and pointed to the two columns of names. "Those on the left are the Play House's employed staff. On the right the theatre company and then those at the bottom are extra staff we have employed for this production."

Kate handed Montgomery the sheet. "Would you mark those that would be unlikely to go backstage, please? I believe you call them 'front of house staff'?"

Montgomery nodded and took an orange highlighter from a pot on the desk. "These are all front of house staff," highlighting names as she spoke, "And these two" creating a little star by each name, "Were the only ones in yesterday."

Kate took the sheet back and thanked Montgomery. "Is the scrubland at the back, part of the Play House?"

Montgomery raised a quizzical eyebrow at the change of direction but answered readily. "It is now. One of the main problems with old theatres in the middle of towns and cities is the lack of parking space but the council has given that back area over to us for parking."

"I notice you have a digger in the back area. Has it been there long?"

Montgomery looked surprised. "A digger? That must be something to do with the contractors, although I didn't think they were starting work until the end of the month."

"Do you have contact details for the contractors, please?"

Montgomery clicked through her screen. "Shall I print them off for you?"

"Thank you."

A previously unnoticed printer in the back corner of the room came to life and began to spit out the information Kate wanted. Montgomery collected it and handed it to Kate. "Is there anything else I can help you with Inspector Medlar?"

"No, that's great. My colleague and I will be using the Falstaff Bar to carry out interviews for the rest of the day."

Montgomery nodded her understanding and was already clicking back through her screen as Kate closed the door behind her.

CHAPTER 8

Kate met Colm and Clare West outside the bar. Clare West looked frighteningly thin and her skin was pallid and waxy in appearance. She looked frightened to death despite Colm's efforts to charm and reassure her. Kate pointed West to the comfy fireside chair and she and Colm sat opposite. The girl perched on the edge of her seat, tension in every sinew.

"Thank you for seeing us Miss West, or may I call you Clare?"

"Clare is fine," the whispered voice was accompanied by a small shrug of the shoulders.

"Thank you, Clare. Now can you tell me how long you have known Joseph Mallory?"

The girl looked up, wide-eyed. "I didn't know him. I've never met him. He didn't come to see me last night." The information gushed from her.

Kate held up her hand to stem the flow. "Joseph Mallory signed in last night at five-forty, claiming he was here to see you."

The girl shook her head vehemently. "I don't know why he did that. I wasn't even here."

Colm donned a pair of gloves and took Stan's ledger from its evidence bag. He began to flick through it and then ran his finger down the columns of names. His finger stopped and he looked up at Kate. "According to this, boss, Clare signed out at three yesterday afternoon."

Clare nodded her head vigorously. "I had a doctor's appointment at three-twenty."

"And you didn't come back afterwards?"

A shake of her head. "No, I went straight home."

"And where is home? You're part of the touring company, aren't you? Are you in lodgings in Eashire?"

"Yes, there's a group of us in a guest house in Eastgate Lane. Mr and Mrs Murphy. Mrs Murphy saw me come in at about four and I offered to help with getting the evening meal ready for everyone." Now on safer ground, the girl was happy to chat. "Mrs Murphy doesn't normally do evening meals but said she would for us, if we helped out with the prep and cleaning up." Having run out of information, she slumped a little in the chair.

"Would one of the other girls have given your name to Joseph Mallory?"

Another shoulder shrug, but this one more defined. "I really don't know. They might have done, but I don't see why."

"Who else lodges with you? All women?"

A nod about the women. "We're all in the chorus line." Colm sat obtrusively waiting for names and Clare began. "I'm sharing with Ellie Marsh. Then there's Jade and Emmie, short for Emerald, they're sisters."

"Last names?" Colm asked quietly.

"Froude, sounds like 'rude'." And then she spelt it out.

"And Kathy Higson has a room to herself."

"Do you get on well with them all?"

Clare's eyes drifted off as she thought about what she wanted to say. "I get on best with Ellie, that's why we chose to share. Jade and Emmie can be," a pause as she tried to frame her ideas, "well, they can be a bit full on and they're both terrible flirts. You know they say sailors have a girl in every port, well they're a bit like that."

"Do they or have they had relationships with other members of the company?"

Clare blushed. "No, Mr Henderson, he's the owner, doesn't allow it. Says it's bad for company cohesiveness." She was clearly quoting Mr Henderson.

Kate sensed some reticence and asked, "but?"

Again, another flush of colour. "Well, in Worthing I did come across Jason and Jade in an intimate position." The girl swallowed noisily. "But a few days later Jade said it was all off. That he, Jason, wasn't worth losing her job over."

Whilst Clare had been talking, Kate ran her eyes down the list of company members' names. "This would be Jason Brooks?"

The girl nodded.

"And what's Jason like? He must have been upset if Jade dumped him?"

Again, that shrug. "I don't know really. He's

a bit of a know it all. I thought he kept giving Jade dirty looks after she told me they'd split up." Again another shrug.

Kate wanted to tackle the drug question but how to drop it into this conversation? The trouble was people felt compelled to lie or edit the truth when you started asking questions where the answers might be seen as wrong, let alone illegal.

CHAPTER 9

Kate leant forward earnestly. "Clare, we sometimes find that some people, when we ask them questions, tend to be economical with the truth because they are afraid of either getting people into trouble or being seen as a grass." Kate held up a calming hand as Clare began to stutter her denial. "I am absolutely sure that you are telling us the truth." Clare relaxed a little in the chair. "I just want you to continue to do so."

Colm also leant forward. "We are only interested in finding out who killed Joseph Mallory. Anything you tell us will only be used, if it helps us. Do you understand?"

Clare sat up straighter but nodded her understanding. Kate sat back to indicate to Colm to continue the questioning.

Colm smiled warmly and began conversationally, "I know that drug taking is part of the scene these days. Is it so in the theatre?"

Kate could see Clare struggling to be truthful and yet still worried about the fall out of any disclosure. Reluctantly, she nodded.

"Do you take anything? A tab when you go out for a party night?"

Clare smiled knowingly. "Detective, the theatre crowd have infrequent party nights, despite what popular media might say. We train all day, work all night and are knackered at the end of the day."

Colm smiled his understanding. "But I don't believe there isn't some use."

Again, Kate witnessed the fight, finally, "Some of the theatre crew smoke weed."

"That's the crew that work for the Play House?" Kate clarified.

"Yes," under Colm's smiling gaze, she continued. "Some of the theatre group take various substances," she said in an attempt to distance herself.

"Like?"

Clare frowned. "Like what stuff or who does?"

Kate intervened. "Let's start with who. Do you?"

Clare shook her head vigorously. "I tried marijuana once and didn't like the feeling or the fact that I ate myself silly after. I have enough problems keeping weight off without adding to them."

Kate wondered if Clare's view of herself was impacted by anorexia, but kept the thought to herself.

Colm again. "And who?"

Clare sighed deeply. Accepting that she wasn't going to get away with skirting what the police wanted from her. "I'm not sure about everyone but I know that Jade, Emmie and Jason used to share drugs. I'm not sure what but it's more than a bit of weed."

"What about the others in the company?"

"Rumour has it that Jan Wey has a coke habit." She hastened to add, "but I don't know if that's true. Otherwise, I think it is just a bit of Molly when we do get time to party."

"Molly as in MDMA?" Colm clarified.

Kate asked, "do you know how these people source their need? If you're moving from town to town, it must be difficult to get a regular supply?"

Clare smiled at Kate's naivety. "I understand that it doesn't take long to have your shopping list filled. Most pubs that cater for youngsters will have someone who can help."

"Do you know which pub in Eashire?"

Clare shook her head. "It's not my scene. White wine is all I want from a pub."

Kate came back to their very first question. "Could someone have used your name when letting it be known they had a shopping list? And that's why Joseph Mallory was in the theatre?"

Clare sneaked a look at her watch. "Do you mind if I go soon? I have a rehearsal in ten. We're getting our positions right now, the props and tabs are set."

Colm looked to Kate who smiled and thanked Clare. Clare, given permission to go, rose fluidly and stepped smartly for the door. Just as she was going through, Kate called, "Clare what is Jason Brooks' role in the company?"

Clare looked surprised. "He's the director."

Kate stood and stretched. "Thoughts?"

"It's a small company, so I think she probably knows more than she's telling."

Kate agreed. "And does it feel like she's directing us to the Froude sisters?"

"Umm. She certainly paints them as the bad girls."

"Well, if there is a rehearsal now, we're not going to see them without creating a furore, so let's try something else."

CHAPTER 10

The 'something else' was noting who was in the theatre when Joseph Mallory signed in and who signed out after his supposed departure. They came up with seven names: Jade and Emmie Froude, Jason Brooks and Daniel Henderson from the theatre company; Calum James and Jon Bell down as lighting technicians and Terry Lennon called in for the malfunctioning trap door.

"Let's see if Bart has given us our normal dream team," Kate said as she flipped open her phone. Seconds later, "Alice! Have we got you and Len? Good. Can you find out where we can find a Terry Lennon - something to do with carpentry and trap doors - and I'll email through a list of staff. I'll ring ones I'd like you to start with. Thanks."

Still holding her phone, Kate said, "Ring those six that were still here after Mallory's arrival and then I'll photograph it and send it through to Alice." The list was soon in the ether and Kate suggested they find Calum James and Jon Bell.

Once again they braved the maze that was backstage. Kate felt that they were getting better at it. Finding a young man in the wings twiddling with a dial on a complex board that Kate thought would not look out of place in a cockpit, she asked for the two men.

The young man momentarily looked up from his board, "Jon's in the booth," he indicated the sound booth at the back of the theatre, "and Calum's up there." His finger pointed to the gantries in the dome of the auditorium. "But you'll not get any sense out of them until we've finished this session."

Kate mouthed her thanks but the young man was already absorbed in the dials before him. Hesitating, she could make herself very unpopular and demand this session stop so she could interview people but then they might be less than forthcoming. In the end she decided to talk with Stan at the stage door.

Once he saw who was at his door, Stan stood and looked ready to undertake any task. Kate smiled her appreciation and asked, "Stan, would you be kind enough to ask Calum James and Jon Bell not to leave this evening until we have spoken with them. We'll be back later this afternoon. Do you know what time this session is due to finish?"

Stan made a note of the names and replied. "Normally about five. It'll get later as opening night gets closer."

Colm and Kate exited and stood in the would-be car park. Kate noted that a couple of Mike's white-clad technicians were just packing away after examining the digger. Kate wandered across. "Anything useful?"

"Lots!" The word was emphasised by a slim young woman, who was struggling to pull the overall off her arms. Kate gave her a hand.

"Finger prints galore on the cab and the pull bars." She pointed to the strap bars that gave someone leverage to pull themselves up into the cab.

Kate felt disappointed. It must have shown because the woman went on to say as she hopped from leg to leg taking the white suit off, "However, there were some interesting marks on the edges of the bucket and some transfer material in the same place. We won't know what it is until we get it back to the lab."

"Thanks for that," said Kate. Maybe her hunch would pay off. As she turned and headed back to the car, her phone rang. "Hello, Alice. Oh great. I think we'll go and visit him now."

Colm looked enquiringly at Kate's phone. As she put it away, she explained, "Alice says Terry Lennon has a sheet. Mainly drunken brawls but one case of ABH."

"ABH? That could just be another brawl but someone made a complaint."

Kate agreed. "But Mr Lennon is obviously not afraid to use his fists. Perhaps he got into an argument with Mallory and it got out of hand."

Colm pulled a grimace that showed his dislike of the scenario but said nothing.

"Anyway, Terry is working on the canal basin site. That's not far from here, is it?"

"Ten minutes but can we stop and pick up lunch, please boss?"

Kate smiled as she checked her watch. "Sorry Colm. I lost track of the time. Now you mention it, I am a bit peckish myself." In all honesty, now she'd thought about it, she was ravenous!

CHAPTER 11

The canal basin was alive with men in high-vis jackets and machinery. Kate wasn't quite sure where to start but Colm pointed out a site cabin similar to the one behind the Play House. Fortunately, the unmade path was dry, otherwise it would have been a wellies job, Kate estimated.

Knocking sharply on the cabin's door, Kate entered with her warrant card ready to show and Colm close on her heels. A grey-haired man was sat at a desk on the telephone. He obviously was more used to outside work as his forehead showed the tan mark from his hard hat and he was fumbling through paperwork on the desk as he spoke. "Yes. We've got them here. Just give me a second." He shuffled more papers. "Gail would choose today to go sick, wouldn't she?" Kate was unsure if that question was directed at them or the person on the other end of the phone.

Clearly not finding what he was looking for, he sighed deeply and said, "Look, I'll have to ring you back in a while. Yes, before the close of play. Yes!" The final with some heat as the receiver was thrown onto the desk. The man stood and held out a ham of a hand. "Police? I didn't expect a detective to come calling about our stolen digger."

Kate introduced herself and Colm before replying. "We're here on another matter, Mr?" She left the question hanging in the air.

"Sorry! Gary. Gary Pugh. I'm the site foreman. No, that's not strictly true. I'm the deputy. Gail is the site foreman but she's off today. That's why I can't sodding well find anything." He ran a hand across his thinning hair. "Anyway, not the digger?"

Kate shook her head. "We'd like a chat with one of your workers, Terry Lennon."

"Terry? What's he been up to now?"

"You sound like it's not unusual for the police to need to talk to Mr Lennon?" Colm queried.

Another run of the hand across his hair. "No. Terry's a good bloke. It's sometimes the drink washes out his good sense. A few too many pub fights. Is that what this is about?"

Kate shook her head. "No, we just need to confirm Mr Lennon's whereabouts early yesterday evening, between five and seven."

"Oh, that's easy. I sent him across to the Play House. They'd got a problem with the trap door mechanism. He left here," a pause as he recalled the time, "about a quarter to six, give or take five minutes and he told me this morning he left there about seven-fifteen."

Colm flapped his notebook closed and Kate thanked Mr Pugh. "If you'd just point Mr Lennon out we'll just confirm those times with him."

"I can do better than that. Hang on." He

stepped across from the desk to a microphone and spoke into it. "Terry Lennon, please come to the site office. Terry Lennon."

Kate could hear the boom of the voice outside the cabin.

"It might take him a few minutes. He's on the far side of the basin but you can use this office. I'm going out to check that we have been sent the right defenders."

With that Mr Pugh stepped from behind the desk and twisted past Kate and Colm and left the office.

Kate was unsure what 'defenders' were but it did mean they had somewhere private to have their chat with Terry Lennon.

CHAPTER 12

Terry Lennon had what could be called a rugged face. Not particularly handsome but aging and experience had made it an interesting one. Although shorter than Colm, he was as broad and the veins seemed carved into his forearms. On arriving and not finding Pugh he looked surprised and not a little suspicious.

"Where's Gary? He said he wanted me here."

Kate and Colm showed their cards and Kate began. "Mr Pugh has kindly allowed us to use his office to have a chat."

Suspicion did not leave Lennon's face. "Whatever it is, it wasn't me."

"So, you weren't at the Play House last evening to mend the trap door?"

Kate watched as some of the tension left Lennon's shoulders. Whatever he'd imagined they were there for, it wasn't this. Lennon looked between the two of them. "Yeh. I was there."

"Could you confirm what time you arrived, please, Mr Lennon?"

"It was dead on six."

"How can you be so sure of the time?"

"Coz I had to sign that damn book Stan has in his cubbyhole and I had to ask him the time."

"Did you go straight to the trap door by yourself or did someone show you?"

"Nah. I know me way around there. Me and some of the lads," he threw an arm in the direction of the site outside, "we did some of the work when they opened the Play House up again."

"Did you see anyone? Talk with anyone on your way or while you were working?"

Lennon shook his head. "Not many about at that time when there's no show on. Different fing if it was a show night."

"You saw absolutely no-one all the time you were there?"

Kate was sure there was a flicker in Lennon's eye as he answered. "Apart from Stan, not a soul."

Colm also must have picked up on Lennon's tell. "Did you hear anything unusual?"

Again, that twitch. Kate was sure that Lennon was debating what to say. "Mr Lennon, there was a serious incident at the Play House last night at about the time you were there, so it is important that you tell us everything." Kate emphasised the last word, "No matter how trivial it may seem to you."

Lennon thought some more and finally, shaking his head, "No. I can't say as I saw or heard a fing. I had my head under the stage for most of the time. You don't hear a lot down there."

For the moment Kate let it go. "What time did you leave the Play House?"

"About seven-fifteen."

"Not an exact time, Mr Lennon?"

"Nah. Old Stan wasn't at his post, was he? And I don't wear a watch. I'd use me phone but I'd put it in my work bag so I made a reasonable guess."

"How did you know it was about seven-fifteen, though?" Colm persisted.

Lennon sighed heavily. "I'd used me phone as a light, to check the springs that was causing the problem. As I put it away it was seven o' nine. I reckoned it took me about five or six minutes to pack away the rest of me stuff and go to sign out."

Kate nodded. It was enough to be going on with. For now. "Thank you for your time, Mr Lennon. We won't keep you."

"Sure. See ya!" Lennon left the cabin.

"He's lying," was Colm's bald statement.

"I agree, but about what?"

"He didn't mention the girl screaming about the spider. That must have been about the time he was packing up to finish."

"Yes."

"I think he heard or saw something or someone."

"That would be my guess, but if so why not tell us?"

Colm shrugged. "What and help the Pigs! Not in his DNA, I guess."

CHAPTER 13

Back in their car Kate called her office. "Len? Can you chase a crime report for me? I'm not sure when, but in this last week someone from Bridewell Civil Engineering will have reported a digger missing. Can you email me the report? Thanks. Colm and I are going back to the Play House for some more interviews."

Negotiating round a dithering motorist, Colm asked, "Are you thinking the digger at the back of the Play House is Mr Pugh's missing digger?"

"Maybe."

"So, is someone covering their backs by reporting it missing or was it stolen for the cash machine job?"

"Not sure but right now we need to be back on focus for the more pressing problem of our murder. I wonder when Gus is doing the post-mortem. I'll give his secretary a quick ring."

Colm parked again in the wannabe car park and Kate made her call. "Eight-thirty tomorrow morning. Gus has invited us."

Colm grimaced. "Nice people get invited to barbeques or parties. We get invited to PMs. I think we took a wrong turn somewhere, boss."

Kate gave him a play punch to the arm. "Just think how much you'll learn."

Colm shook his head as Kate led them back through the stage door. Stan was up and waiting. "Evening detectives. Calum and Jon have just finished and are waiting for you in the green room."

"Thanks, Stan. Green room?"

Stan came out of his office and stood and gave directions with his arm. "Along this corridor, take the second right. Then the first left. You can't miss it."

Kate hoped he was right as they set off. Five minutes later they were sat in the 'green room', although Kate noted that it wasn't green. Calum James was a tall wiry man of about thirty with wild hair desperately in need of cutting. Jon Bell, in contrast wore a shirt that Kate would guess, at the start of the day, had been ironed, a casual jacket and chinos. He was probably also in his thirties and sported a chin-only beard. Both looked a little uncomfortable.

Kate and Colm introduced themselves and Kate began. "I am sure that by now you are aware of the body found in the workshop?" Both men nodded. "We just need to find out who was in the theatre last evening and where and whether anyone saw anything."

Colm flicked the pages in his book. "According to Stan's ledger you were both here after six." Again, both men nodded. "Where were you?"

Jon Bell decided to be the spokesman. "We

were in the lighting booth at the back of the auditorium going through the lighting plan."

"Why just you two?" Kate asked. "Looking at the people employed here several of them are part of the lighting crew."

Jon smiled. "I am the lighting director. I plan the lighting sequence, in collaboration with the director, of course. Calum is in charge of the monkeys."

Kate held up her hand. "Sorry. The what?"

"The crew who climb into the gantries to set the lights. We call them the monkeys." Kate thought this was explained with exaggerated patience. Mr Jon Bell was getting right under her skin. She smiled pleasantly. "Please continue."

"Well, that's it, really. We were going over the plan ready for today's light changes and the rehearsal."

"So you were in the booth all evening? What time did you leave?"

"If you've checked Stan's book then you know that Calum left about six-twentyish and I left a little before seven."

Kate deliberately addressed Calum, who had sat staring at the floor throughout the conversation. "Mr James, did you see anyone, or hear anything when you left the theatre?"

James shook his head but refused to meet Kate's eye. Bell was eager to rush to his aid. "Calum finds social interaction difficult."

"So, how does he cope with giving

instructions to the rest of the crew?" Colm wanted to know.

Calum lifted his head but still wouldn't make eye contact. "I tell them facts. I don't have to make stuff up."

Bell smiled. "Calum doesn't do social chit-chat."

"What about you, Mr Bell?" Colm asked.

"Oh, I do social chit-chat." Bell answered, deliberately misinterpreting Colm's question, Kate guessed.

Colm patiently explained the error. "Hear or see anything or anyone?"

"No. I'm sorry. I didn't. To be honest I thought that I was probably one of the last to leave so I was surprised to see some of the theatre group's names still unsigned out."

Kate felt they would get nothing of interest from the two of them, thanked them both and left the room. Making their way back to the stage door, she couldn't resist a quiet, "Pompous ass!"

Colm smiled his agreement.

CHAPTER 14

Checking the log, Kate saw that Jason Brooks was still in the theatre. "Stan, where do you think I'd find Jason Brooks now?"

Stan scratched his head. "He might be in the workshop. He and Jim have been working out how they use them statues in the play." A pause. "If he's not there and he wasn't in the green room," looking at Kate who shook her head, "then try front of house. He sometimes works in the box office."

"Let's try the workshop first," Kate led the way. She was getting the hang of this warren and soon they were stepping into the workshop. Jim Wheelan looked up from his task of robing one of the statues. White, thin cloth was draped artfully to create a Grecian effect.

"Detective Medlar. What can I do for you?" He smiled benignly.

"We're looking for Jason Brooks, Jim," Colm explained.

Releasing the last of the material that hung in fluid drapes, Jim shook his head. "You've just missed him. He said he was off back to his digs."

"Well we didn't pass him on the way here from the stage door. So, any idea where he might have gone?"

"You could try the girls' dressing room." He

winked knowingly, then shook his head. "Mind you, I'm not sure it's all going as smoothly as he would like."

"I didn't think the company were allowed to have relationships with one another?"

"Well, technically they're not. But who can hold back love? Or is it lust?" Another wink.

"Where do we find the dressing room, Jim?" Colm asked.

"Other side of the stage. Once you're near the wings you'll smell them!"

Kate looked askance and Jim laughed. "No, it's a lovely smell. Face powder, scent and warm talc. A really feminine smell. Very different from the chaps." He pulled a face.

Kate nodded her understanding and they set off for the dressing room. Kate could understand what Jim meant once they reached the left-hand wings. There was a gentle smell of something, and yes she would identify it as feminine. "I thought theatres smelt of greasepaint and sweat."

Colm stopped and listened. Further up the hall, behind a closed door, an argument was happening. Approaching it they couldn't make out the words but they could tell it was a man and a woman and that it was quite heated. Standing outside, they clearly heard the woman say, "I didn't ask you to interfere!" The door swung open abruptly.

Red-faced and teary a young woman stood in

the doorway. She looked shocked to see Kate and Colm. "Good evening, Ms?" Kate left the question hanging.

Kate watched the supreme effort of will that the young woman exerted before replying, "Jade. Jade Froude."

"We're looking for Mr Jason Brooks. Is he here?"

Froude looked back into the room with a look akin to distaste and then turned back to Kate. "He's in there."

"Thank you. Colm, would you take Ms Froude to the green room and check that she's all right? I'll talk with Mr Brooks."

Colm used his hand to indicate that Jade should follow him along the hallway. Kate stepped into the room and closed the door. Jason Brooks was a surprisingly large man. Kate gave her prejudice a tweak. She'd been expecting a more academic or foppish figure. Jason Brooks was an alpha male, reeking of testosterone. At the moment he looked both wary and angry.

Kate held out her warrant card for inspection. "Mr Brooks, I am Detective Inspector Medlar and I am leading the investigation into the body found in Mr Wheelan's workshop this morning."

Brooks merely nodded and barely glanced at Kate's ID.

"I understand you were still in the theatre when Mr Mallory was here?"

"Mallory? Was that his name?"

Kate nodded. "Did you meet him?"

Brooks shook his head. "No. I was in the box office." He vaguely gestured towards the front of the theatre.

"All evening?"

Brooks looked at Kate carefully. Was he evaluating her or what to tell her? Kate wondered.

"We had a technical rehearsal today and I was going through my notes in preparation."

"What time did you leave?"

"I can't remember for sure but Stan will have it in his book. About eight, I think."

"Did you go alone?"

Again, that calculation. "What do you mean?"

"I understand that you and Ms Froude are an item?"

Brooks snorted emphatically. "Did it look like we are an item?"

"That's today. What about yesterday?"

Brooks shook his head. "No. Jade waxes hot and cold and at the moment we're in the freezing stage."

"And what was it you did for Jade?"

Brooks looked intently at Kate. She was sure he was trying to gauge how much they had overheard. "I er." He looked uncomfortable. "I er, had a bit of a drug problem and Jade said she couldn't love a druggie. So I quit." The last was said with some defiance.

"So, Jade doesn't use drugs herself?"

"No." Brooks didn't meet Kate's eye.

"But despite giving up the drugs, Jade still isn't interested, is that it?"

Brooks sighed deeply. "Yeh, that's about the size of it."

Kate was not convinced. Something about Brooks' demeanour didn't ring true. Neither did his assertion that Jade did not take drugs. Kate was reasonably happy that Clare West had been telling the truth. But she was an actress. She would need to double-check that story.

For now, Kate thanked Jason Brooks for his time. As she closed the door behind her she was sure she heard Brooks let out a long and deep sigh.

CHAPTER 15

Colm herded Jade to the green room where she perched on the edge of one of the seats. Colm asked, "is there anything I can get you? A glass of water?"

Jade pointed to a tri-parted screen across an alcove at one side. Behind it, Colm found bottles of water. Releasing the cap of one, he placed it before Jade. She took a grateful sip. Colm noticed that the tissue she had been using for her eyes and nose was now in danger of being shredded and that her hands still trembled as she placed the bottle onto the table.

Leaning forward, Colm began gently, "Are you all right? Mr Brooks seemed to be upset about something."

Jade avoided eye contact and merely nodded.

Colm decided to play the innocent and asked, "Are you and Mr Brooks in a relationship?"

"No!" was said with all the edge of an irritated teenager.

Colm held both hands up. "Sorry. It seemed a bit like a lovers' tiff. I assumed you were an item."

A slight sigh and Jade looked up at Colm through her eyelashes. "We had a bit of a fling a few months ago but he won't let it go."

"Oh!" Colm tried to sound sympathetic. "That must be really difficult, what with you working together."

Jade gave a teenage eye roll. "Tell me about it. I've told him so many times. It was just a fling but he won't listen."

"I suppose it also makes it difficult if you want to go out with anyone else, doesn't it?"

Jade looked up suspiciously. "There isn't anyone else."

Colm tried to placate again. "No, I just meant if you wanted to. It would be difficult. Is Brooks the type to make life difficult for anyone else?"

A shrug of the shoulders and a sullen, "I don't know."

Colm decided to move on. "We're interviewing everyone who was in the theatre when Mr Mallory visited last night. Where were you between five-thirty and seven-thirty?"

"What's that got to do with me?"

"It's just routine," Colm said reassuringly. "We just need to know where everyone was."

There was a long pause. Colm was convinced as he watched her eyes flit around the room that she was fabricating what she was about to say. "I was in the rehearsal room for most of that time. I was having difficulty with one of the tempo changes."

Colm made a point of labouring over his notebook. "So was that for the whole time?"

"Yes."

"Can anyone verify that? Were you practicing with anyone? At any point in the two hours?"

"No, not really."

Colm again made a play with his notes. "Did you hear any screaming? A woman's voice?"

"Screaming. No!"

Colm looked puzzled. "Oh, Stan said one of the girls screamed because there was a spider in the dressing room. I thought that may have been you."

Jade seized the thrown lifeline. "Oh, that! I'd forgotten about that."

"Did Stan sort it?"

"Oh, it had disappeared by the time Stan arrived."

"Where was it?"

"Oh, on the makeup counter. I was afraid to touch any of my stuff."

"Did you know Joseph Mallory? Had he been to the theatre before last night?"

"No, I didn't even know his name until you mentioned it. Never seen him before."

"So you'd have no idea why he was visiting the Play House?"

"Well, he should have written in Stan's book who he was coming in to see."

Colm nodded thoughtfully. "Unfortunately, it looks like he lied. He said he was visiting Clare West but she was not in last night. She had a doctor's appointment and left early."

Was there a slight widening of Jade's eyes? Colm wasn't sure but he thought Clare not being in last night was a surprise to Jade Froude. Colm closed his notebook. "Thank you for your time, Miss Froude. Are you all right for me to leave?"

There was a slight pout. "If you must."

Colm smiled. "I must."

CHAPTER 16

Colm met Kate by Stan's booth. Heading out to the car, he gave Kate the gist of the interview and concluded with, "I'm pretty sure there's more to the argument we overheard than a spurned lover."

Kate nodded. "Yes, I'm sure Brooks was holding out on me, too. She stopped abruptly and thought. Then she said to Colm, "are you up for another interview before we call it a day?"

Colm nodded, "Emerald Froude?"

Kate smiled. "It's nice to know we're on the same page Detective Constable!"

Colm grinned. "Learning from the best, boss."

Kate chuckled as she dropped into her car seat. "Flattery. That's the way to go, until you take your sergeant's exam."

Colm checked for the address of the boarding house where the Froude sisters were staying. Sensibly, it wasn't far from the Play House and less than ten minutes later they were in front of it. In fact, Kate thought, if they'd walked it would probably have been quicker because finding a space to park had taken five minutes.

Kate noted that the boarding house was part of the Georgian expansion of Eashire and the double-fronted building had a short flight of steps leading to a blue front door. The steps were spotless. As were the areas around the basement sections of the house. "Mr and Mrs Murphy, isn't it?" she checked with Colm.

He nodded his agreement.

Kate rang the old-fashioned bell push and inside could hear the definite clang of metal clapper on a bell. Several minutes later a woman of about forty opened the door. "I'm sorry, we have no vacancies," she said pointedly looking at the 'No Vacancies' sign in one of the bow windows.

Kate held up her warrant card, knowing Colm was doing the same. "Mrs Murphy? Detective Inspector Medlar. Could we have a word with one of your guests, please?" Kate's tone brooked no denial.

"Police! Oh! Of course. Come in." The woman stepped back into a brightly lit hall with the original tiles still on the floor. "Not all the girls are back from the theatre yet. Who do you wish to see?"

"Kate made a show of checking her notebook. "Ms Emerald Froude, please."

"Yes, she's in. If you'd like to wait in the dining room I'll go and get her."

Kate acquiesced. The dining room contained several small tables that would comfortably seat two and a third if you were friendly! All were laid ready for a meal and Kate remembered Clare West saying that Mrs Murphy was providing an evening meal. The sound of light steps coming across the tiles heralded the arrival of Emerald Froude.

CHAPTER 17

Where Jade had worn her sexuality explicitly there was something more enigmatic about Emerald. She was a little out of breath. "Hello, is this about that poor man Jim found in his workshop?"

"It is. Would you like to take a seat?" Kate indicated one of the tables and she and Emerald Froude sat at it whilst Colm pulled out a chair from another table.

"Poor man. Someone said he was a druggie. Is that true?"

Kate raised an eyebrow. Interesting. Apart from Clare they had not mentioned drugs with any of their interviewees. "We're still trying to find out why Mr Mallory was at the theatre last night. Is it likely that someone in the company would hook up with a druggie?"

Emerald blushed and hesitated. Colm came in with their standard gambit. "We need to know everything you can tell us. If it doesn't help with our enquiry we'll ignore it. We just want to catch this murderer."

"Do you understand, Emerald?"

Emerald nodded. "Could you call me Emmie. I only get called Emerald when I'm in trouble and it's putting me on edge."

"Not a problem, Emmie. Now are people

liable to want drugs in the company?"

Emmie nodded. "Yes, normally someone makes contact in a new town and we get them to get what we want."

"You take drugs yourself, Emmie?"

A return of the blush. "Only when we're partying. Some of them need to take drugs to keep on the level. I just take them for a fun time."

"What about your sister, Jade? Does she use?"

Another blush. "Yes, but again just for partying."

Kate went fishing. "Was she the one who made contact with a local dealer in Eashire?"

Colm backed Kate up by ostensibly double-checking his notes. Convinced that the police knew, Emmie nodded. "Yeh. She made contact a few days ago. He was due to bring the stuff in..." Emmie trailed off as her thoughts caught up with her words. "Oh my God! Was he? The dead man, was he a dealer?"

Kate gave a standard answer, "We're following a number of leads and are building up a picture of Mr Mallory's life. If he was a dealer, Mr Mallory could have been visiting Jade last night."

Emmie was flustered. "Oh you can't think that Jade had anything to do with his death. That's just ridiculous." Kate could see that their interviewee was close to tears. "We don't think anything of the kind Emmie. We're just trying to get an idea of why Mr Mallory was there last night."

Emmie sniffed loudly and nodded her head.

"When we spoke to Jade earlier she had been having a disagreement with Jason Brooks. Is that normal?"

"Oh my God. He is so jealous! He won't accept that it's all over with him and Jade. Anyone who knows Jade knows she's not the serious type. She just wants to have fun." This was said with considerably more animation than her previous comments.

"How do you think Jason would react if he thought Jade was seeing Mr Mallory?"

"Oh God! He'd go bonkers! There was this time in Blackpool, and this was before he and Jade had their thing. This bloke kept coming up to Jade at a party. He was a bit of a pain but Jade was handling it and then Jason storms in and knocks the poor clown out." In telling the story Emmie's arms and hands re-enacted the blow. A right-handed backhand blow. Not a punch to the jaw as Kate would have imagined.

Once again Emmie realised, too late, what she had just said. "Oh, you can't think it was Jason. He'd fight him. But kill him? No!"

"Is there anyone else Mr Mallory might have been meeting last night?"

A shrug. "I really don't know. What does Stan's book say?"

"That he was meeting Clare West."

"Clare?!" The tone of disbelief said it all. "No.

He wouldn't have been meeting Clare."

"How can you be so sure?"

"No, Clare's too straightlaced. Doesn't really drink, a glass of white wine is her limit. As for drugs!" She allowed her tone to indicate her refusal to see Clare enjoying drugs. "And I've never known her have a boyfriend. Or a girlfriend, come to that."

"Were you in the dressing room when Jade screamed about a spider?"

"Oh my God! Embarrassing. Poor old Stan. Couldn't even find it when he arrived. I'm not sure there was a spider."

Kate's ears pricked up. "Oh?"

Another little blush. "Well Jade does like being the centre of attention and I know she'd just had another row with Jason so I thought it was a just a bit of attention seeking."

"Another row with Jason?"

"Yes. I don't know what about but Jade came steaming in saying that Jason was being a prick and he couldn't keep acting like this."

"Acting like what?"

Another shrug. "I assumed him not wanting it to be over."

"But Jade didn't say?"

A shake of the head.

"Do you remember what time Jade came into the dressing room? Before the spider incident."

"Well, it was after seven." A pause. "Probably about quarter past. I know we had to rush to get back here for supper at seven-thirty, even though it's only five minutes away."

"Why did you stay so late at the theatre last night, Emmie?" Colm asked.

Without hesitation, she replied. "I was getting my stuff sorted. When you're touring and then rehearsing there's not a lot of time for making sure your stuff's okay."

Colm looked puzzled. "Can you give us an idea of what this meant you were doing?"

Emmie flung a hand up. "Oh, you know, putting new taps on my dance shoes; hand washing my silk tunic. Things like that."

"Taps on your shoes?" Colm's face was a picture.

Emmie gave a surprisingly deep laugh. "Taps. Little metal pieces on the soles so that they make a noise when we tap dance."

Colm nodded his understanding and further questioning was interrupted by a brisk knock and the disembodied head of Mrs Murphy appeared around the edge of the door. "Excuse me, Inspector, but will you be much longer? It's seven-thirty and the girls' supper time."

Despite accepting Mrs Murphy's comment, Kate subconsciously checked her watch, before replying. "My apologies Mrs Murphy. I hadn't realised it was so late." Turning back to face Emmie she thanked her for her time.

CHAPTER 18

Back at the car Kate said, "Sorry Colm. I really hadn't realised it was so late. If you would drop me back to the station and then get on home and I'll meet you at Gus's lab in the morning."

"Not a problem, boss." He pulled out from the space and joined the traffic before beginning to hypothesise. "What do you reckon? Jade screamed for attention or for dragging Stan away from his desk and the ledger?"

"It does seem too coincidental that Stan is away just as Mallory supposedly signs out."

"Which means she had to be working with someone. So we're looking for two people?"

"But why kill Mallory?"

"Emmie says her sister was the drug contact for Eashire so it's likely that she did meet Mallory."

"Same question - why would she kill him?"

Colm added to the negative idea, "And could she have moved Mallory's body into the moulding thing? It's quite high off the ground and she's quite small."

"I think Jade gave Mallory Clare's name, pretending to be her."

"Why?"

Kate shrugged. "Security? Malice? Perhaps she feared a sting operation. She's canny enough."

"So, she's not practicing, she's seeing Mallory in the workshop?"

"That would be my guess."

"And then what?"

Another shrug. "If we can find that out detective, we will have our murderer!"

Arriving at the station Kate hopped out. Dipping her head back into the car to say thanks to Colm she added, "And don't forget eight-thirty sharp in the morning."

Colm waved his understanding and drove away. Kate hurried up to the incident room. Somehow room 11 had become her case room and she was pleased to see that Alice and Len, her usual uniformed officers, had already set up the board and that there was a file on her desk of the information Alice had researched on some of their suspects.

Kate quickly checked her emails and also printed off the information about the digger theft. Loading her briefcase she then left the room, switching off the lights as she left. She was just about to turn the key in the ignition when her mobile pinged the text message alert. Checking it, Kate smiled. It was from Jude, Kate's new girlfriend. They were both recovering from former poor relationships and so were content to take things really slowly, but Kate had to admit that her heart lifted when she read the message. *'Hi. Just seen the news. Is this your case? Know you're going to be busy. Ring when you can. XX'*

Quickly Kate tapped her reply. *'Yes mine. Just leaving work. Will ring once I've cooked a ping meal! XX'*

True to her word, once the ping meal was steaming on the kitchen table and Monster, the cat, had been fed, Kate rang Jude.

Knowing that Kate could not talk about ongoing cases, Jude kept the topics light and varied. "Do you think you'll make the picnic on Sunday?"

"I really don't know," replied Kate. "Is it okay to assume that I am and if I have to bail at the last minute that's also fine?"

"Yes, of course. I'll put the hamper together so all you have to do is turn up."

Other inconsequential chatter and then Kate said, "Look I'd better go. I've got some reading to do before bedtime and Monster has decided that he doesn't like sitting in the lounge on his own."

Jude laughed and made her fond farewells.

Kate looked at Monster who stared back accusingly. He was a stray cat who had adopted her at the start of the summer. At first he had been determinedly feral but food and a hands off approach from Kate had led to some domestication. He would normally meet Kate at the gate of an evening and 'talk to her' all the way to the front door. Then he would dart round to the back door and wait to be let in and fed. More recently he had taken to sitting by the closest lounge chair to the kitchen but around ten each night he asked to go out and disappeared until the following evening.

"Okay. I'm coming in but I'm not putting the telly on. I have reading to do." Appearing to ignore the implied reprimand, Monster stalked ahead with his tail saluting her and sat in his usual place. Kate followed, picking up her reading matter as she went. One read through and bed, she promised herself.

CHAPTER 19

Kate and Colm met at the doors to the morgue. "Morning Colm, you're looking very dapper this morning."

Unusually for Colm he was wearing a light grey suit rather than his normal chinos and smart jacket.

He blushed. Something that Kate felt was quite endearing for a man of Colm's size.

"I'm meeting Jenna straight from work. She's got tickets for The Lion King at Bridgewater. Is that okay, boss?"

Kate knew what he was really asking was, could he be away at a reasonable time this evening. "Of course, unless we're actually running down the murderer. Just remind me if time gets away from me."

Colm smiled his thanks as he held the door open for Kate to enter. The receptionist wasn't at her desk but they knew where Gus would be carrying out his post-mortem and made their way to his lab. Peering through the door window, Kate could see that Gus was already underway and so they quickly donned their sterile covers and entered.

Gus looked up. "Good morning detectives. I took the liberty of starting early and getting all the basics covered."

Kate nodded and Gus continued. "Mr Joseph Mallory, twenty-eight. In reasonable physical condition, perhaps a little underweight."

Kate noted that Gus seemed unaware of Mallory's true identity. Probably as well for now. Once their perpetrator was caught, they could amend the paperwork. Gus carried on, "I understand he was part of a drugs ring so I have sent hair off for analysis."

"The body shows little of use in terms of determining the cause of death. There are a couple of bruises on his back," with a nod from Gus his assistant helped him turn the corpse on one side. Gus pointed out three areas of discolouration. "I believe these are about ten days old. They have almost passed through the green/yellow phase of bruising."

With great care, Gus and his assistant lowered Joseph Mallory onto his back again.

"His head is of greatest interest. Come forward and I'll show you." Gus beckoned them over.

Kate looked down at the impassive face of Joseph Mallory. Why did people say that the dead looked like they were sleeping? In her experience people's faces got softer when they slept but the dead became solid, implacable.

"Now note," Gus said pointing, "perimortem I think our victim was hit in the face." He called to his assistant, "Karen, I want some close ups of these marks, please. Can you see Detective

Medlar?"

Kate bent closer, breathing shallowly. She could see that just below Mallory's right eye there was an indentation that had broken the skin. "There was little blood on his face when he was found, which leads me to conclude that this happened close to the time of death."

"But not the cause of death?" Colm asked.

Gus shook his head. "Perhaps when I palpate the skull we will find an injury." He moved round to the head of the counter and gently lifted Mallory's head. Kate could see that he was gently flexing his fingers across the scalp, searching for tell-tale signs in the bone underneath.

Kate hadn't realised that she was holding her breath until Gus nodded to himself and said, "Found it." Kate exhaled and Gus examined the temple. Gus turned to Kate and Colm and explained. "The temple area is the weakest part of the skull. It is known as the pterion." He spelt it out for them. "Now being thin, it is more easily breached, which need not be fatal but underneath runs the meningeal artery. If this is ruptured then your victim suffers an epidural haematoma. Which, if untreated, will result in death."

"Our classic death by blunt force injury," Colm stated.

Gus looked up and Kate thought he was smiling behind his face mask. "That is a workable hypothesis Detective Constable, but until I have examined the interior of the skull I can only tell you that he sustained this injury."

Colm rolled his eyes at Kate as Gus looked away and she smiled in sympathy. Gus was a stickler for facts.

CHAPTER 20

An hour later Gus explained, "Although I believe Mr Mallory would have eventually died from an epidural haematoma this, in fact, is not the cause of death." He looked at Colm. "Back to the drawing board."

Gus next conducted the 'Y' incision. Kate really hated this part, with organs being removed, weighed and measured. Gus began to release the lungs and exclaimed, "Ah ha!" He beckoned Kate and Colm back to the trolley edge and pointed to the remains of the trachea, where he'd separated it from the lungs. "What do you see?"

Kate bent closer and audibly gulped. "It's the silicone, isn't it?"

Colm took a deep breath. "Poor bugger. He was still alive when they put him in that box."

"So, suffocation as the cause of death?"

"That would be my guess. I will need to dissect the lungs to see how deep it went."

"But there's no petechial haemorrhaging," Kate said looking closely at Mallory's face.

Gus shook his head. "It doesn't always occur."

"Why put him in the box?" Colm looked perplexed.

"Muddy the waters? Delay finding him? Who knows what was going through their mind,"

Kate offered.

Colm hypothesised out loud. "So Mallory is in a fight with someone who, probably, accidentally gives him a blow to the temple."

Gus cut him off. "That's not what his body is telling us. If he was in a fight it was one-sided." Gus lifted Mallory's right hand and flexed both the hand knuckles and the individual finger knuckles. "There are no scrapes or signs of bruising. Our victim did not return any of the blows."

"In that case, why did our killer put him in the mould? Did he think he'd already killed him?"

Gus replied, "My thought is that he was breathing shallowly, because of the blow to his pterion. Perhaps to the point that your perpetrator did think he was already dead."

Kate took another look at the silicone in Mallory's airway. "Thanks Gus. You've given us a lot to think about. I look forward to reading your full report later."

"I'll get it to you as soon as possible, Detective Inspector."

Colm was still shaking his head as they threw the coveralls in the bin. "Poor bloke. That's not a nice way to go."

Kate agreed. "We'll head back to the station. Can you let Terry Gilbert know about what we've got so far? Mainly the result of the post-mortem and possible suspects BUT at the moment no motive, drugs or otherwise."

"Yeh. No problem."

"I'll update Bart and check in with Mike. I know it's early days but they might have found something we can work with."

CHAPTER 21

"Sorry, Kate, nothing so far. The cabinet itself was clean. Whether that's because it was wiped down after the body and mix were poured in or because our killer wore gloves, I don't know."

"What about the silicone itself? Anything we can use?"

Another shake of the head. "I've got my best tech on his clothes to see if there was any transfer with his assailant but again, so far, nothing. Zara Bakir is working on his mobile, but again little of interest to your investigation."

Kate turned away in disappointment until Mike offered, "we do have a lot of footprints around the cabinet so two of mine are at the Play House taking shoe imprints."

"Assuming the killer hasn't changed into another pair?"

Mike shrugged good-naturedly at Kate's grouse. "Sometimes it's the little things that show us the way."

Kate waved her hand in part in acknowledgement that Mike and his team were doing their best. She knew the public thought that one advert after the forensic staff have done their stuff at a scene and the results come pouring in. If only.

Returning to the incident room, Colm was

hunched over his computer reading from the screen. He turned as Kate walked in. "Do you want to know what Lennon's ABH was all about?"

Kate smiled her *yes* and Colm read from the screen. "Terence Lennon of 23 Madrigal Street, was arrested following an altercation in The Stag's Head. It is alleged that Mr Lennon thought that Daniel Parker was dealing drugs and assaulted him. Mr Parker claims he was having a quiet drink with some friends when Lennon attacked him."

"Daniel Parker?"

"According to our records, he's one of Phipps' crew, so it's likely he was dealing but Lennon couldn't prove it. Reading between the lines, I think the arresting officer knew this and so despite Parker having to have a stitch in his lip, Lennon was still only charged with ABH."

"So, why's Lennon so anti-drugs that he attacks someone he thinks is dealing?"

Kate shook his head. "See if you can find a reason, Colm. Check with the arresting officer and then we have someone we must go visit. That we should have visited sooner than this."

Colm looked mystified and Kate clarified. "Gary Phipps. If we didn't have the Dutch drugs link, we would have been all over Phipps like a rash. His boy being killed, wouldn't we?"

Colm nodded. "Yes. Once we knew Mallory was part of Phipps' business."

"Ask Alice or Len to follow up on Lennon's ABH and we'll make a move. I'm sure Phipps will be expecting us."

CHAPTER 22

It was Phipps himself who answered the door. "I wondered how long it would take before you lot turned up." He came out pulling the door to behind him. "Look, my boy's home for his lunch. Can you give me ten minutes? Then my mum'll take him back to school?"

Kate saw no harm in playing soft ball and she and Colm went back and sat in the car. "You do know that he could have a stash of drugs in there that he's now getting rid of."

Kate shook her head. "You heard what he said. He's been expecting us. He won't have a single micro dot of illegal substances in his home. And then there's his boy. We know from the Blaiseforth case that his boy comes first."

Colm nodded his head. He could see Kate's reasoning. In a few moments Mrs Phipps, Gary's mum came out of the door holding the hand of a small boy. Kate thought he was about eight and from the tugging he was doing he wasn't keen on holding his gran's hand. She maintained a firm grip.

Passing the car, she scowled at them both and then stomped on, half-fighting the small boy. Kate thought he ought to give in gracefully. There was no way he was going to win against his gran.

Kate returned to Gary's door. He was already there waiting for them. Half-abashedly he said, "Thanks for waiting."

Kate smiled benignly, "No problem, Gary. You know me. You be straight with me and I'll be straight with you." Kate was gently reminding him of their last encounter where Phipps had almost become an accessory to murder.

"Sure! Come through." Phipps led them into the front room. Not a lot had changed since the last time Kate was there. Phipps himself was a little less suave when Kate had her first encounter with him but he still liked to present the face of a businessman. He sat in a single chair and nodded towards the sofa for Kate and Colm, "So this is about Joe Mallory, yes?"

"We are indeed investigating the murder of Mr Joseph Mallory. I understand he was one of your boys, Gary?"

Phipps shook his head, "Nothing that formal. He did a few jobs for me, that's all."

"And what sort of jobs would those be Mr Phipps?" Colm asked.

"Oh, he did a bit of gardening. Helped a mate of mine out with some painting and decorating. In fairness to him he wasn't afraid of hard work."

"So, how long had you known Mr Mallory?"

Phipps sat back in his seat, put one leg over the other and rested his hands on the arms of the chair. A study in relaxation. "Joe moved onto the estate about a year, maybe eighteen months ago."

"From where?"

"Somewhere up north," Phipps said.

"So why did he come to Eashire? Or more specifically the Camworth Estate?"

"He'd got a job with some builder and a flat, well they call it a flat. I'd call it a bedsit, over in those blocks on the Bridgewater Road."

Kate knew the ones he meant. They were ugly things. Probably a '60s development. All brutal concrete and bulky shapes. The road acted as a boundary line between the Camworth Estate and Eashire county town.

"I saw him hanging around at the weekends. Met him a few times in the pub and got chatting. You know how it is."

Kate wasn't sure she did know how it was but it seemed that Mallory/Bradley had done a good job of getting in with Phipps. "Can you think of any reason why Mallory would be at the Play House on Monday night?"

A shrug of the shoulders, "I assumed he had a girl there."

"But you don't know who..."

Another shrug of the shoulders.

"Do you know who he was working for? You said some builder?"

"Oh, he got the sack from that job. Someone complained about him to the management. Said he was dealing drugs. I know for a fact he wasn't."

"Do you know who made this complaint and

the firm?"

"Don't know the bloke who dobbed him in but the business is that one working down on the canal basin, coz Joe was there for most of his time."

"Would that be Bridgewater Civil Engineering?" Colm asked, looking back through his notes.

Yet another shrug, "Sounds like it could be."

"What sorts of jobs did Mr Mallory do for you, Gary?"

"I've told you. A bit of gardening…"

Kate held her hands up. "Okay Gary, let's all agree that you're an ordinary businessman. We take that as read. Now what did Mr Mallory do?"

Phipps eyed Kate speculatively. "Okay. Mallory was a good organiser. He knew where everyone was and what they had. He knew what should be coming in. And he didn't sample the merchandise."

"That sounds awfully like your deputy or assistant."

"Nah. If he was anything, he was a supervisor. I don't need an assistant."

"But he knew about distribution. What about your sources?"

Phipps smiled. "No, Inspector. Some things are classified."

Kate was sure they weren't going to get anything relevant from Phipps, so she just played the game. "Can you think of anyone who would have a grudge against Mr Mallory?"

"Well, apart from the bloke at his work I can't think of anyone. He was popular enough round here."

"And you've no idea who this bloke was?"

Phipps made a real show of thinking hard before shaking his head. "No, sorry. I'm not sure Joe mentioned it and if he did it didn't stick."

Kate stood and thanked Phipps for his time. Back in the car she berated herself. "I said we shouldn't get side-tracked by the drugs thing but that's exactly what we've done."

Colm looked perplexed. "Sorry boss?"

"Where haven't we searched that should have been one of our first ports of call?"

Colm shrugged and Kate supplied the answer. "Mallory's flat." She pulled out her phone. "I'll see if Len or Alice can meet us there with the keys, save going back into town."

CHAPTER 23

If Kate thought the outside of Mallory's flat looked grim, the inside was worse. Dark ungainly stains crept across the concrete walls and floors and the lift smelt like it had been used as the local urinal. Despite the flat being on the fifth floor, Kate was fully prepared to use the stairs, even though Len lumbered behind complaining of the climb.

Mallory's flat was as good or as bad as any Kate had seen before where a young, single man lived on his own. Empty beer cans littered the coffee table and dirty crockery filled the sink. However, the bed did look like the sheets had been changed and the bathroom as though it had been used.

Donning protective gloves and footwear, they searched the flat. They found nothing pertaining to Bradley and very little to Mallory. Colm took his laptop as evidence, otherwise there was little of worth to their investigation to examine.

Sighing, Kate said, "Okay. Len, would you take the laptop and book it in with Mike? Thanks for coming out with the keys."

Len took the evidence bag that Colm held out to him and left.

"Right. I feel better now we've done what we

should have done. Now let's go and find out who had it in for Mallory at the canal basin."

❖ ❖ ❖

The building site was as busy as before but this time the site cabin was occupied by Gail Miller, the site 'foreman'. Kate and Colm showed their warrant cards and explained that they had spoken with Gary Pugh. Miller was thirty-something. Her hair was sensibly short for a hard hat and she wore working jeans and a checked shirt. "Is this about our digger?"

"It isn't, but I noticed that there is a digger behind the Play House. I understand your firm has been awarded the contract for the car park, is that why it's there?"

Miller frowned and flicked through some sheets in a tray on her desk. "That's strange. We've not sent a digger there yet. I'd better go and look."

Kate held her hand up. "You can look and confirm whether it's yours or not but you must not touch it or move it."

Miller went to protest but Kate spoke across her, "I'm sorry but it may have been used in a crime. At the moment it is being examined for evidence."

Her hands ran through her hair; an action Kate recognised in herself when frustration was getting the better of her.

"I assume a digger needs a key to start it? Where are they kept at night?"

Miller pointed to a board screwed to the wall. Piercing its surface were a number of hooks and below each one, a label. Kate walked across to take a closer look. The top row of hooks were for diggers, beneath were trucks and below that, more labels. Most of which she didn't know what the vehicles were.

"I'm sorry about the digger being out of bounds. How many people have access to this office? Would anyone notice if a set of keys was missing?"

"During working hours anyone can come in and out and I'm not always here. At night I check that the keys are there."

Kate looked thoughtful but said nothing more about the digger. "The reason for our presence today is that we understand you sacked a Mr Joseph Mallory and I need to know the details behind it."

Miller frowned in concentration. "Mallory. The name rings a bell but I can't think why. Hang on a sec." She swivelled her chair to face the large computer screen and began to track across several pages. "Yes. Mallory. Joseph. We sacked him June last year. So that's more than a year ago."

"Do your records show why he was sacked?"

Another mouse click. "Ah. He was still on his six months' probation and another worker accused him of both drug taking and dealing. We have a no drugs policy. We even do random drugs tests. So, if true, this was a sackable offence."

"What did Mallory say? What evidence did this other chap have?"

Miller frowned again. "I remember this now. Mallory offered no defence. He refused to take a drug's test or turn out his pockets. I tried to reason with him. Told him his actions were giving credence to the allegation but he just walked."

"What about his pay?"

"Payroll would have sent him a cheque for whatever he was owed."

"Who made the allegation? I assume he was a trustworthy soul if you believed him?"

"Yes. It was Terry Lennon. He's had a real thing about drugs and dealers since his sister's problems."

Kate looked enquiring and Miller continued. "I don't know the details but Terry's sister is in a bad way following years of drug abuse. Terry blames the dealers who kept giving her the stuff even when they could see it was killing her. He's a real crusader."

"Could we have a chat with Mr Lennon, please?"

Miller shook her head. "Sorry, Terry's not in today."

"Is that expected?" Kate's suspicious mind already wondering if Terry was more involved with the murder than he'd led them to believe."

But Miller's next words deflated that thought bubble, "Oh yes. Every so often he needs a day off to take his sister to a hospital appointment. It's a specialist clinic and it's miles away. I'm not sure where but it takes all day."

Kate thanked her for her time and she and Colm left with much to discuss.

CHAPTER 24

"He could be our murderer," Colm said excitedly as they climbed back into the car. "I knew he was lying about his time at the Play House."

"Certainly a possibility," Kate replied cautiously.

Colm carried on with his reconstruction of the crime. "Lennon sees Mallory in the theatre. Thinks he is doing a drugs deal. They get into a fight. We know Lennon is handy with his fists. Mallory hits his temple and Lennon thinks he's killed him. Puts him in the mould thing to cover his tracks and delay the body being found."

Kate nodded. "It works but what about the silicone?"

Colm looked puzzled. "What about it?"

"Jim said you'd need to know the proportions to get the right consistency. Too much of one thing and it doesn't pour. Too little and it doesn't set. Whoever covered Lennon used the right proportions."

Colm slumped but offered a defence, "Lennon uses silicone in his job? Or he just got lucky." It sounded weak even to his own ears.

Kate offered a consolation, "We do need to talk to Mr Lennon. You find his address. I want to check something." Kate reached for the satchel bag she'd thrown all Terry Gilbert's files into and pulled out the one containing a record of all his meetings with Bradley. Starting from the earliest pages she soon found what she was looking for. "Thought so!"

Colm was writing down the address he'd found. "What?"

"The drugs accusation was a set up. Mallory knew about Lennon's obsession and deliberately let him overhear a supposed drugs deal one night in the pub."

"And then didn't offer a defence," Colm nodded his understanding. "That then gets him sympathy with Phipps and a reason to be hanging around during the day. "Clever!" A note of admiration had crept into his tone.

Kate agreed. "But could that trick have led to his death? Lennon isn't one to let go of that kind of thing, is he? And even if the death was an accident, what about the silicone? That's our stumbling block. You can check with Ms Miller about the silicone but I don't think it's something Lennon would have come across."

"So, we've got two drug angles: one involves an obsessed anti-drugs campaigner and the other organised crime."

"Or, we still have the option of it being nothing to do with drugs. I'm still not convinced that we have the full story from Jason Brooks and Jade Froude."

"Well, at least we do have several options," said Colm cheerfully. "We've had some right stinkers where there's no-one to accuse."

Kate agreed. There was nothing more irksome than a case with no threads. Her concern with this case was that she thought they may be led to follow the wrong thread because of Mallory's real identity. "Okay, let's go and see if Lennon is back from his sister's hospital appointment and then we need to speak to Mr Henderson, owner of the theatre company and the only other person who was in the theatre at the same time as Mallory."

CHAPTER 25

Lennon lived in, probably an ex-council house given its state of disrepair, on the Camworth Estate. Only streets away from Phipps' home. Kate wondered if the two had ever crossed one another's paths. Bound to have, Eashire wasn't that big. Colm pointed out the car parked in a marked disabled bay in front of the address. "That's probably Lennon's."

Stepping along the weed-cracked path and avoiding where the stones had disappeared, they arrived at a sagging front door. Layers of paint gave witness to its many lives. There was no doorbell, so Kate used the letterbox knocker and they waited.

At the point where Kate was ready to knock again, the door was tugged open and a harried Terry Lennon peered out. He noted who it was and said sharply, "Go into the front room. I'm just helping my sister get into bed." With that he left the door open for Kate and Colm to follow. Kate saw Lennon disappear into a back room, having opened the door to the front room.

Whilst they waited, Kate assessed the look on Lennon's face when he'd opened the door. It hadn't been fear. Not even curiosity. Did he know why they were back? From the next room they could hear the deeper tones of Lennon but not those of the person he was talking to. Kate could tell that, whoever it was, Lennon was being kind and conciliatory.

Looking around the room, Kate made a guess that the sofa and chairs were second hand and accepted because they were available, not because they suited the room. The only other furniture was the large telly fitted to the chimney breast wall. The paper was faded and in places showed dark lines where pictures may once have hung.

Lennon returned. "Sorry about that. My sister had a hospital appointment and it always takes it out of her."

"I'm sorry to hear that. Is it a serious condition?"

Lennon's eyes darkened. "It's a fatal condition, unless I win the pools," this last was said with a mirthless laugh.

Colm was interested and asked, "What could the money do?"

Lennon sighed and got comfortable in his seat. Kate had the sense that he was used to telling the story to come. "Kelly got in with the wrong sort when she was a teenager. My mum couldn't do anything with her. She'd lock her in her room and Kelly'd climb out the window. Then she found a boyfriend, Simon." Lennon spat out the name with obvious distaste. "He got her hooked on heroin. The only good thing he did for her was to die and that brought her to her senses. She got rehab and has been clean for three years this October."

"But it's left her with health issues?" Kate offered.

"Yeh. She had all these infections and it's messed up her heart valves. Her heart can't get blood around properly any more."

"So is she on the transplant list?" Colm asked.

Lennon shook his head. "Nah. Problem is coz of what they cut the heroin with, she's got all these dead bits on most of her major organs so she's not well enough for the op."

"So why the need for money?"

"There's this special therapy in the States. They reckon they can reverse a lot of the problems Kelly's got and manage to reconstruct her heart valves. But we're talking about thousands, or more like tens of thousands. Where am I going to get that kind of money from?"

Colm breathed out, "Hence the need for money. I get it. Have you tried one of those crowd funder things on social media?"

Lennon shook his head. "All that sort of stuff is beyond me." He shook himself. "Anyway, you didn't come 'ere to talk about Kelly. Is this still about the dead man?"

Kate nodded. "When we asked you if you knew the dead man, you said you didn't."

Lennon scratched at the stubble on his face. "I don't think you did. Or if you did, you didn't give me a name. You was on about what I saw or 'eard when I was working on the trap door."

Kate could have kicked herself. Had they really not mentioned Mallory's name? She tried to recall the interview. She had to concede Lennon could be telling the truth.

"The dead man is Joseph Mallory."

Kate watched as the implications of the name dawned on Lennon. He was either a very good actor or he really had no idea that it was Mallory who had been murdered. "Joseph Mallory! That little toerag who used to work for my firm? You know he's a drug dealer, don't you?"

"We understand you shopped him to the bosses?"

"Too right I did. What with Kelly I don't hold with drugs and drugs on a building site is just asking for trouble."

Kate went in for the kill. "So if you didn't know it was Mallory, what is it you're not telling us?"

"I've told you everyfing!" The mock outrage did not convince any of them. "Look. I'm sorry if you don't believe me but I've had all sorts of run-ins with your lot and you make me twitchy. Maybe that's what's making you think I'm not being straight up."

Kate thought that was a possibility but she could see from Colm's face that he wasn't buying it. "If you change your mind, Mr Lennon, or something else occurs to you," *give him a get out clause*, "please get in touch." She handed over one of her business cards.

CHAPTER 26

As they drove away, Colm spat a "Pah" out. "Lying little sod. He did it. He knew it was Mallory."

"I'm not so sure. Like you, I think he's still lying about something but I think he was being quite genuine about not knowing it was Mallory. I think he heard or saw something that was only made important when he heard there was a dead body."

Colm sighed and Kate could see the disagreement from the tension in his body. "We'll find out what it is. Don't worry. Right," she continued more briskly. "Back to the station and then you go off and enjoy your theatre night with Jenna."

"Are you sure boss? I don't mind hanging on if you want."

"No, you go off. Perhaps by tomorrow Mike and his team will have come up with something."

"Thanks boss. What's the plan for tomorrow?"

"We need to interview Henderson. Mainly because he was in the theatre at the same time as Mallory.

◆ ◆ ◆

Close to ninety minutes later, Kate was swimming up and down the local pool in the adult only session. Jude was steaming up and down the 'serious swimmers' lane. Kept separate for those who just had to power through. Kate knew Jude would join her once she'd done her laps.

As she gently swam breast stroke up and down, she reviewed all the interviews they'd done over the last few days. If Jade Froude was the contact point for getting drugs in Eashire, it made sense that it was her, Mallory had come to see. So, what had gone wrong? And was it related to the larger drug cartel the Dutch seemed to think was being hidden behind the theatre company?

And then there was the digger missing from the canal basin site. Had it really been used in the cash machine heist and she had come across the means by accident? Terry Lennon was a connection between these two crimes: the heist and the murder. Was that coincidental?

Kate jumped as a voice said in her ear, "Penny for them!" Then she laughed as she realised that Jude was swimming alongside her. "How's it going? The case?"

"Early days. At the moment we have more questions than answers but hopefully we will start to get them soon."

"I don't suppose you've thought about a meal tonight, have you?"

Kate grinned. "I'll have you know my ping cuisine serves me very well."

Jude shook her head in mock despair. "How about coming back to my place and I'll cook for us? Shelley's out for the night."

Kate had only met Shelley the once. She was Jude's flat mate. She seemed okay but was a bit too full of herself for Kate's liking. Now the thought of a home cooked meal and time spent with Jude alone sounded like a healing balm to the rigours of her day. "Yes, please."

"Oh good. In that case I'm going to get out now and get off home and make a start. You follow on when you're ready. You've got your car with you, haven't you?"

"I have and I will."

Kate watched as Jude lazily cut through the water to the steps. Her toned body looked fantastic with the water draining from her as she arose from the water. Kate felt her body flush with desire.

CHAPTER 27

Delightful smells of cooking were already wafting through the flat when Kate arrived. "Come and talk to me in the kitchen," Jude said.

Kate followed her into the kitchen diner; although the table and two chairs almost filled the space set aside as the 'diner' end of the combination. The kitchen was equally small, but Jude moved around it with an athletic beauty that Kate found quite mesmerising.

Jude liked to cook and as a fitness instructor she worked hard on eating the right things, which was why she despaired of Kate's hopeless eating habits. She had even volunteered to make up freezer portions so that Kate could ping to her heart's content but eating fresh, unprocessed foods. Kate hadn't yet taken her up on the offer, but she might.

"What are you creating?" 'Cooking' seemed too mundane a word as she watched Jude's kitchen performance.

"It's a sort of vegetarian bolognaise with some additions and we're having it with penne rather than spaghetti. Sound okay?"

"Sounds fantastic. Especially as I'm not the one making it."

In a matter of minutes they were sat at the table for two spooning the delicious mouthfuls in between their chatter. Jude knew to stay clear of Kate's case and so the banter began with Jude's success with a woman who had started to attend the gym last February to lose weight so she could donate a kidney to her sister. "So she's hit her target weight but she enjoys the gym so much that she's going to keep coming once she's recovered from her op."

"Did you get the local paper involved?"

"We did. They ran a piece about the gym giving their services for free in the spring and they want to run another one after, hopefully, the successful transplant."

They'd shared brief details about family and childhood but each time they met a little more was revealed. Whilst Kate helped Jude wash up and tidy the kitchen they talked about childhood tasks.

Kate offered, "My job on a Sunday evening was to clean the kitchen from floor to ceiling, including the oven, so that I could listen to the top forty hits."

"Oh yes. The top forty. Did you used to make tapes of your favourite songs?" They smiled at their shared experiences. "And inevitably at some point the cassette recorder would chew up the tape and you would have to rewind it onto the spool!"

"Using a pencil!" they laughed. They were very comfortable in one another's company. Kate couldn't remember feeling this relaxed around

Robyn, her previous girlfriend. Robyn had been a highflier in London's art scene and Kate, an ambitious detective, working her way through the ranks. The problem had been that she'd had a wandering eye and saw Kate's inability to make opening night parties as an excuse to find other company. Now Kate kicked herself that she'd allowed Robyn to do that to her several times. Eventually she had pulled on her self-respect and left the relationship. Hence her move to Eashire.

Sat on the sofa facing one another, Kate had an overwhelming urge to stroke Jude's face. She reached out her hand and Jude nuzzled it gently before turning away to put her cup on the coffee table. Turning back, she lent in for a kiss. The kiss was soft and sweet, promising more.

"When's Shelley due back?"

"Tomorrow morning."

"Oh good!" murmured Kate as she lost herself in the warmth of the moment.

CHAPTER 28

Kate woke early and felt energised about her day ahead. She had thought about hitting the gym first but she knew Jude would be there and the thought of meaningless chitchat after last night was too much to contemplate. Instead, she readied herself with a brisk walk round the block, being joined on the home stretch by Monster. Kate wasn't sure where he'd come from but one minute she was listening to the distant hum of traffic and the next she was having a one-sided conversation, all on Monster's side.

At the station, Kate's first port of call was Mike's forensic suite. Despite the early hour, Mike, well Kate assumed one of them was Mike, clad in their sterile suits and face masks it was difficult to tell, was already at work. One of the figures was lying on 'his' back shining a strong light through the opaque silicone form that had been Mallory's coffin. Meanwhile another anonymous suit was shining an equally strong light from the top, in the same place.

Kate waited until there was a pause in the work and then knocked at the window. The standing figure acknowledged her presence and switched off the light before moving to the door. Once outside, he removed his face mask. It was Mike.

"Good morning, Kate."

"Morning Mike. Anything?" Kate nodded to the room he'd just exited.

Mike smiled. "Well we may just have some bits and pieces for you." With that he began to shrug his way out of the suit. "Come and see." He gestured when his head and arms were free from their sterile covering.

In his office, Mike reached for a plaster shape. It didn't resemble anything much, Kate decided but Mike looked pleased with himself. "Do you remember that cavity in the silicone where we thought our instigator may have pushed the body's knees down?"

Kate nodded. Mike hadn't thought they would get very much and looking at what he now held in his hands she was sure he was right but he still looked pleased with himself.

Turning the cast a little, Mike began to point out some features. "As I thought, the deeper cavity began to fill with the still liquid silicone but the upper level was more solid, so we have managed to get a cast of a thumb and the little finger."

Now that Mike had pointed out what the two appendages were, Kate could see the two digits. He continued, "Unfortunately, it was still not solid enough to retain finer details like the prints but it does show us a couple of details." He pointed to the thicker protrusion, "I think your man was wearing a plaster or some covering.

Can you see the slightly different texture and the slight ridge on the edges?"

Kate bent her head closer and then could see what Mike was showing her. She nodded. "So, there's every chance he or she is still wearing one or has a cut or scar on their thumb. Well, that's something."

"Oh, but that's not all." Mike turned the object again to have the little finger uppermost. "Your murderer is wearing a ring on his little finger." He showed the elements in the cast. "It's not clear but it looks like it may have a design on the surface. Perhaps something like a signet ring with initials carved on top."

Now Kate stared intently at the area. She could see the ring, but the surface was ill-formed. "The silicone was still too wet to give us more definition," Mike explained.

"Even so, that's two good bits of info. Thanks, Mike." Kate turned to leave.

"Don't rush off. I'll update you on our other results."

Kate stopped and turned back as Mike bent to one of the trays on his desk. He flipped through a couple of sheets as though reminding himself of what they contained and then looked up.

"Okay, the phone is a wash out. Nothing on there to indicate who he was meeting or why he was in the theatre. Most of the traffic is just checking on where people are, what they're doing. But nothing incriminating."

Kate sighed. Phones were often such a good source of information.

Mike continued, "Zara's had a quick look at the laptop Len brought in. Nothing of interest in terms of potential suspects. I'll send through what she's got."

Damn. Another dead end. "What about the silicone cast itself?"

Mike beamed. "Well, there we *may*, and I hasten to add that at this point it is only a *may*, have some better news. We've discovered that by shining a strong light from both sides of the mould we are able to see through its opaqueness. It's not crystal clear but it does allow us to see if anything has been trapped there."

Kate held her breath. She knew Mike was leading up to something.

"And we think we may have detected two hairs."

Before Kate could get excited, Mike held up his hand. "It is too early to tell whether they've come from our victim or our murderer AND we may or may not get DNA from them but there's a chance."

Kate could have hugged him. Forensic evidence was always so important to a jury. Legal argument was one thing but forensic evidence sealed it for them. Mike too was obviously pleased but he did put a warning hand on Kate's arm. "We're still only talking about possibilities, Kate. Don't build your hopes up too much."

CHAPTER 29

The morning was just getting better and better Kate thought, as she took the stairs to her office two at a time. Colm was already at his desk but no sign of Alice or Len. Kate checked her watch. It was still early. "Morning Colm, how did last night go?"

Colm turned from his desk and grinned. "It was wonderful. I've not been to the theatre before for anything more than the Christmas panto but last night's show was amazing. Jenna loves the theatre so I reckon I'm going to be seeing much more in the future."

"I am pleased. Did you go for a meal as well?"

"Yes. Jenna had organised a pre-show meal at the restaurant next door. It was just two courses and I kept looking at my watch in case we over ran but it worked out really well."

"If Jenna's such a theatre fan you ought to arrange a weekend in London and grab one of two shows while you're there." As she said it, Kate thought it was an idea she might also think about for her and Jude. She'd need to check that she liked theatre first though. And even if she didn't, they could still do a weekend of sightseeing. Or show Jude all her old haunts.

"That's an idea, boss."

Further comment was stopped by the arrival

of Alice and Len. Kate called a quick meeting and updated them on Mike's forensics and what she and Colm had found out so far. "So, in summary, we have a possible suspect in Terry Lennon but I didn't notice a ring on any of his fingers, did you Colm?"

Colm shook his head and Len offered, "Some building sites don't allow jewellery on Health and Safety grounds so perhaps he takes it off when he's working."

Colm shook his head again, "No. In that case he'd have been wearing it yesterday. He wasn't working at all yesterday." He added as an afterthought, "Much as I like Lennon for it."

The meeting was interrupted by the ring of Kate's desk phone. Alice, being closest, answered it. "One minute, sir, I'll get her." She mouthed 'Bart' as she handed the receiver over.

"Good morning, sir. Oh no. Yes, we're on our way. Has Mike been informed? Right. Thank you, sir."

Kate put the phone down and looked at her team, "Jim Wheelan has just called in to say that there was another body in his moulding cabinet!"

Stunned faces looked back at her. Colm asked, "Does this put the Dutch angle out of the frame, then?"

Kate mused a moment, "I think that's going to depend on who we find is the latest victim."

"I thought the cabinet was coming in to the

labs," Colm said as he reached for his jacket from the back of his chair.

Kate nodded. "Yes, I thought so, too. I'll need to ask Mike about that. Okay. Alice, Len. Keep on with the background searches of the theatre company. Have you looked at the owner, Henderson, yet?"

The pair shook their heads.

"Right, Alice, you take a close look at him. And Len will you do the same for Jason Brooks, the director? I want everything there is to know about those two."

Kate followed Colm out of the room and turned back as she reached the door, "I'll let you know as soon as we have an ID."

CHAPTER 30

This time they entered the theatre from the back. Stan was at his desk and stood as they arrived. "I have copied the names of people who were here late last night. There's more of them than last time because rehearsal went on later."

Kate acknowledged his comment and carried on through to the workshop. This time there was no need to ask the way. A familiar scene met her eyes as she entered. The cabinet was taped off and scenes of crime were paddling about inside it in their paper shoes and overalls. Jim Wheelan was over by the headless statues.

Wheelan turned as he heard Kate and Colm approach. His face was grey and Kate saw that his lower lip was trembling. Kate reached out a hand to steady him and accidentally knocked one of the statues. To her surprise it wobbled. They were much lighter than she had expected. "I thought these were solid."

Wheelan smiled weakly. "No they're hollow. I shall need to create a plug for the bottom so we can fill the bases with sand to steady them."

"Why a plug?" Colm asked.

Patiently Wheelan explained, "So that when we have to pack them up for transit they're not too heavy!"

The conversation seemed to have steadied

Wheelan and Kate felt it was now reasonable to ask her questions. "Can you take me through what you found this morning Mr Wheelan?"

Wheelan took in a deep breath and exhaled slowly. "I came in and put on the lights. The cabinet was there behind the tape. Then I noticed that the mess your chaps had cleaned up was back so I went to have a closer look. Not over the tape," he hastened to add, "and then I saw the blood." He pointed to the far side of the cabinet where the photographer was crouched low and snapping shots. "That wasn't there before."

Colm put a hand on Wheelan's shoulder. "Thanks, Jim. Would you like to go up to the Falstaff Bar? The boss and I will have a look down here and then come up."

Wheelan nodded and walked away. His gait was slower and his shoulders sagged. Finding two bodies will do that, Kate thought.

Once suited up, Kate and Colm ducked under the tape. Keeping to the edge, they made their way round to the pool of blood, now being sampled by another suited person. Close by, Kate saw a piece of timber with obvious blood splatter on one end.

Colm hazarded a scenario, "Looks like our victim was hit, probably around the head with that wood and then into the mould like Mallory."

"Umm!" Kate agreed. "But this time I think there was a lot more pre-meditation. Mallory's death and immersion I can see as panic over an accidental death, but this I think was planned. So why?"

"We'll probably have a better answer for that when we know who it is."

Kate agreed. She went and spoke with Mike, ensuring that she crossed as little of the crime scene as possible. "Morning, again, Mike."

He acknowledged her presence with a nod. "How come the cabinet was still here and not at the lab?"

Mike sighed. "Sorry, Kate. That's down to me. The cabinet wouldn't go in our normal vehicle so I organised the larger one to collect it today."

Kate understood. "I'm going to be upstairs interviewing. Will you ring when you're at the release stage?"

"Sure. No problem." Mike went back to his minute examination of the surface of the cabinet and Kate crossed back under the tape.

"Okay Colm, you go and take a statement from Jim Wheelan and I'll ask Montgomery to check staff lists."

CHAPTER 31

Mr Wheelan's story about the previous evening was similar to that of the Monday. He caught his normal bus. Other people were in and out all afternoon. And no, he had no idea who could be in there. Montgomery's list also told the same story: no-one appeared to be missing.

"Let's go and talk with Stan and what his log can tell us."

Even here the story had its repetitions. Most staff had been in until later because of the rehearsal but by seven-thirty only a few remained. This time, however, no-one had signed in."

"So there were no strangers yesterday at all?" Kate asked.

Stan clarified, "We had a domestic supplies delivery yesterday afternoon but they were gone by three-thirty, look." He pointed to an earlier entry that showed a John from Eashire Solutions had been in and out in under ten minutes.

"That was our only stranger," Stan emphasised.

"So it's got to be one of those still signed in that's dead," Colm suggested.

"Apparently everyone has signed out but the same thing happened to that other fellow, Mallory, didn't it?" Stan offered.

"Or our victim arrived after the theatre closed. Stan what time did you leave?"

"Eight thirty precisely," Stan stated, almost standing to attention.

"And did you lock up?"

Stan explained, "The stage door was locked so anyone still here would need to leave by the front door and have keys to them."

"Do you know who was still here when you left last night, Stan?"

Stan checked his log and pointed, just those four."

The names he pointed out were, Jason Brooks, Julia Montgomery, Jon Bell and Daniel Henderson.

"They've not signed out at all. Why's that?" Kate looked at Stan.

"Once I've gone off duty," he said, "and this area is closed down, they go out the front but there's no record of the times because they have to have keys. Do you see?"

"Well, there are our suspects, boss," Colm said cheerfully.

Kate turned back to Stan. "Is there anyway, at all, that someone might have come into the theatre without you seeing them?"

Stan solemnly shook his head and added, "Not even for a loo break. Since what's happened, I've locked the stage door if I've had to leave my post even for a second."

"Could someone have let someone in after

you've locked it?" Kate persisted.

Stan looked uneasy. "Well, I suppose so. See it's a fire exit so it's got to be able to be opened from the inside at all times."

"So, if someone wanted to, they could have opened the door and then re-latched it?"

Stan nodded miserably. "But they'd have to have been in the theatre already." Apparently, it was only just occurring to Stan that the murderer was someone he knew.

CHAPTER 32

A call from Mike dictated their next move. This time, he had all the necessary tools close at hand and was already cutting through the middle point of the cabinet. As the two halves were separated and the body was released, Kate was aware that this time the sound was much wetter than when Mallory's body had been released.

"I thought so," said Wheelan, who had come to the edge of the tape to view the process.

Kate could see that the top part of the mould was ill- defined and that some of the silicone was still viscous. She looked to Wheelan for an explanation.

"I haven't ordered any more curing agent. Looking at it," he nodded his head towards the cabinet, "I would say that he mixed one amount, using the right ratio but needed more for the top part and didn't have enough curing agent."

Kate understood. She now moved in for a closer look, "Oh bugger!"

Mike looked at her, "Do you know the victim, Kate?"

Kate nodded slowly, "Yes. He was a suspect. His name is Terry. Terrance Lennon. He was in the theatre Monday night."

Kate could see that there was blood visible in the mould. It had seeped and mixed in with the liquid. Glowing a translucent pink as the lights of the team moved around the cabinet.

Colm exhaled noisily, "There goes my only theory."

Colm and Kate stepped back to talk quietly as the forensic team carried on with its work. Mike had explained that Gus couldn't make it so they were going to transport the body in situ to the morgue so that Gus could see it before releasing the body from the mould.

"We'd better go and see the sister. Kelly, wasn't it?"

Colm checked his notes and nodded. "How the hell did he end up dead?"

"Best guess? He saw or heard something Monday night and tried to blackmail our murderer."

"Blackmail? Why?"

"You heard him yesterday. He's desperate for money for Kelly's treatment."

"Silly sod," Colm sighed under his breath as Kate took her farewell of Mike.

"Off to see the next of kin, Mike. Can you tell Gus to go ahead with the PM? We just need to know if it was the blow to the head or the immersion that killed him."

Mike acknowledged her comment and returned to instructing his team.

"Come on then, Colm. We need to find out when and why Lennon was here. And I'll ring HQ and let Alice and Len know the identity of our new victim. I'll also arrange for a Family Liaison Officer to come to the Lennon house. I think Kelly is going to need some support after we've been there."

CHAPTER 33

It took a while for Kelly Lennon to answer the door and when Kate saw the hospital drip stand, the oxygen cylinder and heard the wheeze from Kelly, she understood why. Kelly barely glanced at the warrant cards before turning back and leading the way inside. Following her, excruciatingly slowly, back to the front room, Kate wondered how Kelly would cope on her own.

Finally, sat in a chair with her equipment and medicines close to hand, Kelly removed her oxygen mask. Her voice was weak and rasped, "I'll try and talk without this," jerking at the mask, "otherwise you may not work out what I'm saying."

"Ms Lennon, we came to see your brother late yesterday afternoon and he had just helped you to bed. Was that the last time you saw him yesterday?"

Kelly looked afraid, "He's dead, isn't he? I knew when he didn't bring me my breakfast this morning that something must have happened."

Kate spoke slowly and softly, "I'm afraid a body has been found at the Play House and we think it is your brother."

Silent tears ran down Kelly's face and through them she said, "What's he got himself involved with now? Another get rich quick scheme?"

"At this stage we don't know why Terry was killed, but I'm sorry to say it is murder," Kate said.

Kelly didn't seem surprised by this revelation. She said, more to herself than her company, "He was doing it for me. I know he was, but I wish he hadn't."

Kate seized on this, "What was he doing, Kelly?"

Kelly leant back in the chair, slipped the mask on and breathed deeply with her eyes shut. Several breaths later she was respiring normally again and removed the contraption. "It doesn't matter now. I can tell you everything. He can't get into any more trouble, can he?"

Kate and Colm waited as she closed her eyes again and started. "Terry came into me last night and brought me supper and a drink. Whilst I was eating he told me he had a plan. He'd heard and seen something that someone would pay a lot for not having it in the open." She opened her eyes and looked directly at Kate, "I knew he meant he was going to blackmail someone, but he didn't tell me who or what it was he'd got over them."

"So, I'm assuming Terry went out last night?"

Kelly nodded and explained, "I have my emergency line," she pointed to the pendant around her neck. "So Terry knows someone will come if he's at work or out."

"What time did he go out last night?"

"I'm not sure exactly but it was sometime during Eastenders. I heard the front door slam."

Colm used his phone to check television listings and Kate carried on with her questioning.

"Were you not worried this morning when Terry didn't turn up?"

"Of course," said with some asperity.

"And you didn't try his phone?"

"By the time I woke up and realised Terry hadn't been in, it was too late to phone. They don't like them having their phones on at work. Too much of a distraction, they say."

Colm put his phone away and Kate raised a questioning eyebrow. "Eastenders was on between seven-thirty and eight last night."

"Kelly, is it all right if my colleague searches Terry's room, in case he's left any evidence of who he was meeting last night?"

Kelly nodded her agreement, "It's the front bedroom."

Colm left the room and Kate offered to make Kelly a hot drink. "Have you had breakfast if Terry didn't bring it in?"

Kelly nodded to an empty plate on the side table. "I can get my own food, but Terry likes to bring me tea and toast in bed," she smiled as more tears rolled down her face.

Back with a hot drink, Kate asked, "Is there anyone we can call to come and be with you?

Parents? Aunt or uncle?"

Kelly shook her head. "Did Terry tell you what a waste of space I was as a youngster?" She didn't wait for a reply, "Terry was the only one to stand by me."

"Will you manage on your own?"

More tears and a shake of her head. Kate's heart went out to her. All right she had made some pretty major mistakes in her life but wasn't she paying for it now?

"Look, I have arranged for a Family Liaison Officer to come and stay for a while. She should be here soon. Perhaps you need to think about contacting Social Services. They could probably organise a care package so you can stay in your own home."

A lacklustre shrug and more tears. The silence that descended was broken by a firm knock on the door. Kate offered to answer it. It was, as she expected, the FLO. Val Owen was an experienced FLO and more than used to the situation that was now before her. In hushed tones, Kate gave her the background to the situation and then introduced Val to Kelly.

Whilst Val was getting to know Kelly, Kate went and waited at the bottom of the stairs for Colm. When he came down, he had Terry's laptop in an evidence bag.

"No sign of his phone but that's probably on him."

Kate looked in through the door to see Val

and Kelly deep in conversation.

Kate called out, "Okay Kelly, we're going now. Val you have my contact details?"

There was no response from Kelly but Val smiled her acknowledgement.

Colm echoed Kate's own thoughts. "There must be someone she can call on."

"Perhaps when we get back to the station, Alice or Len will have found out a bit more about Terry's family background.

CHAPTER 34

Lodging Terry's laptop in the boot, Colm said, "I don't think we're going to find anything useful on it. It's not password protected and his search history is either porn or the therapy treatment that might help Kelly. He was looking at in excess of fifty thousand pounds and that was without the flights and accommodation for him."

Kate looked thoughtful and Colm continued his monologue. "Where was a bloke like Terry Lennon going to get that kind of money? You know, I don't really blame him for trying a bit of blackmail."

Kate looked surprised and Colm tried to explain himself. "No, I'm not condoning it, but you can understand where he was coming from."

"Did you notice that Kelly asked if it was 'another get rich scheme'? Any thoughts about what other schemes Terry might have tried?"

Colm shrugged.

"How about an ATM heist?"

Colm digested that and said, "Oh wow! That would make sense. He had access to the digger." Colm was quiet a moment but then contradicted himself, "No. How did he get his hands on the keys if they're checked each night?"

"I have a theory about that." But Kate said no more.

Colm waited until Kate said, "Let's go back to the canal basin. We need to let them know about Terry's demise and we might get to talk to some of his workmates."

"Or fellow conspirators, do you think?"

"May be," Kate agreed.

As Colm drove, Kate contacted someone she had met before in Social Services and explained Kelly's situation. The friend assured her that someone would contact Kelly before the end of the day.

◆ ◆ ◆

The moment Gail Miller saw Kate she launched her attack, "What did you say to Terry that's scared him away? He's not in today if you've come for another 'chat'."

Kate waited until Miller had settled herself back in her chair before explaining, "I'm sorry to inform you, Ms Miller, but Terry Lennon's body was discovered this morning and his death was not from natural causes."

Miller's mouth opened and closed a few times before she managed, "Dead? What the hell happened?"

"At this early stage in our enquiries we are just trying to gather evidence and understand the sequence of events."

"What about Kelly? God, she can't live there on her own. Terry did everything for her."

"I've contacted Social Services and asked for their help but do you know of any other family Terry had?"

Miller thought but shook her head. "I only know about Kelly because he had to have days off for her appointments."

"Was Terry close to anyone here, at work? Someone he might confide in?"

Again Miller thought. "There's Gordon Connell. They were pretty close. I know they'd go drinking together." As an afterthought, "I suppose you'll want to have a word with him?"

"We will," Kate confirmed.

Miller rose from her seat, "I'll go and get him."

"What about the tannoy?" Colm asked.

Miller shook her head. "If it's okay with you I'll tell him about Terry. I think he'll be upset and will need time to get his head together before he sees you."

Kate agreed with the action, much to Colm's surprise until Miller had left the office and then Kate removed from her pocket a small set of keys. She held them up.

"They're not exactly the same but I want to try a little experiment." With that she removed a set of digger keys from the board and replaced them with her own small set.

Colm had to agree, at a glance they didn't look too dissimilar to the ones Kate had removed.

"You think that's what Terry did. Replace the digger keys with a similar set and then returned them the next day?"

Kate smiled. "We should find out when the site closes this evening. Miller says she checks the board every night. Let's see how closely she does that inspection."

CHAPTER 35

Gordon Connell was from the same mould as Terry Lennon. Small and rugged, however, he boasted a drinker's nose and hands like shovels. Kate had expected to see sorrow or even puzzlement in Connell's eyes. What she hadn't expected was fear. "Mr Connell, I'm sorry for the loss of your friend."

Connell looked at her blankly. He tried to speak and then cleared his throat. "What happened to him?"

"I'm sorry. Mr Connell, at this stage we're not at liberty to give out details. All we can say with some certainty is that it was not an accident."

Again, Kate was thrown by his reaction. She'd expected surprise but instead she thought she saw resignation.

"Mr Connell, is there anything you can tell us about Terry that may explain why he was a victim in this murder?"

"When he'd had a drink he could be a bit..." Connell searched for the word, "wild!"

"So you think Terry was involved in a fight that got out of hand?"

"Wouldn't surprise me."

Kate felt like her interviewee was slipping away from her. Her gut instinct told her that Connell had, if not useful, at least interesting information about Terry.

"How has Terry seemed these last few weeks?"

"Seemed?" Connell looked puzzled.

"Was he happy? Down? In a mood? Anything that might explain why he was murdered?"

A shrug. "He was just Terry. He had all these mad plans about getting money for Kelly, his sister!" He looked at Kate for confirmation that she knew who he was talking about.

Kate nodded. "So what sort of schemes were they, these money making ideas?"

Another shrug. "I didn't really pay a lot of attention. They were all pie in the sky stuff." Connell's avoidance of eye contact during this statement left Kate convinced that he was lying through his teeth. Had Connell been Terry's partner in the ATM crime? Kate was now sure that Terry had been part of the gang who did the raid. But he must have had others with him and, given the silence from the residents in Peace Way, one of them must have connections with one of the local gangs. Enough of a connection to keep the residents silent.

With this thought process came an answer to Connell's fear. He thought Terry had been killed by someone linked to the failed heist. She needed to get him talking but fear was keeping his mouth closed.

"Did Terry get involved with some of the less law-abiding members of Eashire?" Connell's eyes flitted everywhere but in Kate's direction.

Colm intervened, "Look Gordon, you want us to catch whoever did this to Terry, don't you?"

Connell gave an almost involuntary nod. "So anything you can tell us we will treat in the strictest confidence and only use if it helps with our case. No-one has to know where we got our information from."

Connell stared at Colm for several seconds before turning back to Kate. "I don't know who Terry got involved with, if he got involved with anybody at all. He just had these desperate schemes because he needed money for Kelly."

Kate and Colm tried several other tacks with Connell but he was no more forthcoming. Finally, Kate offered one of her cards. "If you think of anything at all Mr Connell, please ring me. We want whoever killed Terry to be brought to justice."

As the door closed on Connell, Colm said, "He knows something but he's scared to death. Should we have told him how Lennon died? That it's probably related to the theatre, not whatever he and Terry had got themselves involved with."

"Once we have the forensics back we'll talk to Mr Connell again. See if we can persuade him to be honest with us. As you say, he's clearly scared to death."

CHAPTER 36

Kate was pleased to see that Mike had sent her several forensic reports. In addition, Len and Alice gathered information on some of their key players so Kate called them together for an exchange of information and ideas. Kate began, "Let's start with the forensics on our first body, Joseph Mallory."

Bart had organised that a laptop projector was now part of room 11's equipment and Kate made good use of it now with Mike's reports.

"In essence, forensics had a lack of fingerprints on the cabinet and the silicone itself. However, they have managed to make a partial cast of the killer's hand." A three-dimensional model slowly rotated on the large screen. Manipulating the image, Kate pointed out the possibility of a plaster on the thumb and a ring on the little finger.

"On a more definitive note, Mike has been able to remove a hair from the silicone, which may or may not belong to our killer, and extract DNA. He's sent this off but as we know it's going to be a while before it's back and really is going to be more use as a confirmation when we have a suspect than pointing us to the suspect.

"Our suspects for Mallory's death seem to be the six people who were still in the theatre after

Mallory supposedly signed out. Three of those names appear again for Lennon's death, if we assume he was killed after most of the cast had left last night."

We haven't yet managed to interview the theatre company's owner, Daniel Henderson. However, we have interviewed Jade and Emerald Froude, Jason Brooks, Jon Bell and Calum James. Brooks and Bell were also at the theatre late last night; along with Henderson and Montgomery. So far no-one has a watertight alibi but equally no-one has an obvious motive.

Kate turned to Len and Alice, "What have you managed to dig up on our suspects?"

Alice took the lead, "I have tracked down as much as I can on Lennon. Eashire man born and bred. Parents still alive and living in Hopton, on the far side of Camworth."

"We'll need to talk to them about Terry and Kelly. Colm that needs to be our next task."

Further sharing was interrupted by the phone on Kate's desk ringing. She got up to answer it, listened carefully and then said, "I'll be straight there, sir."

Replacing the phone, she turned to her team, "Someone has put two and two together and made five. The local paper is asking for confirmation that two bodies have been found in the theatre and that they have been mummified!"

Surprised silence greeted her remark and

then Len said, "I bet someone saw that cabinet being taken out. It looks a bit like an Egyptian coffin thing."

"Sarcophagus!" Alice helpfully supplied.

"Whatever it is, Bart is not happy and wants some kind of disclaimer. Colm will you go and see Mike's team and see if they've got anything from the digger. Len and Alice, can you continue with the research? I particularly want you to look at Henderson and Brooks for the moment."

Kate walked out of the office. She really didn't want to put too much information out into the public realm. She hoped Bart had an idea about what they could say to refute the mummification angle but without giving out real details.

CHAPTER 37

Colm and Kate met at the doors to the car park.

"How did it go with Bart?"

"Okay, I think. We came up with a form of words that he's going to let the media department have a look at. How did you get on?"

Colm grinned and waved a sheaf of papers around. "In summary: Lennon's fingerprints were all over the controls of the digger. There are fragments of brick and metal, consistent with the ATM surround, on the bucket. There is more of a jumble of prints on the door and pull bars. But it does put Lennon in the frame."

Playing devil's advocate, Kate offered, "Unless Lennon was a regular driver."

"Yes, but Mike's team is pretty sure that Lennon was the last person to operate the digger. There are no smudges or overlay of prints on the controls."

Colm passed Kate the papers as he hunted in his pockets for the car keys, "Lennon's parents now?"

"Yes. We need to let them know about Terry and Kelly."

During the drive, Kate read through the forensics report, "Even better!"

"What's that?"

"There are marks on the wall around the ATM

that have the same pattern of paint and rust as the bucket has."

"So no-one can claim the paint could have come from any old digger!"

"Indeed! They're a clever bunch in that lab."

Colm grinned, "Don't go telling them that though, will you?"

Kate grinned her response.

Hopton, like many districts around Eashire had once been a small village, or maybe even a hamlet. Now its pre-Victorian main street was intersected with roads off to small estates from various periods in the past hundred years. Each one merging into the next until Hopton was a large conurbation.

The Lennon's house was the left-hand side of a post war semi-detached. There was nothing remarkable about it; it looked exactly the same as the forty odd other houses in the road. Kate knocked on the door holding up her ID.

Peter Lennon was a greyer version of his son. A little bit taller maybe, but the same stocky build. He seemed disinterested in their ID and merely stepped back to widen the doorway and pointed with his right hand to the door through to the lounge. Sitting at one end of a leather sofa was Mrs Joyce Lennon.

Kate introduced herself, "Mrs Lennon, I am Detective Inspector Medlar and this is my colleague, Detective Constable Hunter."

Before she could speak further, Mrs Lennon

burst out, "She's dead. Isn't she? I've been dreading this day for years and now it's arrived."

Mr Lennon came and stood at the end of the sofa with a hand on his wife's shoulder. Kate made to sit close to Mrs Lennon and said quietly, "Kelly is still alive but I'm sorry to inform you that your son Terry's body, was found this morning and we are treating it as a suspicious death."

Both parents looked at Kate blankly until Mr Lennon cleared his throat, "Terry? Our Terry?"

"We will need a member of the family to officially identify him but we are certain that it is Terry, yes. I'm sorry for your loss."

Mrs Lennon turned her head to look at her husband and then back to Kate, "Kelly's still alive?"

"Yes."

"How is she?"

"Her health is not good," Kate felt that there was an unasked question there, "and she's clean. I know this is a bad time for you, but can you tell us when you last saw Terry?"

Again, husband and wife shared a look. Mr Lennon cleared his throat, "We've not seen either of them since Terry decided to take Kelly in and that must be two or more years ago.

"We got so tired of the stealing, the lies and the broken promises. We just couldn't take any more but Terry was all for trying again." There were tears in Mrs Lennon's eyes. "I remember when I brought Kelly home from the hospital and introduced her to Terry. I said, 'You're her big brother and big brothers take care of their little sisters, and he took that to heart.

"Always looking out for her; from her first day at school to the first lad who broke her heart, Terry was always there for her." Mr Lennon looked into the distance to stop his tears from falling.

"How will Kelly cope without Terry?" Mrs Lennon asked.

"To be honest, I'm not sure. She was putting a brave face on it when I spoke with her but her health is very poor and I understand Terry did a lot for her."

Mrs Lennon turned to her husband with a determined look on her face, "We need to bring her home."

Whether she was expecting an argument or not Mr Lennon acquiesced, and Kate and Colm left them making arrangements to go and see Kelly straight away.

CHAPTER 38

"Where to now, boss?"

"Bridgewater's. I want to see if Ms Miller spots the key swap."

Colm checked his watch, "Do we have time to stop for a coffee and a sandwich on our way?"

Kate checked her own watch, just after four-thirty. She couldn't see the site closing much before five, maybe even six. "We can and goodies on me."

Sat in their car, parked a little distance from the site's gates, Colm and Kate sat and enjoyed their food and drink. The site was still busy but to Kate's eye it was the busyness of putting things away and clearing up for the day.

Blowing on her coffee, Kate asked, "Okay, Colm, I need a rundown of the local gangs or crooked groups in Eashire. I'm assuming Phipps runs all the drugs in the area? No-one trying to muscle in? Big boys from the metropolis? County lines?"

Colm frowned in thought, "If you want details, you're going to need to talk to Terry Gilbert but Phipps has always been the King of Drugs. As far as I know no-one's ever attempted to topple him. There again, if he has contact with whoever is supplying the theatre company perhaps he's got the back up of bigger people."

"That would make sense. But Phipps is not going to be behind the ATM theft, is he?"

Colm shook his head vigorously. "No! A theft like that would have to involve one of the Mafia families."

"Mafia? Really?"

"No," Colm grinned and then his face became more solemn. "There's the Winchelsea family. They have their fingers in lots of pies but it tends to be 'off the back of the lorry' type stuff *and*," Colm emphasised the word, "they don't do the strong arm stuff that's keeping the residents of Peace Way quiet."

"Just honest to goodness crooks?" Kate said a little sardonically.

"Well, in a way, yes, that's exactly what they are. Your wicked crooks are the Marshalls. They moved into the area about ten years ago. We think they're into the protection business judging from the number of broken shop windows and the number of falls shop owners had when the Marshalls first arrived."

"What do we know about the Marshalls? Is it a family?"

"A couple of brothers. Think they're the inheritors of the Krays."

"But couldn't make it in a real city?"

"May be but they're a right couple of bastards and only employ those who work along the same lines."

"I'm surprised they haven't tried to take over

Phipps' business then. Drugs is where the big money is?"

"Sort of lends credence to the idea that Phipps has big muscle at his back, doesn't it."

Kate nodded but her mind was onto their next matter. Whilst she and Colm had been talking, workers had begun to drift out of the canal basin site.

"Time to go and see Ms Miller."

Colm drove onto the site just as Ms Miller was locking the site office. Her shoulders drooped when she saw Kate and Colm get out of their car.

"Inspector, I thought we were done. Can whatever it is, wait until tomorrow?"

Kate merely looked and Miller answered herself, "Of course it can't." She turned back and unlocked the office door and Kate and Colm followed her in.

CHAPTER 39

Miller sat resignedly behind her desk and waited for Kate to begin. "Did you check whether the digger at the Play House was yours?"

"I did and it is but I was told I couldn't move it."

"No, not for the moment. It's part of another crime we're investigating. Have you any idea how it got there?"

"No. I told you none of the keys are missing," Miller nodded to the key board on the wall.

Kate walked over and removed the set of keys she had placed their earlier, "But these aren't machinery keys, are they?"

Miller rose and went to stand beside Kate, "Show me."

Kate showed the cuckoo set of keys, "From a distance they look similar don't they." Kate then delved in her pocket for the missing keys and replaced them."

Miller looked surprised and maybe just a little angry. "You swapped my keys?"

"I did. I think this was how the digger was removed from your site without you knowing it had gone."

"But what about the site gates?"

"How many people have keys to those gates?"

"Um, myself and Gary Pugh. Steven

Gainbridge from the council and..." she paused, clearly already making connections, "...and Gordon Connell."

"Why does Gordon have a set of keys?"

"He lives the closest and offered to be on call. You know, in case the police needed access or saw something suspicious." Miller was clearly placing pieces of the puzzle together. "What did Terry and Gordon use the digger for? Was it that ATM on Peace Way?"

"Why do you assume Terry and Gordon did it together?"

"They were as thick as thieves," she gave an ironic laugh at her choice of simile, "and Gordon doesn't drive the digger but Terry can. Could." She corrected herself.

Kate felt a great deal of satisfaction. The ATM case was coming together pretty much as she'd thought. "I would appreciate it, Ms Miller, if you would not mention this conversation with anyone else until we have interviewed Mr Connell."

"You won't find Gordon tonight. He's out on a stag do. Half a dozen of the men have asked for a half day tomorrow." She explained further as Kate looked mystified, "So they can get over their hangovers and have the alcohol out of their systems before they come back into work. I can't have them on site still having the effects of the night before."

Colm's phone rang and he took the call

outside. Kate finished up with Gail Miller.

"As I said, Ms Miller, if you could keep this conversation to yourself until we have spoken with Mr Connell. It may well be that we'll catch him here tomorrow."

Miller nodded and made a show of checking her watch. Kate thanked her for her time and joined Colm outside. He was just finishing his call. As he put his phone away he smiled, "We have another one of those delightful social invites."

Kate smiled as well, "PM? Tomorrow morning?"

"Yes. Now where next?"

Kate looked thoughtful, "We're going to have trouble finding Connell and if we do will he be in a fit state to interview?"

"There's always Henderson," Colm offered.

Kate nodded but said, "I think I'd like to interview him when we have better information about Lennon's death. I think it's home time. Drop me off at the station so I can pick my car up and then go home."

CHAPTER 40

Pulling up outside her home, Kate was surprised not to be met by Monster. In the last few months he had made a point of meeting her at the gate and 'talking to her' until he got his food. Worried that he may be hurt, she hurried around to the back door only to be met with the sight of Jude and Monster communing on the back step. Kate's heart quickened but she didn't engage her brain, "What are you doing here?"

Jude looked up guiltily and Monster continued to rub his head against her thigh. Kate noted that Jude was possibly surprised by the tone of the question, so she tried again, "Sorry that didn't come out the way I meant. I was just so surprised and to see Monster allowing you to stroke him."

During the ramble, Jude rose from the step and placed her finger against Kate's lips and then replaced it with her own lips. Pulling back gently she said, "I brought supper!" and she held up a bag of groceries. "I saw on the television that your case was getting more difficult, so I thought I'd come and cook for you."

Kate smiled, "That's really kind of you but I could have been out for hours. There's no set times when we're on a case."

"I must admit that hadn't occurred to me

until I was almost here so I was going to give you until eight. In the meantime, Monster and I have become good friends."

Kate took on a mock disapproving tone, "So I noticed. He hasn't let me stroke him yet."

Jude grinned. "It could have something to do with the salmon nibbles I picked up for him," she pulled an opened packet from her pocket.

"Cheat!"

Jude laughed and Monster meowed. "Okay. Come on then. Let's get food sorted."

Having fed Monster, Kate began to help Jude prepare their meal. She was given the task of preparing a salad whilst Jude seasoned two fillets of fish and placed them beneath the grill. Whilst they were cooking, Jude made up some couscous and added all sorts of ingredients.Whilst Jude served up, Kate went to her desk and removed an item.

They sat at the kitchen counter, eating. Kate had to agree it was better than any ping meal and she realised how much she enjoyed company when she ate. Having finished, she slid the item from her desk across to Jude. It was a front door key. "Just in case I'm out whenever you arrive." Was she being too forward? Would Jude think she was moving too fast?

Jude smiled, "Thanks, Kate. I won't abuse using it, but it does mean I can make sure Monster is fed if you're out really late."

Kate also smiled. Monster got fed when she

got home but it was a good excuse for Jude to have the key.

Pots cleared and washed, Kate and Jude retired to the lounge and Kate's extravagance, a large comfy sofa.

"If you've got work to do I can either sit here quietly or disappear completely," Jude said anxiously.

"No, please stay awhile. I'll need an early night, but I could do with some switch off time. It sometimes helps to put things into perspective."

They spent an hour or so chatting around all sorts of subjects. Monster had declined to join them on the sofa, even with salmon nibbles as a bribe. He sat, as he always sat of an evening, by the chair closest to the kitchen door. At ten he made his move to the back door. Jude took this as her signal to go as well.

A chaste kiss and a waved farewell and Kate was alone. Relaxed and content, she went to bed. She knew her dreams would hunt through the evidence of the cases and may come up with some ideas.

CHAPTER 41

Kate had a distinct sense of déjà vu as she met Colm outside the morgue. Colm must have felt it as well, "We must stop meeting like this, boss!"

Gus had started the postmortem when they arrived, clothed in their sterile coveralls. He waved a bloodied hand in acknowledgement of their presence but continued with his assessment of Lennon's organs. Having reached a satisfactory point, he beckoned them both closer to the trolley.

"Good morning. Another interesting case, Inspector. Terrence Anthony Lennon, aged forty-three. Cause of death was blunt force trauma."

"He was definitely dead before he was put in the silicone?" Kate clarified.

"He was indeed. Mr Lennon experienced three separate blows to the back and left side of his head. I would suggest that the two blows at the back of his skull were delivered whilst he was stood upright but the final blow I think was delivered when he was already on the floor."

"Was it the third one that killed him?" Colm asked.

Gus looked thoughtful. "I think there was sufficient damage dealt with the first two blows to cause death, but perhaps not instantly."

"So, if the blows are from behind, he

wasn't involved in a fight?" Colm was trying to reconstruct the scene.

"No, his knuckles and hands are unmarked. He was taken unawares."

"And the blunt force object?"

"A two-by-four length of wood was recovered from the scene. It was untreated wood and some splinters were left in all three wounds. In addition, blood on the wood comes back to Mr Lennon here."

"Other than that, he was in good health?"

"Well, I think, given the state of the liver; there are signs of scarring, which is normally an early sign of cirrhosis."

"We understand he was a bit of a drinker."

Gus nodded his agreement.

"Any idea of time of death?" Kate asked.

"It's a little difficult to be exact because the silicone maintains some of the body heat but I think it was probably between about ten the previous night to two yesterday morning. And probably the earlier end of that timescale given the state of digestion of his evening meal."

"Thanks Gus. We'll let you finish up here."

Leaving their coveralls in the bin provided, Kate and Colm exited the morgue.

"Right, we need to find out what was on his phone. Who did he contact Wednesday evening? Where did he go between leaving home between eight and eight-thirty and ending up dead between ten and twelve?"

"Mike had Zara Bakir on the phone so she should have something to tell us."

"Okay. First, the station and then we'll go and interview the theatre crew again."

CHAPTER 42

"It doesn't make sense," Colm said for the umpteenth time since they'd received Bakir's verbal report on Lennon's phone. No calls from his mobile Wednesday evening. "How did he let whoever it is know that he wanted to meet with them?"

"Just turned up at the theatre?" Kate mused.

"No. Stan would have locked up by the time he got there so he would have had to be let in by someone. And how did they know he was there to be let in?" Colm's exasperation was palpable.

Kate had to agree that it was a conundrum. She put her faith in all such things eventually having an answer. "We'll start with Mr Daniel Henderson."

Stan was his usual font of information and Kate and Colm found Henderson in the box office as Stan had predicted. He was on the phone and merely looked bored when Kate showed her ID and continued with his call. Kate tried not to let her irritation show. Mr Henderson was ticking all her prejudice boxes; swept back hair, held in place by aviator sunglasses, a blazer and, for goodness sake, a cravat. He was like something from an Agatha Christie novel.

Eventually, the call ended and Henderson deigned to give them his attention. "I assume this is about the dead bodies?" His accent was a strange mix of East London overlaid with an American twang. Quite discordant on the ears.

"It is indeed, Mr Henderson?"

"Yes." He stood and shook their hands. Kate felt like she had just witnessed a personality change. "How may I help you? I'm afraid I didn't know either man."

"We're just trying to establish a timeline and place for everyone who was still in the Play House on the evening of each murder, Mr Henderson. So could you explain your movements for Monday evening? I understand you were here until after Mr Mallory's supposed departure."

Henderson sat back down and invited Kate to take the only other chair in the room. Colm leant against the door; notebook ready.

"I'm not sure, Monday evening?" he looked thoughtful. "I spent most of that Monday in here on the phone to future venues and confirming dates."

"And that took all day? Until after eight that evening?"

"Most of the places we perform are not as palatial as the Play House. They're little local drama clubs that are often staffed by volunteers. Consequently, they're often not open until the evening when they have performances on. I do most of my calls in the evening."

"Can you give us a list of who you called that

evening, please sir?" Colm's pen hovered over the notebook.

Henderson sighed and reluctantly pulled his tablet towards him. Swiping through a number of screens, he then held it up for Colm to read. Colm wrote the information down assiduously whilst Kate merely noticed that it was a diary page with names and numbers. She nodded to the screen, "These people will be able to confirm what time you rang on Monday evening?"

"Yes, they should be able to. Perhaps might not be able to pinpoint it to the minute but they'd have a rough idea."

"Thank you. And were you doing a similar task Wednesday evening?"

Was that a slight hesitation? May be even a touch of embarrassment? He cleared his throat and then offered, "I was meeting with Julia, Julia Montgomery."

"During what times would that have been, sir?"

"Well, I watched the rehearsal. What a shambles that was! So, after that. About seven-thirty?"

"Until when. Sir?"

"I'm not sure of the exact time. Julia might have a better idea. I think nineish."

"How did you get into the theatre business, Mr Henderson?" Kate asked conversationally.

Henderson gave a negligent shrug, "A friend of mine wanted someone to organise a theatre group he'd 'inherited'. He said it was chaos and needed someone with a business head."

"So you had a business background?"

Another off-hand shrug, "I'd worked in a number of jobs as a troubleshooter. You have to be able to see where the problems are and what the answers are. I've always been able to do that."

"So is this company a good one now?"

Henderson nodded, "It's not bad. We have a solid core of performers, a reasonable director, although don't tell him I said so. We get asked back to places, which is always encouraging and we make enough to cover our costs and a bit more."

Carrying on the interested party performance, Kate asked, "Do you just tour this country?"

"Mainly, yes, but we do have a link with a youth programme in Amsterdam. Every three months or so we go over and perform a traditional play; normally Shakespeare, for their schools."

"Is that tough or fun?" Kate genuinely wanted to know.

"A bit of both. But it's profitable and that's the main criteria."

"Blimey, how do you get all your props and stuff over there each time?" Colm chimed in.

"We have it down to a fine art. We have a particular storage unit and everything goes in there. Would you believe it's actually cheaper and quicker to do it that way than take a lorry across?"

Being unable to think of anything else at present, Kate took their leave but added, "We may need to come and confirm some times with you later."

Henderson was already dialling another number from his tablet and waved his hand in acknowledgement of Kate's statement.

CHAPTER 43

"What do you think? Customs get used to them going backwards and forwards. See a unit full of props and looks no further?"

"Certainly a possibility. If they are moving drugs, I'm sure they're quite well hidden but yes, Customs being familiar with them might make them a little less thorough."

"A bit slimy wasn't he?"

Kate smiled. She hadn't warmed to Henderson either. "I'll go and check timings with Montgomery. You use the bar and contact some of those numbers. See if you get any replies. If Henderson's right, we may need to do that later this evening."

Colm turned and walked away. He'd make the calls from outside. He'd only gone a few steps when Kate called out, "Colm!"

He turned and headed back. Kate stepped to meet him. "Henderson's probably telling the truth about these places only being staffed of an evening. Instead, would you ring Terry Gilbert? Ask him to send whatever they've got on Henderson through to Alice. He must have become a person of interest with the Dutch intel."

Colm nodded his understanding and strode off.

Kate made her way to Montgomery's office where she found the manager working her way through a thick folder of papers, which she was marking up with a coloured highlighter pen. Kate thought she actually looked relieved to be interrupted. When Montgomery saw it was Kate she threw her pen down, "I hate financial papers."

Kate grimaced her sympathy, "Sorry, to interrupt you again."

"I know, another body. Is this going to stop the play opening next week?"

"I don't think it should have any impact. Obviously, I can't say for sure until we have caught our murderer."

"Well, anything I can do... let me know."

"At the moment we are trying to establish a timeline of who was where and when. According to Stan, most of the cast left at about seven-thirty but you, Daniel Henderson, Jon Bell and Jason Brooks were all here after Stan left. Do you all have keys to the front doors?"

"Yes, we do."

"And Mr Henderson said he was meeting with you once the rehearsal was over."

Kate could not identify the look that flitted across Montgomery's face before she replied, "Yes, he arrived just before eight and left just after nine."

"Do you mind me asking what your meeting was about?" There was that look again.

Montgomery hesitated, "I assume that anything I say will be kept confidential?"

Why did people never understand that she couldn't give that kind of assurance? "Unless your information is pertinent to our case it will not be disclosed to any third party."

That seemed to satisfy Montgomery who gave a slight shake of her head before explaining the looks that her face had given away. "Henderson turned up here, in my office, with a bottle of wine and two glasses. Admittedly a very nice wine but his intentions were far from subtle. He'd asked for a meeting, and I'd assumed it was business. He had other ideas."

"And it took you an hour to explain he'd got the wrong idea?" Kate tried to keep her scepticism out of her voice.

Montgomery rested her arms on her desk and clasped her hands, "You have to understand that the Play House relies on entrepreneurs like Henderson. We need his company to perform as much as he needs a venue. So I tried to be diplomatic with Daniel. That took the time."

"What time did you leave Wednesday night? Were Bell and Brooks still here?"

"I wasn't far behind Daniel. I don't know whether Jason and Jon were still here. We each set the alarm as we leave. It is only triggered to the external doors so we unset and reset as we leave."

"Thank you." Kate made to leave and then

turned back, "By the way, if you have your own technical staff does that mean the theatre groups that visit just bring the cast?"

"In the main, yes. Sometimes they might have a specialist but, no, generally they use our staff."

"And that's the case with Henderson's company?"

Montgomery was nodding as her finger was negotiating her computer mouse. "No, hang on a minute." A few more clicks and she said, "I'd forgotten Henderson has a couple of lads that are sort of roadie type characters." Her fingers ran down the screen in front of her, "Yes, here we go. Josh Campbell and Max Harper."

"So what's their role whilst here?"

"I don't really know. Henderson seems to manage them directly. I saw him sending them off on errands this morning."

"I'll check them with Mr Henderson. Thank you for that. Hope the papers are not too much of a headache," inclining her head towards the financial file Montgomery had been perusing when Kate entered.

CHAPTER 44

Kate found Colm in conversation with Stan. Spotting his boss, he made his farewells and came out of the booth to talk with Kate.

"Terry's got quite a file on Henderson, which he is sending to Alice and also two characters called Campbell and Harper."

"Josh and Max!"

Colm raised an eyebrow. "Yes. Stan says they're regularly here at the start of the day but disappear for the rest of it."

"No idea what they're up to?"

"Wellll!" Colm drew the word out, "Stan does have a theory."

Kate raised an eyebrow, waiting for Colm to disclose his nugget, "Stan thinks they may be couriers. He says they've always got rucksacks on that look heavier on the way out than in."

"You're thinking drugs, aren't you?"

"It would make sense."

"And if I add to that theory that they only seem to associate with Henderson."

"Henderson is the man behind the supposed drugs trafficking!"

"Right. We need to be careful that we don't get led away from our murder investigation. So, if I take Brooks, will you find Bell? And we'll meet back at the car."

Colm held one hand up whilst the other reached for his notebook. "Hang on, Terry also had some info on Brooks," he flipped some pages. "Apparently, one of his ex's had to get a restraining order against him and the address he was registered at during their relationship had three call outs for suspected domestic violence but no charges were ever brought."

"So the argument we overheard is not out of character for Brooks. I wonder if his volatility led to Mallory's death."

Colm suggested a scenario. "Jade Froude is detailed off to make a drugs contact. It's Mallory. He sees it as a perfect opportunity to have a sniff around. For some reason Jade has used Clare West's name. They meet in the workshop in a bit of a huddle, Brooks comes in. Sees the girl he still wants with Mallory and fights him as a love rival?"

"It works," Kate agreed. "Brooks accidentally knocks Mallory out but thinks he's killed him and so puts him in the cabinet."

"But why do that?"

Kate is warming to her theory. "To give him time to pretend that Mallory's signed out."

"Jade must be in on the act. She saw Brooks murder Mallory but doesn't tell us. Why?"

"Worried about how she'd explain what Mallory was doing there?"

"Or afraid of Brooks?"

"Either way works," said Kate. "And I think

Terry Lennon heard or saw something and tried to blackmail Brooks. That has to be premeditated murder."

"But how did Lennon contact Brooks to be let into the Play House in the first place? He didn't use his own mobile so who's did he use and why? And why haven't they come forward to tell us?"

"Jade Froude is a name that springs to mind. She already may not have told us what she knows about Mallory's death."

"Did Lennon know Jade?"

"We need to know where Jade went after rehearsals Wednesday evening." Kate checked her watch. "First Bell and Brooks and then we'll meet back at Stan's booth rather than the car and find out where Jade and co are."

CHAPTER 45

Kate found Brooks in the auditorium going through a scene with three of the main cast. Kate knew he would not relish the interruption, but he would need to understand that her murder enquiry trumped his rehearsal. Walking down the main aisle, she called out, "Mr Brooks could I have a word, please?"

Kate walked to the stage so that Brooks could see clearly who was wanting him. If she thought it would help, she was wrong. Brooks scowled. "This will have to wait Inspector. I'm in rehearsal."

Kate stood her ground, "I'm sorry, Mr Brooks, this cannot wait. I'm sure your cast would appreciate a five-minute break."

For a moment Kate thought he was going to argue his case but he clearly thought better of it. He turned back to the waiting actors, "Okay, take five. Jack, you and Izzy need to check that last part of the scene. You're arguing viciously. You're making it sound like a children's spat." With that he walked to the side of the stage, sat on the edge and then slipped down into the aisle. He passed Kate and strode halfway up the aisle before taking a seat. Kate allowed him his little show of power and followed. She sat in the row above Brooks so that he was forced to sit sideways in his seat.

"Thank you, Mr Brooks. I know you must appreciate the urgency of my work, with two murders in less than a week."

It seemed to Kate that Brooks' nod was a reluctant one. "With the death of Mr Lennon, we are once again trying to establish people's movements during the relevant time."

Brooks neither acknowledged nor denied her statement and Kate continued. "Did you know Mr Lennon, Terry Lennon?"

"No. Should I have? He didn't work in the theatre, did he?"

"He was in the evening of Monday, when Mr Mallory was killed, mending the trap door."

"Oh right. I knew someone had come in, but I didn't know his name."

"So you didn't see him on Monday evening?"

"No. I would have said when you interviewed me last time."

Kate nodded and continued, "What time did you leave the Play House on Wednesday evening?"

Brooks looked unsure and Kate gave him a little more, "I understand you were still here after Stan locked up the stage door."

"Oh yes. I must have just missed him. I used my keys and went out the front."

"And what time would that have been, sir?"

Brooks was clearly calculating. Did he know what time Stan finished?

"I'm not entirely sure of the time."

Kate played helpful, "The rehearsal finished about seven-thirty, but you didn't leave then. What were you doing?"

"I was working in the auditorium. Marking up the script with points I wanted to go over with the cast. That sort of thing but I don't know how long that took."

"Did anyone call you? That might help with timings." Was it her imagination or did he visibly jump when she mentioned a call?

"No, no-one called."

"Did you go straight back to your lodgings or go for something to eat?"

"I went for a drink. I'm not sure what the place is called. It's on the way to my place."

"Don't worry, we'll see if we can pick you up on CCTV. We know it must have been after eight-thirty."

That also seemed to make him twitch and he hastened to add, "I also spent some time checking that the statues would work. I collected one from the workshop and tried it in different positions around the stage."

"So you hadn't just missed Stan leaving?"

"No, it was because I'd just missed Stan that I decided to try out the statue."

"And you didn't see anyone hanging around? Mr Bell for example?"

"Jon was in his lighting cupboard when I left the auditorium, but he'd gone by the time I left."

"Because he wasn't in his booth?"

"Yes."

"Thank you Mr Brooks, we'll check with Mr Bell and CCTV and see if we can get a better timeline established for you."

Kate was convinced that Brooks looked far from happy at this piece of news. Her gut was telling her she had her murderer. Proving it was going to be the stickler.

CHAPTER 46

Colm found Jon Bell in his lighting booth. Through the window he could see Kate interviewing Brooks. He smiled as he watched Kate establish the winning move. In the meantime Bell had not even looked up from the panel in front of him. Colm saw a screen with pulsating lines and dials and sliding knobs that you always saw in the typical sound studio set.

"Good morning, Mr Bell, I need to check some information with you."

Still no response. "I appreciate that you're a busy man, Mr Bell, which is why I am trying to interview you at your place of work. We could always try my place of work!"

The comment had the desired effect. With an aggressive sigh, Bell pushed himself away from the desk.

"Ask away!"

"We understand that you stayed on in the Play House after the rehearsal on Wednesday evening?"

A mere nod and Colm persevered, "What needed doing that meant you had to work on so late?"

Another exaggerated sigh, "A rehearsal is my opportunity to start programming in the light display. I wanted to run through what I'd made and see if it worked."

Colm shook his head, "So you don't move the lights manually on the night?"

"It's a mixture. We couldn't do it entirely pre-programmed because the actors are not robots, taking exactly the same amount of time everytime they perform." More's the pity seemed to be the subtext to this.

"Okay. So how long did you stop for and did you see anyone else?"

"Well, Brooks was working in the auditorium. He had his script ranged across the front of the stage. He got a call about eight-thirty, and before you ask, I checked my watch then."

"Surely you couldn't hear it ring in here?"

"No, but whatever it was he was very agitated and was striding up and down the stage like a thing demented. It broke my concentration on the lighting."

"Okay, so then what?"

A negligent shrug. "I went back to my programme and when I next looked up, Brooks had gone. That made me check my watch again and I saw that it was after nine, about ten past, I think, and I decided to call it a day."

"We know Stan left and locked up the stage door at eight-thirty so how did you leave?"

"I have a key to the one of the front doors and the alarm code. After Stan leaves, the alarm is on all the external doors so you have to come out the front and unset and reset it as you leave."

"Do you know how many other people have keys and know the alarm code?"

"Well, obviously Julia, as the manager."

Colm decided this was very much in the tone of *teaching your Granny to suck eggs*, but he persevered. "So, just the two of you? How would Brooks get out if he was still around?"

"I believe, although you will need to check with Julia, that both Henderson and Brooks also have guest keys."

"Is there a danger that someone else will get hold of a key and try a little burglary?"

"They would also need to know the code and we change that after every company leaves. Now, if there's nothing more, I need to carry on working."

"No, thank you, sir, for your valuable time." Bell looked up sharply, but Colm merely gave one of his winning smiles.

CHAPTER 47

Comparing notes in Stan's booth whilst Stan made a point of being busy, Kate pounced on the news that Brooks had received a call.

"I knew he was lying!"

"Whoever it was that called caused him a lot of agitation, according to Bell. Marching up and down the stage."

"Do you think it was Lennon directly or someone on behalf of Lennon?"

"Could Lennon know that Jade Froude was involved and he tracked her down?"

"Are we getting a little too focused on a theory we have no proof for yet?" Kate put the brakes on their surmising.

Deflated, Colm puffed out his cheeks, "Yes, may be."

"Let's find out where Jade was after rehearsal Wednesday. Is she in now?"

Colm checked the log book. "No, but Clare West is. Worth talking to her first?"

"Why not?"

Kate called to Stan, "Stan, where are we likely to find Clare West at the moment?"

"If she's not on stage, try the practice room. Up the metal staircase on the left of the stage."

Clare was not on the stage and they followed Stan's directions to the practice room. Long before they arrived at the door, they could hear the rhythmic pounding of feet on boards. Kate guessed that there were at least two of them in the room. She quietly opened the door. To one side a floor to ceiling mirror and a ballet rail indicated the room's use. In the centre of golden floorboards three young women were co-ordinating their moves. As the door opened fully one saw them and stopped. Three pairs of eyes turned to stare.

Kate smiled and called out, "Hello Clare, it's Detective Inspector Medlar."

Clare came forward. A worried expression on her face. "I don't know anything about this other man. It's just too horrible. We're all upset." The other girls nodded their agreement and clustered around Clare as though giving her support.

"It must be very upsetting for you all, I'm sure. We just wanted a quick word."

"With me?" Clare looked frightened.

"Well with all of you, if you don't mind?"

A hesitant, "Okay," from all three of them.

"Your names are?" Colm asked.

A young woman with fair hair and a pointy chin answered first, "I'm Christie Mason."

The third young woman, as dark as Christie was fair, dimples when she smiled and a buoyancy about her that Kate found attractive, "Lucy Grainger, the clumsy one of this trio!" She laughed.

"Well thank you for being available. We just

want to clarify where people were on Wednesday evening. I understand that the rehearsal finished about seven-thirty. Is that right?"

All three nodded. "So, was it straight back to your lodgings or a drink at the local? You probably deserved it." Kate kept her tone light.

Clare shook her head. "I went straight back to Mrs Murphy's and so did Ellie."

"But we went to the pub, didn't we Christie? There was a whole crowd of us."

"Did any of you see this man?" Kate produced the photocopy of the image they had on the police system for Lennon. "Sorry it's not very good quality."

Clare took the paper and looked, shook her head and passed it on. Lucy took it and stared for a while, "Isn't this the bloke that was pestering Jade, Christie?"

Christie took the photograph and held it away from her, squinting slightly. "I think it might be."

"So, what was this man doing to Jade?" Colm asked.

"I remember him coming into the bar. It was quite crowded and I noticed he seemed to be looking for someone. I thought poor chap come for a quiet drink with his girlfriend and us lot are in there," Lucy said. "Then he, sort o' barged his way through to where Jade was and I pointed him out to Christie, didn't I Chris?"

"Yes. I love people watching, don't you?

Anyway, Jade tried to shrug him off but then he said something. No idea what it was but she looked at him and nodded."

"After that, other people stepped between us and our view of them and next time it was clear he and Jade had gone," Lucy concluded.

"Any idea what sort of time this was?" Kate probed. Perhaps their surmising wasn't so far off the mark.

"Well, we went straight to the pub and it's only five minutes away. It's that one on the end of the road."

"The White Hart?" Colm supplied.

"That's the one. We'd just got our drinks and found a seat so about quarter to eight?" Lucy looked to Christie for confirmation.

"That sounds about right." Christie nodded her agreement.

"Did you see Jade or this man again that evening?"

Three shakes of the head.

"Not even Jade back at Mrs Murphy's, Clare?"

"No. I went straight to my room. Had a shower and straight to bed. I didn't hear anyone else come in."

Kate turned to Colm who mouthed, "Jade now!"

Kate subtly shook her head and Colm put his notebook away. Kate turned back to the young women. "Thank you all. You've been very helpful."

Walking back down the stairs, Kate talked over her shoulder to Colm following closely behind. "Check and see whether The White Hart has CCTV and also what there is on the street. I expect there is something as that's a really busy corner. We want signs of Lennon and Jade Froude.

"But not going for Jade now?"

"No. I have an idea. Tell you on our way back to the station."

CHAPTER 48

Colm settled back in the seat as he drove them back to the station. "Come on then. What's your idea?"

Kate got her thoughts in line before beginning. "We seem to have three overlapping crimes." She ticked them off on her fingers. "The ATM, the murders and the potential drug business."

Colm nodded. "And we seem to have potential answers for two of them, the ATM and the murders."

"If we 'solve' the murders we no longer have an excuse to visit the Play House, which means the drug thing is out of our hands."

Colm was incredulous, "So, are you suggesting we don't solve the murder case?!"

Kate smiled at his tone. "No, merely postponing it. Froude and Brooks aren't going anywhere until the show is done, so we could wait another couple of weeks."

"And you're sure it's Froude and Brooks we want?"

"Run through the case for me."

This time it was Colm's turn to gather his thoughts. "Okay. Jade makes contact with Mallory for a drugs hook up. For some reason she uses Clare West's name. Mallory turns up,"

"With the goods?"

"We didn't find cash or drugs on him so our murderer took them?" Colm said.

"Seems a reasonable conclusion."

"Mallory and Jade are having a chat and Brooks comes in and puts two and two together and makes five."

"We know he has a temper on him and is not accepting that things are over with Jade."

"So, Brooks attacks Mallory and accidentally kills him when he hits his head."

"Or thinks he's killed him."

Colm nodded. "Yeh, poor bloke was still alive." He shuddered at the memory of the silicone in Mallory's airway. "So did Jade help him hide the body and why hide it and why the signing out?"

"I think it was panic and then to cloud the waters. I think Brooks got Jade to scream to pull Stan away from his book and give him time to forge Mallory's signature. Otherwise, Stan would be searching the theatre before he locked up, looking for Mallory."

"So what did Lennon see?"

"Jade and Brooks planning their subterfuge or Brooks coming back from the false signing? Kate said. "Whatever it was it gave Lennon ammunition for some blackmail."

They were both silent and then Colm offered, "Lennon didn't know how to contact Brooks, so he went looking, knowing that the theatre company's social life was centred around pubs."

"Yes. He could have been looking for Brooks but instead found Jade."

"Which means he must have seen her and Brooks together in the theatre."

"Good point," Kate conceded.

Warming to his scenario, Colm continued, "So Lennon found Jade and frightened her into calling Brooks who, Bell says, was greatly agitated by the call."

"Lennon came to the theatre and Brooks let him in and then murdered him and hid him like he did Mallory."

"It would be tight timing for him to be out just after nine, which is what he said."

Kate agreed. "Have them look out for Brooks as well when checking the CCTV on the streets around the Play House. We have the theory. We now need the proof."

"Or a confession."

"But not yet, I think."

CHAPTER 49

Back in the incident room, Alice had collated her own information and that from the drugs' team on Henderson and his runners, Campbell and Harper. Kate decided to read through the files before she went to talk to Bart about her idea. If he thought it could run they would need to meet with DCI Wakeford and DC Terry Gilbert from the drugs unit.

The file on Henderson made interesting reading. Underneath the veneer of respectability, Kate could see the connections to the less than salubrious elements of the London crime world. She had worked there long enough to know some of the names that appeared on Henderson's CV. She called across to Colm, "If you add 'crime world' to most of the names Henderson worked with in London you won't be far off the mark."

Colm acknowledged this piece of information and added, "He doesn't seem like a candidate for a cultural ambassador, does he? Even without that bit of information."

Kate agreed. "No, he's a front man. Looking at this I'd be quite sure that the theatre company is a mask for some kind of illegal activity. And it could as well be drugs as anything else."

Alice offered, "Campbell and Harper are also not your average theatre workers. Both have crime sheets. Nothing outrageous but both have drugs related offences."

"Perfect for making contacts in each new venue."

"So, how are they hiding the stuff?"

Kate was thoughtful again, going over her conversations with Jim Wheelan. "Alice, do you have the company's itinerary? When are they next in Amsterdam? And what are they performing?"

"Leave it with me," Alice said.

Colm and Kate went back to their reading matter. "Harper, in particular, sounds like a thug," Colm offered.

"Umm. I wonder if Phipps deals directly with Henderson or with these two?"

"I can't see Henderson getting his fingers dirty."

Their contemplations were interrupted by Alice, "Okay, the company is off to Guildford and then Newcastle before a ferry crossing to Amsterdam."

"Does it say what they're performing?"

"All venues are showing the same play as here."

Kate smiled. Colm looked across, "You have another idea, don't you?"

Kate's smile broadened into a grin. "What did you notice about the statues that Wheelan had made?"

Colm thought and then shrugged, "They're

of the present cast members?"

"They're hollow. Wheelan said he would make plugs for the bottom so he could put sand in them to make them steadier."

"And then take it out to make them lighter for travelling, yes?"

"What if something else was secreted inside the statues that wasn't removed until they'd crossed back to Britain?"

Colm gave a silent whistle. "Oh perfect. We might not know how they've done it in the past but that's certainly a future project. Very clever."

"It's only a guess at the moment. We could really do with some more intel from the company now."

"And not arresting our suspects yet is part of that?"

"A major part but not the only part. I need to go and talk with Bart." Kate picked up her desk phone to contact him. She would need to put forward her very best arguments to get this past Bart and the drugs team.

CHAPTER 50

Kate knew it would be a hard sale with Bart but her heart dropped lower and lower as she watched him jot cryptic notes on his pad and listened without interruption to the information Kate and her team had gathered and her intention not to close the murder case. Finally, running out of steam, Kate finished and Bart looked up. His face betrayed no emotion, but his pen began to scratch at different notes he had made as he had listened.

"Let's start with the ATM job. You think Lennon was involved with the assistance of Gordon Connell. So why hasn't Connell been arrested?"

"Peace Way residents are mainly shop owners who live over the shop. No-one is talking, which leads me to think that someone else was also involved in the job, probably the Marshall Brothers. I'd like to try and get the other person or people involved."

"And Connell isn't a flight risk?"

"I don't think so. He may think Lennon's death was because of the ATM job, but we can set his mind at rest about that."

Bart nodded and wrote something alongside one of his former notes. "And what about the murder suspects, are they a flight risk?"

"Again, I don't think so. They're both involved in the show, so unlikely to leave until the theatre company does."

"And you want to continue to have access to the Play House in case you can get anything more on the drug angle?"

"Ideally, we could do with someone on the inside but at this late stage I can't see how we can do that. My concern is that if we arrest our suspects then the theatre company will leave prematurely. I'm not sure they could continue with this production without their director."

A quiet nod of the head was Bart's only response before, "I think your idea about the statues for the next Dutch visit is viable but how are they getting the stuff in at the moment?"

"As I said, we really need someone on the inside. Perhaps get close to Campbell and Harper."

"Not Henderson?"

"I get the impression that he's a bit of a ladies' man in a smarmy sort of way so we either put a female officer in a difficult situation or a man is unlikely to get close."

"And how much do you think this undercover worker will find in a couple of weeks?"

"I don't know, sir. May be something, may be nothing at all," Kate said. "I'm not sure how viable an action it would be."

Bart made a few more notes and then said,

"Leave this with me Kate. I need to decide what I think are the best moves and then we have to convince Wakeford if it's going to impact on their investigations."

"How soon do you want us to meet with them?"

"Well, if we're not rushing into arresting anyone, I think we can wait until Monday. Go and tell your team to enjoy their weekend."

"Thank you, sir."

Kate left with a lighter heart. Bart hadn't dismissed it out of hand or bitten her head off about not arresting their suspects immediately. Oh well, a weekend to wait and worry.

CHAPTER 51

The good thing about Bart's delay was that it gave Kate a chance to catch up on domestic jobs and she would be available for the picnic. Jude had been delighted when Kate had rung her that evening to say she was free. "Oh, great. I thought, with this case you'd be up to your eyebrows in work. Is it solved?"

"Sort of. I'm waiting on a decision from my DCI about what the next steps should be."

"I'm working tomorrow, early shift, so do you want to do something tomorrow evening?"

Kate suddenly found her mouth uttering sentences she hadn't censored first, "Why don't you come to me for food, stop over and we'll go to the picnic from here? I'm closer to the park than you are."

There was a pause and Kate wondered if she had rushed things, but Jude said, "That sounds lovely. I'll go home after work and freshen up and pack all the picnic stuff I've bought. Your fridge should be big enough." There was another pause and Jude asked, "Had you any plans for food tomorrow evening?"

Kate laughed, "Are you asking whether I'm doing ping cuisine?"

Jude echoed her laugh, "Just wondering!"

Bravely Kate said, "I will cook something

from scratch. Do you like coconut and fresh ginger?"

"Sure do. Right, I have two recipes in my repertoire and since your lasagne is better than mine you get the other one!" Kate had her fingers crossed as she said this. It had been a long time since she'd cooked her ginger and coconut curry. On that happy note they ended the call. Already Kate was panicking about cooking for Jude. She knew her limitations in the kitchen and compared to Jude she was in the pre-beginners class. Kate tried to console herself with the thought that Jude already knew she was useless at cooking. The task now was to make a list, do some shopping and tidy up if Jude was going to be staying over.

◆ ◆ ◆

To Kate's great surprise her cooking went better than she had anticipated. She'd already set herself to accept failure, but it was going surprisingly well. She sniffed appreciatively as she stirred the vegetables in their golden ginger sauce. She would add the coconut when she reheated it later. Ping rice was her only cheat as everything else was from scratch. Happy that she had done her best, she switched the flame off and put a lid over the curry. Time now to spruce herself up. Jude said she'd be here for fourish.

Monster was happy to be in and out of the

house on the rare days when Kate was home and he followed her now upstairs to her wardrobe. She wasn't going to glam up, something comfortable if they were going to spend time on the sofa. She'd picked up a couple of new release DVDs she hoped Jude may want to watch.

Looking now at the contents of her wardrobe, she felt depressed. Work clothes or scruffs. One decent pair of jeans but she wanted something a little more relaxing. Finally, she opted for a loose pair of harem pants that she'd bought on a whim several years ago and had never worn. A simple white t-shirt would be fine. Or would it?Kate hesitated. Jude would be here soon. Monster was no help. Whatever she tried on, he just sat and watched. His green eyes offering no sign of agreement or disapproval. Kate heard a car. So did Monster, and if Kate wasn't sure it was Jude's, Monster was. He disappeared from the doorway, off to greet his latest friend. Or, perhaps that should be only friend, as Kate was sure she was regarded merely as the purveyor of food.

CHAPTER 52

Kate stretched quietly, aware that Jude was still asleep next to her. Last night had been a great success. Jude had been impressed with the curry and had not thought it a cheat to have a shop bought trifle for dessert. They'd watched one of the DVDs but spent most of the evening chatting until romance took a hand.

In her shopping mode yesterday, she had bought pain au chocolate, easier to eat in bed, she had decided when contemplating croissants. Now, she crept out of bed and went down to the kitchen. On opening the door Monster was sat on the step waiting. Kate fed him first and then proceeded to brew coffee and warm the pastries. She didn't see the going of Monster and assumed he had gone back outside. She'd leave the door ajar so he could come and go as he wished again today.

Balancing the tray carefully, she climbed the stairs quietly, wanting Jude to awake to the surprise of breakfast. However, on entering the bedroom, Kate found Jude sat up, with the sheet tucked across her breasts, and Monster head butting her hand until she stroked him. Kate tutted and Jude smiled, "My very own wake-up call!"

Balancing the tray on Jude's bedside table,

Kate bent to move a cup and plate of pain au chocolate onto the coasters. She was aware that her dressing gown had slipped open and blushed when Jude smiled at her view. Making much of getting her own food and drink on the other bedside table, Kate slipped quickly out of her dressing gown and under the sheet pulling it up tightly. It was still too new a relationship to feel comfortable walking around naked.

♦ ♦ ♦

The picnic was in Eashire Park, a bequest from Lord Eashire in the 1850s. It boasted a fairy dell, a bandstand, flowerbeds and lawn. The nineteenth century cricket pavilion had been renovated as a café. When Kate and Jude arrived, picnic rugs and folding chairs were already being placed on one of the lawn areas. Kate with her red hair and fair skin opted for the shade of a tree, an oak she thought. Its spreading roots gave crannies for couples to set up in and the wide boughs gave plenty of shade. People called out to Jude as they passed and she waved and passed a few words. Kate felt a little out of it and sat nervously under the tree.

Perhaps sensing her nerves, Jude sat with Kate and friends and acquaintances came to them. Soon Kate was as involved as Jude with the chatter and relaxed into the event. She watched as mums and partners took it in turns to watch the older children in the children's play area whilst babies and toddlers crawled in the safe space created by rings of blankets. Kate felt it was quite idyllic.

Suddenly, the peace and tranquillity was broken by the hectoring tone of two women travelling in opposite directions to each of the groups gathered, "Come on, rounders time!"

Although there were a few groans, most people willingly got to their feet and teams were soon mustered. Jude pulled Kate to her feet, "Come on."

Kate followed and was soon fielding for her team as each batter took their chance as the ball fired at them. Suddenly, one was coming in Kate's direction. Shouts went up, "Catch it!"

Oh God! She was hopeless at ball games. All fingers and thumbs. She saw the ball dropping from the sky. She just stood and watched and then it was in her hands. A mighty cheer. Kate was the most amazed amongst them. And her heart lifted when she saw Jude grinning at her from the third base. She threw the ball to her and shouted, "That was pure fluke!"

Kate's luck did not last when her team were into bat. She missed all three throws and barely made it to first base. Jude followed her and whacked the ball. Throwing down the bat, she shouted at Kate, "Run! All the way round!"

Jude was so fast she almost overtook Kate and they collapsed in a laughing heap at the final base. Jude grinned. "We'll soon get you playing like a natural."

Kate wasn't convinced but had to admit the friendly rivalry and good humour of the group was a wonderful tonic to the pressure of work.

CHAPTER 53

Kate groaned as she got out of bed and realised she had used muscles playing rounders that she'd not used in a long while. Standing under a hot shower, she felt the warmth unknot them and stretched her shoulders and revelled in the heat. She didn't dare spend too long under the water. She'd received a text late last night from Bart asking her to attend a meeting with the drugs team at nine and a pre-meeting with himself at eight.

Despite the muscle ache, Kate felt good about the weekend, about the picnic and, most importantly of all, about Jude. Today, her mind felt clear and sharp. The more she thought about it, the more she thought her ideas would work if she could just get the bosses' backing. Ensuring Monster had been fed and gone out, Kate locked up and headed for her office.

At the station she was asked to go directly to Bart's office and was surprised to find PC Alice Giles already there, talking with Bart.

"Good morning sir, Alice."

"Morning boss," Alice replied, smiling whilst Bart waved his hand in acknowledgement of her presence.

Kate was intrigued. Why was Alice here? She was a very good member of her team and

Kate had been encouraging her to try for her sergeant's stripes but why would Bart want her in this meeting?

The reason soon became clear. "Kate, I have had long and involved discussion with the superintendent over the weekend and she is adamant that the murder case is resolved as soon as possible."

Kate's heart sank. They weren't going to allow her to get the drugs as well.

Bart continued, "I've asked PC Giles, Alice, here this morning to propose she become our undercover operative at the Play House. The Super did okay that idea."

Kate wasn't sure if her mouth had dropped open, but her shock would certainly have allowed for it.

"Alice?" Kate gathered her thoughts, "No disrespect to you Alice but you're not experienced in this line of work. It's very specialised."

Bart didn't give Alice chance to respond, "I believe Alice will be perfectly able to undertake this task. It is, as you yourself have said, only for a matter of two weeks. Alice will be a volunteer at the Play House. Home from uni and wanting space to think about her future."

"Alice is in her late twenties, sir and although she looks younger when in mufti, she won't look like a twenty something."

Alice answered this objection, "I'm going to

say that I took a few years out before uni. Perhaps community volunteering, something like that."

"You're going to have to have your back story really solid before you go in."

"And that's where you come in DI Medlar. You and Alice will prepare her backstory and rehearse it. Alice can start volunteering tomorrow."

"We'll need to run this past Julia Montgomery, the manager at the Play House. She will need to be in the know."

"Already done!" Bart said flatly. "Ms Montgomery is perfectly happy for Alice to volunteer and has suggested that she shadow Jim Wheelan as the theatre company's props are all in his workshop. Maybe Alice will be able to find out how they've been smuggling the drugs in."

Kate felt she now knew how it was to have the wind taken out of your sails. True, she was getting her own way with some of her plan for the three cases she was overseeing but Bart was taking it in a slightly different direction.

"What about DCI Wakeford?"

"That's why we're meeting early. I want to forestall any problems they might want to offer as a reason not to go down this route. He won't like having his thunder stolen but he's a good officer and will do what it takes to nail this group. Now, shall we get down to details?"

CHAPTER 54

As Bart had predicted, DCI Wakeford and his second in command, DS Bell were far from happy with the proposed plan to begin with but after much discussion and concessions on both parts, the plan was agreed. Kate would be Alice's contact point and her panic/problem word was 'Scarborough'. To be used either verbally or by text.

Returning to the office, Kate and Alice were met by two pairs of eyes, desperate to know what was going on. Kate called an immediate team meeting and updated them all on the state of play with all three cases and Alice's undercover role.

Colm gave a silent whistle. "So when do we bring in Froude and Brooks, boss?"

"Tomorrow. Today I want you and Len to go visit Gordon Connell and explain, obliquely that Lennon's death was connected to the theatre, not the ATM job."

Len coughed and offered, "I sort of know Gordy. He's come through with a bit of info now and then."

Kate's eyes lit up. "Has he now? Perhaps you could get him to come clean about who else was involved in the job. I am positive it wasn't just him and Lennon."

"Might it be better if I absented myself for part of your chat, Len?" Colm suggested.

Len nodded, "Maybe. We'll play it by ear."

"Okay, you two go off and do that and then when you're back, Colm, if you could chase forensics and see if they've got any news on that hair Mike found in the silicone and then begin to put the case together against Froude and Brooks. Len, you'll need to take over the murder book. Alice and I will be creating her back story."

As the two men left, Kate said, "Team debrief at five, okay?"

Both men nodded and Kate and Alice got down to work. As far as possible Kate and Alice needed to use Alice's real background for as much of her new identity as they could without revealing too much. "What's one of your grandmothers' maiden names?"

"You mean for my identity? I always liked Nicholls."

"Fine, Alice Nicholls it is. Where did you go to school?"

"Local primary and then on to Eashire Comp."

"You should check whether your class teachers in primary were still there five or so years after you left."

"What about the years off before uni?"

"I thought I'd say I'd done VSO, you know, Voluntary Service Overseas. I did do this, but only for a year. I'll extend it by three."

"Make sure you have dates clear in your head. Most people can recall key dates, even if they're a bit hazy about exact moments.

"So, which uni did you attend and what did you study?"

"Portsmouth and I studied Business Studies and Economics."

"Did you really? How come you ended up in the force?"

"I decided I didn't want to go down the corporate route and thought my skills would be useful in the police. I actually attended a careers day organised by the Students Union and chatted to a local detective constable. She was really upfront about some of the gender issues in the service but said she'd always felt it was more effective to knock things down from the inside rather than throw bricks from the outside." Alice blushed a little. She'd never really explained her reasons before, and certainly not to a superior officer.

Kate waved a hand, "Sorry, I didn't mean to be so nosey about your personal thoughts."

"No problem," Alice smiled. "Obviously I shall say the bit about not wanting to go down the corporate route and now I'm just trying to find what I want to do with my life."

"Where do you live?"

"Ah, ideally it ought to be with my parents, but I'd rather keep my family out of this. What do you suggest?"

"Where do you really live?"

"I rent a flat out towards Westergate."

"You could use that. Perhaps invent a flat mate or two?"

"Yes, I can use my final digs share at uni. There were three of us sharing. Yes, I can do that."

"Hopefully, most of this you won't have to use but you need to go away and memorise it all. Check on a few facts and we'll reconvene just before our team debrief."

CHAPTER 55

Gail Miller was no more pleased to see Colm and Len as she had been last time Kate had visited. Colm explained that they were there to speak to Connell again. This time Miller did use the tannoy. Having instructed Connell to come to the site office she said, "The lads are doing a collection for Kelly and they want to know when the funeral is to be."

"The body has been released so you may want to give Kelly a ring. I don't know whether she's at home or gone to her parents for a while."

"Her parents? Terry said they wanted nothing to do with either Kelly or himself since he took Kelly in."

"I think they may have had a change of heart."

Any further discussion was interrupted by a brisk knock on the office door and Connell's face appearing around the edge as he opened it.

"Come in Gordy," Miller said, "These officers want another chat with you."

Connell's face blanched and Colm thought there was a fight or flight moment, but Connell steeled himself and stepped inside. He looked warily from Colm to Len and then his face brightened as Len said, "Morning Gordy, how you keeping? I heard about Terry. I'm really sorry about it all."

Connell dropped his head and shook it slowly from side to side. Len continued, "Come and sit a moment, we've just got a bit of news for you and then we'll be out of here."

Colm looked at Miller who took the hint and grabbed her jacket and hard hat before leaving the office. Connell looked from Len to Colm and back again.

"What's this bit of news then?"

Colm pulled up another chair and sat knee to knee with Connell. "We just wanted to let you know that we believe we know who the murderer is. We hope to make an arrest in the next few days."

Connell lifted his drooping head and looked Colm in the eye, "Who is it?"

"We're not at liberty to tell you but I can say that it is in connection with..." It wasn't Colm's imagination Connell tensed as though waiting for a blow, "another murder at the Play House."

Connell sagged like a deflated balloon. "The Play House, not the..." he stopped himself.

"Not what Mr Connell?"

Connell shook his head. "No, nothing!"

Just then Colm grabbed his jacket pocket and then pulled out his phone. He said to the room in general, "Sorry, I'd better take this." And left the office.

Len took Colm's seat and began conversationally, "You and Terry been mates for long?"

"Yeh. Long enough. He was a good bloke. A bit handy with his fists when he'd had too much but a good bloke," he shook his head again.

"Before this Play House link we wondered if Terry had got himself in with some of the bad boys with one of his get rich quick schemes. You ever discuss anything like that?"

Connell shook his head but with not a lot of vigour and Len continued, "You see, we think Terry was behind that ATM job on Peace Way."

Connell tensed and said quickly, "I don't know nothing about that."

"Well, it occurs to me that Terry would be bright enough to know that tackling anything in Peace Way would upset the Marshall Brothers, unless they were involved as well. Don't you think?"

Again, Connell claimed ignorance.

"See, the thing is, my boss is only really interested in the big players. I think she'd quite happily come to an arrangement for the right information."

Connell remained quiet and the silence was broken by Colm's return. "Okay, Len. I don't think we should waste any more of Mr Connell's time."

Len got up, leaving space for Connell to leave. As he was closing the door, Len called, "Remember what I said, Gordy."

With the door closed, Colm looked questioningly at Len who said, "I'm not sure, but

I laid it out for him."

CHAPTER 56

Tuesday morning Kate met Colm outside Mrs Murphy's guest house. Her stomach was jittery and she'd managed nothing more than a cup of tea that morning. Were they doing the right thing letting Alice go undercover? She'd never forgive herself if she got hurt and if she was rumbled there was every chance that could happen. Now she and Colm were waiting for signs of life from the guest house before going in and getting Jade Froude. They'd decided at this stage that she was going to be asked to come and make a formal statement about both evenings in question. That way, Kate hoped, any news that went back to the Play House would not alert Brooks that they were on to him.

Colm nudged her. She looked and could see what he'd spotted. Jade was coming out of the door. They hadn't expected that. They had thought they would collect her after she'd breakfasted. Kate and Colm crossed the road and Jade noticed them. Was it Kate's imagination that the girl blanched?

"Good morning, Ms Froude. I'm glad we've caught you. We'd like you to come down to the station and make a formal statement, please."

Jade now looked like a trapped beast. "Couldn't this wait? I have a lot to do today.

That's why I'm up so early."

Kate tried to put a look of regret on her face. "I'm afraid this can't wait. We can let someone know if you were planning to meet them."

Jade shook her head. "No, it's okay. But will this take long?"

"To be honest, Ms Froude, I'm not sure. But if at any stage you need to let someone know where you are we can arrange for that."

◆ ◆ ◆

Colm escorted Jade to an interview room. The greyness of the place would have an impact on the soul of even the most hardened of criminals.

"Am I under arrest?" she asked Colm as she was shown to a seat, bolted to the floor.

"No, you are helping us with our enquiries," Kate answered coming in behind them, "but if you wish to have a solicitor present, we can organise that for you."

Jade looked doubtful. Would she look guilty if she asked for a solicitor? But she'd seen all these police dramas. Would it be more stupid not to have one present? Finally, she made her mind up, "I'd like a solicitor, please."

Kate kept her face neutral. "Do you have someone in mind or would you like me to contact the duty solicitor?"

"The duty solicitor is fine."

"I'll arrange that for you now. Obviously

there will be a bit of delay while they get here. Would you like anything? Tea and toast? You don't look like you had any breakfast this morning."

"Yes please."

Kate and Colm left, and the supervising officer went into the room. Kate organised the drink and snack. Returning to the office she said, "Do you think she's brighter than we gave her credit for? Or guiltier?"

Colm lent back in his chair. "I think everyone today thinks they know how we work because of all the police shows on the telly. The duty solicitor is on her way. It's Constance Styles."

"Oh well, a decent duty solicitor. What about forensics?"

"Nope. Mike is chasing. I've just got off the phone from talking to him."

"Why is it that in all those police things there's always tonnes of forensics and they have the results immediately? I want to live in that world."

Colm grinned, "You and me both."

CHAPTER 57

Constance Styles was sat alongside Jade Froude. She had discussed some of the key points with Kate and then her client. Now they were ready to begin. Kate introduced herself and then asked each of them to give their names for the benefit of the tape.

Kate had decided to lead with the second murder. "Ms Froude what did Terry Lennon say to you in the White Hart on Wednesday evening?"

Whatever Jade thought Kate was going to ask her, this was not it. She looked at Kate blankly, "Who?"

"The second man who died. Terry Lennon. He spoke with you in The White Hart around eight on that Wednesday evening." To pre-empt a denial, Kate slid a poor-quality photograph across the table for Jade to see. Despite the grainy texture, it was clearly time stamped and dated and showed Lennon leaning in to talk to Jade.

Jade stared at the still. She hadn't known that The White Hart had CCTV. Only the bar area, but it had picked up Jade and Lennon. "I didn't realise that was his name or that he was the second man murdered."

"What did he say?" Colm reiterated.

"Oh, he was just trying to chat me up. I told

him he was too old for me." Jade gave a nervous laugh.

Kate feigned mock confusion. "And yet we have witnesses that say you and Lennon left together. Where did you go?"

Jade's already pale face greyed as she sat there. Kate became more conciliatory. "Let me help. We know that you and Lennon went outside and that you made a phone call." Kate slid another still across. This was much better quality despite it being an outside shot at night. It clearly showed Jade making a phone call and Lennon gesticulating beside her. "Who did he ask you to phone?"

Jade's body sagged. Styles leaned across and spoke quietly to her client. Jade nodded her head and Styles spoke to Kate.

"My client wishes to draw up a statement about the events of the night in question."

Kate terminated the interview and she and Colm left.

◆ ◆ ◆

Back in the interview room, Styles read Jade's statement.

> *"Mr Lennon asked me to contact my boyfriend. At first I didn't know who he meant but then realised that it was Jason Brooks he was referring to. I telephoned*

> *Mr Brooks who arranged for Mr Lennon to go to the Play House immediately. Mr Lennon was to knock four times on the stage door and Mr Brooks would let him in. I don't know what Mr Lennon wanted to talk to Mr Brooks about or what happened after Mr Lennon arrived at the Play House."*

Styles laid the paper down and looked at Kate.

"Thank you. That does help clarify some of our ideas. Could you explain why Mr Lennon thought Mr Brooks was your boyfriend?"

Again, Jade looked like a rabbit caught in a set of headlights. "I don't know."

"I'm assuming that Mr Lennon must have seen you with Mr Brooks at some point prior to Wednesday. Would that have been Monday evening when he came in to fix the trap door? Did he see you and Mr Brooks arranging for you to create a distraction for Stan?"

Jade bowed her head and her shoulders began to shake. Kate pushed the obligatory box of tissues across the table. Blindly, Jade's hand groped for them without raising her head. Pulling out a handful, she buried her face in them. Kate allowed her time to compose herself.

"Do you want to tell us what happened on both evenings?"

Jade shook her head, face still down but Kate heard the mumbled, "He'll kill me!"

"Not if he's been arrested he won't."

Again, Styles spoke quietly to her client and then nodded to Kate to continue. Step by step Kate led Jade through the events of Monday evening. The meeting with Mallory to do a drugs deal, the little bit of flirting, Brooks' explosive temper and the death of Mallory.

"I did want to call the police," Jade wailed, "but Jason said I would be an accessory and that it's my fault things had got out of hand and he'd get away with it being a crime of passion because I was such a tease."

Jade looked up and any sign of the pert young woman was gone. Kate had heard film critics call such outbursts 'ugly crying' and this was certainly true for Jade.

Kate then led Jade through her contact with Lennon again before finishing the interview. "Jade I am going to keep you here, at the station, to make a formal statement. You will be charged as an accessory..." Anything else Kate was planning to say was drowned in the wail from Jade. Kate waited for her to control herself before continuing, "However, given the circumstances and a good solicitor you may well receive a minimum sentence."

Kate and Colm stood to leave and Kate addressed Styles. "I'll give you time with your client before sending someone in to take a formal statement."

Styles nodded. "Thank you, Inspector. I agree

with your summary about sentencing and I can recommend a barrister to take Ms Froude's case."

CHAPTER 58

Before going to arrest Jason Brooks, Kate sent Colm off to organise a warrant and search party for both Brooks' lodgings and any space in the Play House. Kate decided to look in on Mike. She could see from the cheery wave of his hand beckoning her into his domain that he had good news.

"Detective Inspector Medlar. You must be a mind reader. I have just received the email we were waiting for," he tapped his keyboard. "Yes, they were able to extract DNA from the hair but no, it does not belong to our victim. All we need now is a suspect."

"You may yet get your wish," Kate smiled. "We're about to make an arrest and I've got a search party organised so you may have some shoes to match your footprint as well."

"Oh Inspector, you spoil me!" Mike fluttered his eye lashes and Kate gave him a playful punch. "Don't get too excited. We may have forensics for the first murder but precious little for the second."

"Tell the search team to bring in trousers and jackets. The amount of force used on Lennon's head would have resulted in splatter. If there's a drop of his blood on your suspect's clothes, I will find it."

"Thanks, Mike. I'll let them know."

Back in the incident room Colm was talking to the search team. Kate added the clothes to their list of items to be seized. Len was to lead the group and Kate was pleased to see his enthusiasm. He certainly was living down his former reputation of being a lazy officer.

The team left to search Brooks' lodgings first and would catch up with Kate at the Play House. Colm stretched. "Just waiting for the warrant. It shouldn't be too long."

Kate updated him on Mike's DNA news. "My only concern is, as yet, nothing but Jade's phone call ties Brooks to Lennon. Some forensics would be nice. You know how a jury loves the science."

"Hence the clothes to be examined. Mike reckons there would have been splatter?"

"Yes. We can but hope."

"Don't forget we'll also have Brooks' and Jade's phone records that ties it up."

"Umm. I'm just worried he'll claim he sent Lennon on his way and had nothing to do with the murder."

"There's CCTV on the front of the theatre but nothing by the stage door that'll show Lennon coming and going."

Kate shook her head. "Remember, Jade said Lennon was sent to the stage door. So Brooks clearly knew how to take the alarm off that. No-one knew Lennon was in the theatre."

"So, if he's clever, Brooks will claim that

Lennon went on his way from the stage door and it's not his fault if we then can't find him on any CCTV in the area."

"I'm hoping we pin him for Mallory's death and he coughs to Lennon's."

The office printer began to whirl. "That's our warrant. Come on."

CHAPTER 59

Kate had to admit she rather liked taking the arrogant Mr Brooks down a peg or two. On their arrival in the auditorium, Brooks was, again, directing some of the cast members. When he saw Colm and Kate, he forestalled them with, "I'm sorry Inspector you've missed the lunch break. Whatever you want will have to wait."

Kate stayed where she was at the top of the raked seats whilst Colm strode down to where Brooks and his papers were. There, in a clear, strong voice that carried beautifully in the theatre, Colm began the Miranda rights.

Brooks was speechless. Less so the cast on the stage. Whispers began immediately and Kate noted a few mobile phones being surreptitiously used. She sighed. Social media. Everyone could know everything at the touch of a button. In this case it didn't matter.

Colm insisted that Brooks be cuffed and he was protesting as much about this indignity as he was about the arrest as they joined Kate at the back of the auditorium. Despite his noise, Kate could see the fear in his eyes but she was under no illusion that Brooks was going to be an easy nut to crack.

◆ ◆ ◆

To begin with, Brooks demanded that he wanted his own solicitor but changed his mind when he understood he would spend the waiting time in a cell. So, some ninety minutes after his arrest, Brooks was sat in the same interview room as had been used for Jade Froude, talking with the duty solicitor, Jon Hynd. Who also pointed out to Brooks, who was still complaining that he couldn't use his own solicitor, that unless his solicitor was familiar with criminal law, then a duty one may be better.

Whether it was the use of the term 'criminal law' that brought Brooks to order was not clear, but he seemed to change. Gone was the belligerence Kate and Colm had witnessed. Now he was "happy to clear this matter up".

"Before we begin, Mr Brooks, I would like to take a saliva sample for DNA matching. Are you happy to do that?"

Brooks looked far from happy but an affirmative nod from Hynd made him give his assent. Colm took a sample tube from its sterile wrapper and asked Brooks to wipe the inside of his mouth and cheeks. He then sealed the container and passed it to the officer standing waiting outside the door.

Once again Kate asked everyone to identify themselves as the interview was being recorded. Brooks sat attentively, his body language conveying helpfulness. Kate began with some routine questions, asking Brooks to talk her through his activities on the Monday evening. Then she began her slow paring down of his defences.

"Mr Brooks, would you say you have a volatile temper?"

"No, not particularly. I can be short with people if they don't do things the way I want. But that's the role of a director." Brooks was clearly finding the need to establish his status.

"But what about in your private life?"

Brooks evaded the question, "I don't have much of a private life, being on the road for much of the time."

"What about your relationship with Ms Emily Lansdown?"

Brooks looked at Kate through half-closed lids. Kate wasn't sure he was going to answer. "You did have a relationship with Ms Lansdown, didn't you?"

"Yes, but it was rocky from the start. I shouldn't have continued seeing her."

"In fact, you tried to continue seeing her even after she'd asked you to leave. Isn't that so, Mr Brooks?"

"That was just a misunderstanding."

"A misunderstanding that led a court to issue a restraining order on you. And how many times did the police visit you with reports of domestic violence when you lived with Ms Lansdown?"

"There were never any charges. They were just heated arguments."

"Heated arguments that led to," Kate checked her notes, "a broken television, a damaged bathroom door and cries for help from Ms Lansdown."

Kate let the information hang in the air. Brooks made no reply and looked down at his hands resting in his lap. Kate could just see the whiteness of his knuckles. Looking through her papers again, she selected one to place on top. "Witnesses have said that you used to have a relationship with Ms Jade Froude but that you were unable to accept that it was over."

Brooks' hands now gripped the edge of the table and Kate could see the white extending to the tips of his fingers. "I love Jade. I just wanted her to see that. That's all." Whilst his hands gripped the table Kate also noted that Brooks had a pale band of skin on the little finger of his right-hand. A ring? She would need to check.

"Would you say you were a jealous man, Mr Brooks?" Again, flicking through her papers. "Because witnesses have said you knocked out a young man who was trying to chat Jade up once and that you were constantly hounding her."

"I was not hounding her. And that bloke was a nuisance. It's not my fault he couldn't take a punch."

"So, you are a jealous man? Is that what happened on Monday night when you found Jade talking with Mr Mallory? You thought this was another man trying his luck and you weren't having that, were you?"

Brooks threw his hand up into the air and looked at his solicitor, Hynd. "I have no idea what they are on about." He turned back to Kate, "What evidence do you have, Detective Inspector Medlar?" The sarcasm was unmistakeable.

"At this moment in time, Mr Brooks, your lodgings and any private areas or lockers you have in the Play House are being searched. Shoes and clothing will be part of the forensic seizure. A footprint here, a stray hair there. It all adds to our evidence."

Brooks looked uncomfortable and asked, "Am I entitled to a comfort break?"

Kate confirmed this and formally suspended the interview. An officer escorted Brooks and Kate and Colm left the solicitor to await the return of his client. Once away from the interview room, Kate asked Colm to check Brooks' personal effects logged at the desk and if there was a ring, to take it to forensics. Something like a ring had made a mark on Mallory's face. Perhaps there was evidence of Mallory on Brooks' ring.

CHAPTER 60

On returning to the interview room, Kate was met with a speech from Brooks' solicitor, Mr Hynd, "Inspector, my client feels you are on a fishing trip and, unless you can offer concrete proof of my client's involvement with this murder, I have advised him to answer with 'No comment'."

Kate was tempted to send Brooks back to his cell and hope that forensics came up with some answers before their twenty-four hours was up. Although, she thought they had a good chance of getting an extension on Brooks' custody. But no. She'd try the evidence they had for the Lennon murder.

Kate slid the still of Jade and Lennon making a phone call outside The White Hart. "Mr Brooks, do you recognise the people in this image?"

She turned so that the image faced Brooks and he pulled it towards himself for a closer look. "That's Jade Froude. I don't know who the chap is."

"Are you sure, Mr Brooks?"

Brooks made a point of having another look, "Yes, quite sure."

"Do you see the date and time stamp on this still? It's taken from a CCTV camera outside The White Hart, which I understand is a frequent stopping place for the company."

Brooks stayed silent.

"You see, the interesting thing is that Jade's phone records and your phone records show that at this precise time she was phoning you at the behest of Mr Lennon. Terry Lennon, the man in the image." Kate waited before asking, "Can you tell me what you and Jade discussed in that phone call?"

Brooks looked Kate straight in the eye and said, "No comment."

"You see I have the problem that firstly you lied to me and said you'd not received any calls on Wednesday evening and secondly, we have a witness that says this call, and it's the only call you received on Wednesday evening, made you very agitated. Can you explain why that was?"

Again, "No comment."

"Jade Froude has given us a signed statement where she claims that you made arrangements for Mr Lennon to come to the Play House and be let in through the stage door. And that is the last time anyone saw him, alive. Is her statement accurate?"

"No comment!" with particular force.

"Why would Ms Froude make up something like that?"

Brooks couldn't help himself, "Because she's a neurotic, attention seeking tease!"

"By 'tease', do you mean a flirt?"

Brooks merely looked at Kate, the anger

evident in his eyes and in the tension of his neck muscles. Hynd must have sensed the temper that was boiling and placed a restraining hand on his client's arm. Brooks looked down at it, took a deep breath and shook the hand off."

"Why did you hide the bodies in the silicone? First Mallory and then Lennon."

"No comment." Brooks was looking intently at his hands, clasped in front of him.

"Did you know that Mallory was still alive when you covered him?" Brooks' head shot up. His face disbelieving. Kate continued, reading from the post-mortem report. "The deceased has signs of inhaled silicone in his airways. The trachea and bronchi are lined with it and approximately eighty percent of his alveoli were occluded with the material."

"If you'd called an ambulance, Mallory might still be alive," Colm added.

Brooks hung his head and muttered, "No comment."

Kate brought the interview to a close. She wanted her final comment to Brooks to make him think. "Mr Brooks, we will find forensics to link you to both these crimes. I would suggest that you talk with your solicitor and discuss the advantages, to you, if you confess rather than the police having to prove. Because I promise you, we will prove your involvement."

CHAPTER 61

On her way back to the incident room, Kate popped in to see if Bart was free. He was and she briefly updated him on Brooks. "At the moment our evidence is circumstantial or hearsay, but I am sure Mike will find forensics."

Bart agreed but began another topic. "Just in case you are fretting, I have contacted Ms Montgomery this morning. Alice arrived punctually, has been introduced to various staff as she was escorted down to Jim Wheelan's workshop. Mr Wheelan is happy to have an additional pair of hands and, apparently, was chuffed that a young woman was interested in the more technical side of the business."

"Oh good," Kate said, although she was still worried about Alice's position.

Bart saw this. "She's a professional, Kate. She'll be fine."

Kate murmured her agreement and returned to her incident room. Colm was tapping at his keyboard but turned when Kate arrived. "I had a thought about why he used the silicone."

Kate nodded for him to continue. "Do you think he was trying to confuse the time of death?"

"How do you mean?"

"Well, you can use silicone to preserve

things, can't you? So, did he think that being encased in silicone we wouldn't be able to tell when Mallory died?"

Kate was thoughtful. "It would work for Lennon but what about Mallory. We could pin the time of death because of him signing in and out."

"Unless he thought Mallory's signature would be the last one and hadn't reckoned on Lennon being in."

"To be honest Colm, I'm not sure. Perhaps Brooks will deign to tell us when we have the forensics to start pushing him from his *No comment* stance."

"Just a thought!"

"We'll keep it in mind. I think now we need to start compiling our case against Brooks and also what we charge Jade Froude with."

"At the very least she has obstructed a police investigation. Do you think we could have her as an accomplice? Or it could even be a conspiracy?"

"That's what I'm not sure of. Let's start getting our ducks in a row."

The next hour or so was focused work. Kate began her detailed report on the steps in the investigation and the evidence they had compiled. She had to admit, sure as she was that Brooks was their murderer, unless forensics came up with something, it was a slim case.

At some point Len returned and detailed the items he had logged with forensics. "Everyone down there is working on our items and Mike says he'll get information to you as soon as he can."

"Okay. I'm going down to have a chat with the custody sergeant about Brooks' arrest and then I think it's time for us to go home. We can't chase anything until either Mike and his team or Alice have something to report.

CHAPTER 62

Even though she had finished earlier than usual, Monster was still waiting for her by the gate as she drew up in her car. Kate wondered if it was the sound of her engine that alerted him. Whatever it was, he never missed a greeting unless Jude had arrived before her. Kate was in two minds about whether to go out again and attend the adult only swimming session. It would mean she would see Jude but having arrived home she was reluctant to go out again. She decided to text Jude and if she was going to the session she would turn up as well.

Jude only took a few minutes to reply and the answer was *yes* to the swimming session. "Well, that's decided then, Monster. I'm off out for a swim." Kate moved around her home, changed into casual wear and found her swim bag and ensured that everything she needed was in there. Monster followed, adding an occasional comment as Kate spoke to herself as she got ready.

It was a long time since Kate had attended the adult session from the beginning. Jude was in the 'serious swimmer' lane and Kate decided that she too would do some serious strokes. Two lengths of the pool later she decided that the leisurely breast stroke she had adopted was doing her muscles a lot more good that trying to power up and down in a crawl.

At some point she was aware that Jude had joined her but sensing Kate's semi-meditative state as she swam, she just shadowed her. Finally, Kate pushed off from the deep end and turned to float on her back. She smiled at Jude who was still keeping pace with her.

"Hello, there." Kate's smile deepened.

"I didn't like to interrupt. You seemed to be in a world of your own there."

"Umm. I was thinking things through. Have you got any plans for after the swim?"

"Not particularly. What had you in mind?"

"I want to walk a potential route for a crime. I'll treat you to pizza after?"

Jude grinned. "How could a girl turn down such a romantic offer!"

Kate turned again and splashed a little as they then headed for the changing rooms.

Coming out of the leisure centre, Kate's phone rang. Seeing that it was Alice she said, "I have to take this. We'll take my car and I'll drop you back later?"

Jude agreed and they walked towards Kate's car as she took Alice's call. "Hi, Alice. How did you get on?" Kate clicked her car open and Jude got in whilst Kate remained outside.

"Nothing much to report but did you notice a large reinforced container in Jim's workshop?"

Kate thought back to the room. Yes, she

remembered the unit. "Blue and padlocked."

"Yep. That's the company's travelling storage unit and only Campbell and Harper ever go in there. Jim reckons they're in and out at least once a day."

"A good chance that's where the drugs are stored, do you think?"

"That's pretty much where my mind was at. I'm going to get in early tomorrow. Jim says they're normally there about nine. So, I'll see if I can chat to them."

"Just be careful. Remember their rap sheets. Neither is a choir boy!"

"I will, I promise. Any news on the murder? The place is buzzing with all sorts of theories. Neither Jade nor Brooks have been seen since this morning."

"Jade has moved to another guest house. Her sister's with her. Brooks has opted for 'No comment' so we're waiting on forensics."

"Do you think you'll get supporting evidence?"

"I hope so. Mike seems quite confident."

"Okay then boss. I'll ring again tomorrow."

"Take care, Alice."

CHAPTER 63

Getting in the car, beside Jude, Kate said, "Sorry about that. Work."

Jude asked no questions and Kate was grateful for that. She would either have to lie or avoid the question.

"Right! We're going to the Play House car park."

A smile in her voice, Jude repeated, "The car park? Not the Play House, just the car park. What a treat!"

Kate grinned as she put the car into gear and drove out to their venue.

The back of the Play House was dark. The area behind the place was undergoing regeneration. The old warehouses were making way for more housing, but it was early in the development, so only the occasional street light ghosted the once busy streets. Kate got her torch from her glovebox. "Let's go!"

Leading the way to the street running along the side of the Play House, Kate played the light up and down, commenting, "No residential buildings and no CCTV."

On the main street the road opposite was Peace Way.

Kate pointed out, "That camera was put out of action and none of the premises here have any." She took Jude's arm and they crossed into Peace Way.

"You have plenty of residents here," Jude said, pointing at the lighted windows above the many shops in the road."

"Umm! Unfortunately, nobody heard anything!"

"What?" Jude was shocked. "That can't be true."

"We think they're too frightened," Kate said stopping in front of the ply board cover. "This is where they took the ATM from."

"But it must have weighed tonnes. What did they use?"

"Six hundred and seventy odd kilos, apparently and I think they used the bucket on the front of a digger."

Jude nodded as she considered this. "It would work. So," she had been listening to Kate's commentary as they walked to the scene of the crime, "Your gang used the digger I saw at the back of the Play House. They brought it here avoiding all but one camera that they'd disabled. Made a hell of a noise, that no-one heard, and then what?"

"I think they went back the way they came."

"So, is the cash machine still in the bucket or did they load it onto a truck or something?"

"I don't know, but whichever way round they did it I think they went back to the car park. Come on."

Back there they got back in the car. "Will you mark on this street map where we go now?" Kate asked as she reached for her book. She had desperately needed it when she first moved to Eashire.

"Sure, you got a pen?"

Kate reached into her inside jacket pocket and handed a biro over. "Okay. They must have turned left out of the car park otherwise one of the cameras along Commercial Street would have picked them up." Kate turned the car left. The road continued into the development area. At the first crossroads she asked, "Which way, would you guess?"

By the light of her phone screen Jude said, "Left again. If you go right you hit the A-road and out of town."

"Wouldn't they want to get out of town?"

"Yes, but undetected, right? There will be masses of cameras on the A-road."

"Well done! I'll make a criminal of you yet!" Kate turned the car left again. The road was still going out of town but on smaller roads. Roads, Kate pointed out, that did not have traffic cameras.

At a roundabout neither of them was sure which exit to take. "The first exit looks like it bends back into town but the second and third are both heading for the edge of the expanse of the town. Straight across is one of those light industry estates and the third goes to that out-of-town development, White Spirit."

"So, what do you think? Exit two?"

"Yes, go for it."

They were soon in a maze of roads that encircled and criss-crossed a large industrial estate: garages and showrooms, storage units and building merchants, painters and decorators and plumbers' merchants. Kate stopped the car.

"They could have driven anywhere in here. But have you noticed there are several CCTV cameras on these businesses? Perhaps we could find them as they drove past."

Jude tried to smother a yawn and Kate was contrite, "I'm so sorry. I'll drive you back to pick your car up and we'll get pizza on the way." Kate turned the car around, "But you're going to have to direct me back to where we started. I'm completely lost."

CHAPTER 64

Whatever Kate had planned to do with the ATM job had to be put on hold as she was met with a message from the custody sergeant: Brooks had been demanding to see his solicitor since seven that morning and that Mr Hynd was, at present, with his client.

Kate phoned down, "Hi Dave, Kate Medlar. What's the state of play with Brooks?"

"Good-morning Inspector, Brooks and his solicitor are in interview room two."

"Has Brooks had breakfast and a shower yet?"

"Nope."

"Would you arrange for that to happen and then put them in interview room one." Kate thought interview room one was the gloomier of the two; just to twist the metaphorical knife a little.

If Brooks was yet to breakfast, Kate thought she would have time to talk with Mike. As usual, Mike was crouched over a computer screen in his lab. At Kate's entrance, he looked up, "Morning, Kate. I've just emailed you."

Kate thought he looked like he'd slept at his desk. A day's stubble and a crumpled shirt spoke of hours of work. Kate smiled, "It must have passed me on the stairs! Anything useful, please!"

"Your wish is my command. Hang on a minute, I'll pull up the report." A few clicks later, "We managed to match one of Brooks' shoes to the footprint in the evidence for the first murder."

"A hundred percent?"

"Yes. Same make, same tread and, most importantly of all, same wear pattern."

"Still no news on Brooks' DNA but I have called the DNA lab this morning and begged them to put a rush on it. They said they'd try for lunchtime today."

"Fingers crossed I have enough evidence by then to either charge our suspect or apply for an extension. What about the second murder?"

"A bit more tentative but potential DNA. We found blood in the leg seam of a pair of Brooks' trousers and in the tread of a shoe. At this stage we can say that it's not Brooks'. His blood group is O positive and the blood we retrieved is A positive."

"And the blood group of Lennon?"

Mike grinned, "A positive!"

Kate returned the grin. "Enough to put him in the frame. Brilliant!" She was tempted to punch the air. "DNA will be the clincher but if he won't confess, we can certainly make a case against him."

Mike gave a mock bow in his seat, "We're here to please!"

"Thanks Mike. And thank your team as well. I saw the log Len brought in for Brooks' stuff. Have you even been home since yesterday?"

"Home? What is that?"

"Sorry, Mike."

Mike waved her away, "Give over! I'll head home in an hour or so and get spruced up and then only pop back for a few hours."

"Don't your family miss you? Seriously."

Mike switched mid-smile, "Yeh, fortunately Sophie is a nurse and works shifts and understands that the job doesn't stop when your shift is up. The kids are both in uni now. But, yeh, I think I missed out on their childhood." He swept a stray lock of hair back and continued with a smile, "But at least when they're home we have more quality time with them and less of 'turn that music down!'"

Kate returned the smile, remembering her own parents' shouting up the stairs when she played Bowie too loudly.

CHAPTER 65

Brooks' hair was still damp from his shower and he had declined the use of the razor. His stubble showed the grey that he clearly dyed out from his hair. Mr Hynd, looking a little less spruce than yesterday was in attendance. Colm waited for Kate to take a seat before sitting next to her. Once again, Kate asked everyone to introduce themselves for the tape.

Mr Hynd ostentatiously rattled a sheet of paper. "My client would like to make a statement with reference to the two deaths at the Play House." He adjusted his glasses and began to read,

> *"I first saw Joseph Mallory in The White Hart last Saturday evening. He was annoying Jade and I told him to clear off. The next time I saw him was on Sunday evening at the Play House."*

Kate's heart lifted. He was going to confess.

> *"He and Jade slipped into the theatre workshop. I thought he looked furtive and was worried about Jade, so I followed them. In the workshop Mallory and I got into a bit of an argument, which resulted*

> *in me pushing him. He fell over and hit his head as he fell. I felt for a pulse and couldn't find one. I panicked and put the body in the moulding cabinet. I thought he was dead. At that point I was just trying to hide the body. Then I thought that if I poured the silicone in, it would destroy evidence and confuse the time of death."*

Kate bit her lip to stop herself from repeating the truth that Mallory had still been alive at that point.

Mr Hynd continued,

> *"I forced Jade to create a diversion so that Stan would leave his booth, and then signed Mallory out. I didn't know that Mr Lennon was still in the theatre and could prove the time of Mallory's supposed departure. I did not mean to kill Joseph Mallory. It was an accident. I panicked and know I should have told the police everything from the start. I have no knowledge of Mr Lennon's death."*

Mr Hynd put the paper down with a flourish. For a moment the only sound was the slight buzz from the recording device.

Kate looked at Brooks a moment before speaking and then she said, slowly and clearly, "Thank you Mr Brooks but I am afraid your accident became murder the moment you drowned Joseph Mallory in the silicone."

Hynd interrupted, "My client has explained that he panicked and had been unable to find a pulse."

"I know, but it doesn't alter the facts, Mr Hynd. You know that." A pause, "And we still have the problem with Mr Lennon's death."

"My client has already explained that he has no knowledge of Mr Lennon's death."

Kate ignored Hynd and looked directly at Brooks, "But we know that's not true, don't we Jason?"

Brooks looked away and Kate pressed on. "You see, creating blood when you kill someone increases the likelihood of us finding evidence. Minute droplets of blood can hide in the creases, the seams, the patterns on the soles of your shoes. A hundred places, and we can find them, analyse them and get DNA from them."

Brooks looked at his solicitor who nodded his head. Kate didn't know whether Hynd was acknowledging that they could do these things or that Brooks needed to come clean. She pushed her point, "What blood type are you Mr Brooks?"

Brooks looked at his hands, "I'm not sure. O positive, I think."

Kate smiled brightly, "Quite right, O positive.

So can you explain why we have found A positive blood on your clothes and shoes?" Another pause, "Which so happened to be Mr Lennon's blood group."

Still no response from Brooks. Hynd leaned in and spoke softly in Brooks' ear. He nodded. Hynd asked, "Could I have some time with my client, please Inspector?"

"Of course," Kate and Colm rose, "Interview suspended at the bequest of Mr Brooks and his solicitor at nine-forty," Kate double checked her watch, "seven. DC Hunter and DI Medlar exiting the room."

CHAPTER 66

The grin that had wreathed Colm's face as they had waited for Brooks and Hynd to consult, disappeared as they re-entered the interview room. Once again, Hynd held a paper in front of him but the fanfare of the previous statement was missing.

> *"My client agrees to co-operate fully with any questions you may have in relation to the death of Mr Lennon."*

Kate looked at Brooks. He looked resigned. Kate knew they had their suspect and that he was reeled in tight. This next bit was for form's sake. "Thank you for your co-operation, Mr Brooks. If we can go back to Wednesday evening?"

Brooks nodded and Kate consulted her notes. "You received a call from Jade Froude that evening. What did you discuss?"

"She told me that a man had sought her out in the pub and wanted to talk to me. Apparently, he hadn't asked for me by name but rather 'the man you were talking to in the theatre when that chap was killed'. Jade was in bits. This man, who I later found out was called Terry Lennon, said he knew all about the murder and would go to the police, if firstly Jade didn't phone me, and then the same threat if I didn't meet with him that night."

Kate could hear the disgust in Brooks' voice. Was it because Lennon had dared to threaten him?

"So, you planned to meet him at the Play House? How did he get in?"

"I knew Stan would have gone by nine so I told Jade to tell Lennon he should rap four times on the stage door."

"Wasn't the door alarmed?"

"Yes, but I know the code because I have a key to the front entrance."

"What about a key to the stage door?"

"It's a fire exit. It doesn't have a key. You can open it from inside but not from the outside."

Colm made notes as Brooks spoke. "And it's the same code for both doors?" He now asked.

"Yes. It's all on the same system."

Point clarified, Kate continued, "So what happened when Lennon came inside."

"I wasn't sure who else was still in the Play House so I took Lennon into the workshop. No-one was likely to go in there."

"And what did he want?"

"Money! What else?" It was a rhetorical question and Brooks continued, "He'd seen me coming out of the workshop and then arguing with Jade. Later, he saw me signing the log book. When the body was discovered and you went to talk to him about it he put two and two together."

"So, he had no proof, as such?"

"No, but he said you lot would soon have evidence, especially if he pointed them in the right direction."

"How much did he want?"

"Twenty thousand."

"Not a fortune then?" Kate queried.

Brooks looked at her disdainfully, "We both know that wouldn't be the end of it, would it? He'd constantly be coming back for a little more. He'd bleed me dry."

"So, why not just tell us then that Mallory's death was an accident?"

Brooks looked like Kate was speaking another language. He ignored her comment and continued with his narrative, "He was such an arrogant little man. Before I knew what I was doing, I lifted a strut off the wood pile and hit him across the back of the head."

"Just one blow?"

"Oh yes!" there was a note of, if not glee, then certainly satisfaction in his voice, "I put all my weight behind it."

"You intended to kill him?"

Brooks shrugged, and Hynd put a warning hand on his arm. Briefly, Brooks looked at him and then turned back to Kate, "I suppose I must have. I know I just wanted to get rid of him."

"So why the cabinet again?

Another shrug, "I thought I might as well do the same thing as last time."

"Like a signature?" Colm offered.

"Brooks' face brightened, "Yes, a signature."

Kate's heart froze. He sounded like others might have ended the same way as Lennon and Mallory in the future if they'd dared to cross Jason Brooks. Had she managed to nip a potential serial killer in the bud?

CHAPTER 67

Both Kate and Colm blew their breaths out as they sat back in the incident room.

"Wow!" said Colm. "That was chilling. Do you think he might have killed again? I certainly got that impression."

"Yes, me too," Kate agreed. She sat up straight in her chair. "Right, I'll send everything we've got to the CPS and check that we go for murder on both counts. In the meantime..."

Kate was stopped by the arrival of Len. "Morning boss. I think I might have a lead on that ATM job."

Kate could see he was bursting with something that he thought was important. She allowed him his moment in the sun. "Go on then."

Len sat at his desk and swivelled his chair round to face the room. "I went for a drink last night and came across Gordy Connell," Read, *I went looking for him*, Kate thought. "Anyway, he let slip that Paul Marshall has a lockup on the Handley Estate."

Kate held a hand up, "Hang on Len, where's that?"

Colm walked to the street map of Eashire on the wall of the room. He peered at it for several minutes and then began to trace a route. He tapped the map. "This is the Play House and this," he traced a route that Kate thought was similar to that which she and Jude had travelled the previous evening, "is the Handley Estate. Light industry, small businesses."

Len reclaimed the limelight. "Well, I went out to the estate this morning and I think we have a couple of options for a lock up and both pass a traffic camera on the road into the estate. The one I favour is in the Best Storage. It's run by an ex-con I recognised as one of the Marshall Brothers' gang."

Kate kept her own sleuthing secret, "Well done, Len!" She was pleased to see the glow of confidence on his face. "Colm you take a look at camera footage. And Len can you see if you can trace the ownership of the Best Storage? See if the Marshall Brothers are owners. Let me know when either of you have something, while I tie up this murder enquiry."

For the next hour only the sound of mouse clicks and tapping keyboards were heard in the office. Occasionally, Colm puffed out his breath. Then, "Oh yes!"

Kate looked over and saw the smile that lit up Colm's face, "You've got something?"

"I think I may have. One of those covered flatbed models drove past the camera at three twenty-six. It seems to be quite low on its axles, as though carrying something heavy."

"Can you see the number plate?"

"Not clearly enough. The techs might be able to clean it up."

"Anything else?"

Colm bent back to the screen and then smiled as he looked up again. We've got a dark coloured car. Not sure about make but it looks high end."

"Check to see whether either vehicle returns." Kate said before turning to Len, "What about the ownership of that business?"

Len shook his head. "It seems to be owned by companies who are owned by another and so on. Not clear who the buck stops with."

"Keep on it."

Again, there was silence apart from the occasional pained sigh from Len. Then Colm pushed back from his computer. "The car comes back twenty-three minutes later but no sign of the flatbed."

"Someone coming to pick up the driver of the flatbed?" Len offered.

Kate nodded. "Which means the flatbed was, or maybe still is, somewhere on that estate." Kate looked thoughtful and then said, "Okay Len, leave that for now. You and Colm go back to the estate. Now we know what vehicle and time we want, see if any of the businesses out there have their own cameras that may have caught more information."

Pleased to leave his desk, Len was up and waiting by the door as Colm closed down his computer and reached for his jacket.

CHAPTER 68

Colm and Len sat companionably in the car, Colm driving. "Okay, how did you manage to get the information out of Connell?"

Len smiled complacently, "Oh, I commiserated with him over the loss of his friend; bought him a few drinks; sat and listened."

"I really didn't think he'd give up anything about the Marshall Brothers."

"No, well he's dead scared. So, not a word from anyone about where we got the info from."

Colm mimed zipping his lips closed and Len nodded.

Once on Handley Estate, Colm asked, "Right, which way now?"

"Head left and then follow the bend. There's the camera that clocked our flatbed," Len said, pointing out the traffic camera on the junction.

Colm drove slowly, noting the businesses that lined the way. "See any cameras?"

Len had his notebook out. "That builders' merchant has one. It's trained on the gate to his yard, but it might give a partial view of the road."

"Yes, and that Tile Market has one. It looks like it's directed to the road."

"Right! Turn right here. That's the storage business and the lockups are on the far side."

Colm turned onto the storage front apron and then followed the cement road that led round the back. "No cameras at all," Len observed.

"That strikes me as a bit fishy. Wouldn't you want to cover this in case of sticky fingers?"

"Not if you know who owns the place and I'm sure anyone with sticky fingers is more than aware of that fact."

Colm turned the car round. "We're going to need to access the records for these lockups."

"You reckon Marshall will have it listed in his own name?"

"Um, good point. What's opposite this back?" Colm stopped the car and got out. The back of the storage building was fringed by a row of straggly trees. Beyond them was another road and then more buildings. Colm got back in the car, "Let's see if any of them have cameras facing this way."

"Bit of a long shot, isn't it?"

"Yep! But what else do we have? I think we should stop off at the office and make enquiries about hiring a lock up and the lack of cameras for security. See what he says."

"I'd better stay out of sight. I know the bloke from previous encounters."

The office was typical of something from the 1970s, complete with the topless girls' calendar. According to his badge, the man sat in there was the manager. He was a large man. A thug if ever Colm had seen one. Complete with shaved head and tattoos that disappeared under clothing on every limb.

"Hi, I've just been looking at your lockups. How much do they cost per week?"

"We only do monthly lets," was the surly reply.

"Okay, monthly?"

"One fifty and a fifty quid deposit. You get that back if there's no damage."

"I notice that there's no CCTV at the back. Doesn't that mean anyone can try their luck on the doors?"

"Nope. Never had even an attempted break-in here."

"Okay. Thanks for the info. I'll chat with my wife and see what she says."

"You do that!" The sneer was not hidden.

Back in the car, Colm relayed his conversation. "Don't worry, he's always been moronic. I think his second brain cell escaped when he was still quite small."

Colm grinned. "Right, let's start asking about footage. We'll go to those businesses behind here, first."

CHAPTER 69

At lunchtime Kate got told that she could keep Brooks beyond the twenty-four hours with a view to charging. She let the custody sergeant know and asked him to relay the information to Brooks' solicitor, Hynd. By mid-afternoon she had been given the green light for two murder charges to be brought against Jason Brooks.

She was arranging Brooks' transport to the local remand centre when her desk phone rang, "DI Medlar."

"Hi boss, just a quick call."

"Alice! Are you okay? No-one can overhear you, can they?"

"Don't worry boss, I'm out running an errand for Jim so I'm not at the Play House, but I've quite a bit of news."

"In relation to the drugs?"

"Sort of. This morning, Henderson announced that he was thinking about taking the company back to London and not performing in Eashire at all."

"How did that go down?"

"Lots of mutterings. I hadn't realised that the whole company is on a retainer but then get paid per performance, so being on just a retainer until their next booked gig is not going down well."

"Is it the lack of director that's caused the

move?"

"Yes. Henderson thinks he has a director he can use but he isn't available for a few weeks and doesn't feel confident that the cast can do the play without Brooks. As you can imagine, Julia Montgomery is furious. She even mentioned something about breach of contract. So, Henderson may change his mind. I don't know. But my real news is..." There was a muffled sound that Kate couldn't make out.

"Sorry, boss. Anyway, as I was leaving the theatre I went out through the front doors and saw Henderson take Harper and Collins into the box office. My shoelace needed tying, so I bent down to do it." Kate could hear the smile in Alice's voice. "I couldn't hear it all but I did hear Henderson say 'it will all have to go out tomorrow'."

"So you're thinking the last of the drugs are going to be moved tomorrow?"

"Yes. I thought DCI Wakeford needed to know."

"Good thinking. I'll get on to Bart and set up a meeting with Wakeford and Gilbert. Take care Alice. Perhaps if the drugs are gone we should pull you out?"

"Let me know what Bart says. Bye boss."

Minutes later, Kate was in Bart's office setting up a video conference with the drugs team. Fortunately, for both Bart and Kate, Bart's secretary, was a dab hand with the technical knowhow. Once Wakeford and Terry Gilbert's faces and voices were present in the office, she left. Kate gave Alice's news and then began the discussion about what the drugs team wanted to do about it. Nothing, for fear of alerting the players higher up the chain. Arrest Harper and Collins and maybe get them to give up Henderson, but they would still lose the higher players. Or follow the pair and see who they delivered to, in the hope it was Phipps, and close down the Eashire end of the drugs line.

In reality, Kate and Bart were the audience as Wakeford and Gilbert tossed ideas back and forth. Finally, they decided on the last of the three options. Their reasoning was that they could shut Phipps down without endangering the possible links to the Dutch intel.

The final decision was Alice's role. All were agreed that she would serve no further use if the drugs were leaving the following morning and that she should be pulled out. Kate was tasked to convey that message.

CHAPTER 70

Colm and Len entered the building merchant's yard. It was unlike Colm's previous visit to such a place. There, everything had been within a large metal warehouse with everything neatly stacked on miles of aisles of shelving. Here, pallets of stones were littered amongst baulks of wood and a pile of loose sand tumbled from a half-sided shed. The office appeared to be a small hut towards the rear of the premises. A small rotund character emerged, wiping a grubby handkerchief across his brow.

"Morning gents, how may I help you?"

Colm pulled out his warrant card and introduced himself and Len, "Are you the owner?"

"James Birch, owner, manager, labourer and sweeper upper!" he laughed good-naturedly.

"We'd like to have a look at some of your CCTV footage for last Saturday night into Sunday morning, if possible."

Birch immediately looked uncomfortable. "Ummm, what are you after?"

"We just want to check if a vehicle passed this way."

"Not sure you'll get a lot. The camera is pointed towards the gate, not the road."

"Well, if we could just have a look. You never

know," Len encouraged, walking towards the hut, "It's in your office, is it?"

Birch hurried after him. "Yes. Look, do you have to report everything you see on the camera?"

Colm halted and looked back, "As long as it's not illegal, Mr Birch."

Birch appeared even more flustered;. "No! Nothing like that." He moved in front of Len and led the way. His office was as shambolic as his yard; papers and receipts were scattered across his desk and an enormous old-style computer sat on a table to the side. Birch dragged his chair, the only chair, across to it and sat. He fiddled with the controls and the screen came to life. A poorly lit and grainy image of the yard's gates and a section of the road appeared. Birch turned to Colm, "Do you know what time you want?"

"If you'd let PC Goodfellow take a seat, he can scroll through to the relevant times." It seemed Birch relinquished control with some hesitation, "It won't take me five minutes."

"No, thank you sir," Len said standing rather closer than strictly respectable to the chair.

Birch got the message and moved. Within a few minutes Len had the time gap they were interested in. Birch was correct, most of the screen was taken up with the yard gates but there was a part of the road in the top left quadrant. A vehicle appeared within seven seconds of the traffic camera image.

"There it is," Len said, freezing the frame. Colm made a note of the time whilst Len fast forwarded to the second vehicle. Again, little could be seen other than another car having passed. "We're not going to get their return journey," Len said as he scrolled through a little more, "The camera's not picking up anything from the other side of the road."

Just as he was about to stop the footage, the top of James Birch's head appeared in the bottom left of the screen. Soon joined by a woman's. As they came further into frame, Colm and Len could see that both were dressed to go out and that both were the worse for drink. Before they left the screen, a passionate kiss was exchanged.

Colm raised an eyebrow and looked at Birch who was blushing furiously. "You don't have to tell anyone about that, do you?"

Colm shook his head, "No, Mr Birch. Your private life is entirely your affair."

As they left the yard, Len smirked and said, "You wouldn't have thought he had it in him, would you? What do you reckon, Mrs Birch waiting patiently at home?"

Colm merely shook his head. "Who's to say that wasn't Mrs Birch and they were just enjoying a little spice?"

Len's turn to shake his head, "Nah! That's his bit on the side. I'd lay money on it."

"Well, it's none of our business. Let's go and see what the tiling place has got."

CHAPTER 71

The answer to Colm's question was, not a lot. Like Birch's camera, the Tile Market's was focused on their forecourt. Being on the opposite side of the road from the builders' yard it only caught a glimpse of the second vehicle leaving the estate.

After these comparatively fruitless tasks, Colm was feeling dejected. Rather than going back to the car, he paced the road through the estate. Where else might have a camera that picked up the cars that night? Desperately, he searched the fronts of buildings looking for possible CCTV. Nothing. However, just as he was heading back to the car, he noticed an office block. One of those glass and steel affairs. The reception area was clear to see from the road and the reception desk had a bird's eye view of the junction their suspects would have to have used.

Waving Len over, Colm stepped across the road to the building. As he thought, for a place like this, there were several cameras in the foyer. Would any of them catch the activity outside? Only one way to find out, Colm decided as he pulled open the door.

A young man was sat at the reception desk. Very young and very pink, Colm thought. Smartly dressed in a suit and tie. The image spoilt, to Colm's mind, by the multiple studs in one of his ears.

Colm showed his ID just as Len joined him in the building. The young man looked excited as Colm explained his need to see what the foyer cameras had recorded.

"I'll have to ring for Mr Springer, head of security."

Colm nodded and he and Len waited whilst the young man phoned through to him.

"He's on his way," he said to them as he put the phone down. Any further conversation was prevented by the phone ringing and the young man went into his telephone spiel.

A few minutes later, Mr Springer arrived. He did not fit Colm's idea of a head of security. He was a small, maybe wiry man who looked to be trying to grow a beard and moustache but was failing miserably, as testified by the scarcity of hair on both his chin and head. However, Mr Springer was all efficiency. He held out his hand, "Jack Springer. I understand you wish to look at our camera footage."

"If we could, yes please," Colm said as his hand was gripped in a vice-like handshake. Was Springer trying to establish dominance?

"I'm happy to let you have a look but if you want a copy, you will need a search warrant."

"Thank you," Colm said. He wasn't going to get into a tussle over legalities at this stage.

Springer led them through into a service corridor. Quite stark and dark in comparison to the décor of the foyer. In a small office a bank of screens showed what all the cameras in the building were filming. "You want the three in the top row, to your left," Springer said pointing out the individual screens.

Colm scanned them. Cameras one and two were of the interior of the building, but, bingo! Camera three filmed the door and also caught the junction they were interested in. Before he allowed himself to become too excited, he checked, "How long do you keep your data for?"

"A month."

"And they screen twenty-four hours?"

"Yep, so when do you want to view?"

Len pulled out his notebook and read off the date and the times they were interested in. With nimble fingers, Springer played with buttons on the console and soon they were looking at a night scene of the junction. The cabbed flatbed came into shot. With the glare of the streetlight hitting the windscreen they couldn't make out who was driving or how many people were in it. But the winner was they could clearly see the number plate.

"Yes!" Len crowed.

Len gave the next time and soon they were watching a dark BMW enter the junction. Again, the same problems but a clear number plate. Len wrote down the details. And finally, the return of the BMW. "I can't see who's in it but there must be more weight," Colm said, "look at how low the chassis is at the back. I'd say a couple of big bodies but not the cash machine."

Turning to Springer, Colm thanked him, "And we'll have a warrant issued for copies of camera three for these times."

"Not a problem."

Back outside, Len was immediately on his radio to the station to find out who the vehicles belonged to.

CHAPTER 72

Kate had just finished speaking to Alice when Colm and Len returned to the office. They seemed to be in good spirits and Kate hoped that they had some positive news to report. She finished her telephone conversation and nodded to Colm as he mimed *Did she want a drink?* Minutes later, drinks in hand they sat around the main table.

"Spill the beans then," Kate urged.

Colm indicated for Len to take the floor. "In short there are no cameras in the lockup area. However," a deep breath, "we have found a number of cameras that recorded the passing of a dark, probably black, flatbed truck, and..." Kate felt he wanted a drumroll, "...we got the number plate!"

"And guess who owns it?" Colm wanted in on the excitement.

"One of the Marshall Brothers?" Kate hazarded a guess.

"In one!" Len clapped his hands. "In fact, Paul."

"Good work!"

"Oh, but that's not all," Len charged on. "Someone came to give the driver of the flatbed a lift and we got the number plate of that as well."

"Okay," Kate smiled at their simmering

excitement.

"And that belongs to John Marshall. We've got them both!"

Kate looked thoughtful.

"What's up, boss?" Len asked.

"We have proof of our theory that Paul Marshall was involved but we don't have enough for a warrant for either his place or the lockup. We have no evidence."

"But what about catching him on CCTV? Surely that's enough?"

"Driving around an industrial estate late at night, visiting your lockup, is not illegal. We have no *evidence* of criminal action." Kate put in the emphasis.

Both Colm and Len looked down-hearted and Kate hastened to mollify them. She knew a lot of leg work had gone into them finding this result, "But, it does mean we have the upper hand. They don't know what we know. So, we're a step ahead. What we've got to think about is how we get this info to work for us."

There was silence for a few moments and then Colm said, "If we can't link the flatbed to the cash machine job then we've not got anything for a warrant for the lock up or its register."

Kate agreed and then offered, "Do we think the cash machine is still in the lock up?"

Another silence and then, "It's got to be. It would be madness to move it about yet. Knowing the Marshalls, they'll wait until the heat dies down and everyone's forgotten about it and then the machine'll be found in some dump somewhere. One without CCTV!" Len suggested.

A plan was forming in Kate's mind and she began to voice it, "What if we rattle Paul's cage and let him know that we suspect him. What do you think he'd do?"

"Sit tight?" Colm said.

"Nah! He'll move the machine as soon as possible," Len argued, "Worried that we might have enough evidence for a warrant."

"It'd be a night job?"

Both men agreed and Kate continued, "So if we staked out the lockup we might catch him in the act?"

"That's going to cost," Colm worried, "Do you think Bart will go for it?"

Kate put down her mug and stood. "Only one way to find out." She hastened to the door and called over her shoulder as she left, "Keep everything crossed!"

CHAPTER 73

It took Kate longer than she'd expected to convince Bart that the stakeout was the only way they were going to get Paul Marshall in the frame for the ATM job. Then he had insisted that she talk it through with the Super who gave a provisional green light, dependent on Kate having a foolproof plan on the table by eight the next morning. Which was why Kate was now parked at the junction where Colm and Len had been able to read the number plate of the vehicles they were interested in. She had thought about calling Colm but she'd noticed he was wearing one of his best jackets, which normally meant he had a date with Jenna. And it wasn't like she couldn't do this on her own.

Apart from streetlamps, there was little light. Which Kate thought worked in their favour. She left her car and walked to the car park of the office building Colm had gained the footage from. Although there were no trees it did have a shoulder height hedge and no nearby lighting. Kate stood in the bay closest to the junction and imagined she was in her car. The position gave a good view of the intersection and at this distance the number plate would be readable. So, she'd have a unit here. They could follow the suspect's car to the lockup, lights off.

She drove to the lockup. It was a rectangular fenced compound with locked double gates. Kate drove round the area and also walked the perimeter. The gates were the only entrance and the access to the lockups at the back was to turn right once through the gates. The left held caravans, motorhomes and fast food mobiles. In fact, these types of vehicles spilled over into the space behind the storage unit. Kate noticed that the only external lights the storage unit boasted were at the end, where these were and, as far as she could see, no CCTV. Unusual for this kind of business.

Kate returned to the front gates. Although the street was pretty deserted, it wasn't completely car free. A few vehicles were parked up outside various retailers' units. Kate decided that two units would wait in the street and silently follow Marshall into the lockup area. The first unit from the junction observation could act as blockade should Marshall manage to get round the other two units. Could she sneak a fourth unit actually into the compound, hidden amongst the motorhomes at the back?

Finally, she needed an observation car that had a clear view of the lockups who could give the signal to go in once the pickup was out. Kate, again, drove round the compound and found a place she thought would work. Tree cover meant it was dark but gave a clear view. Once Kate had her plan clear in her mind, she headed for home.

Now all she had to do was to convince the Super.

CHAPTER 74

Alice was back in uniform the following morning and Len and Colm between them brought her up-to-date with the developments on the Marshall Brothers. There was no sign of Kate. She had not returned to their office before they'd left the night before so they were still waiting to hear the outcome of her meeting with DCI Bartholomew. Having plenty to do, they each sat at their post and began work, Colm with an ear cocked to listen out for Kate's arrival. And there it was.

Colm guessed she had good news as her steps were light and hurried. She breezed into the room. "Morning troops! Gather round. We have a busy day ahead of us." As she spoke, Kate unfurled a cylinder of paper she'd been carrying under her arm. "Okay, mugs to weight the corners down, please."

Instructions carried out, the team gathered and peered at the paper.

"That's Marshall's storage unit and estate, isn't it?" Colm queried, crooking his head to get a better view.

"It is and it is going to be the scene of our stakeout tonight."

Excitement rippled round the team and Kate set to and explained her plan. "Now the trickiest part is I want a car in here before they close for the night," Kate tapped the compound area. "There are two motorhomes and a caravan parked around the back, opposite the lockups. Colm, I want you and Len to be in position from five. The place closes at five-thirty."

"Won't they check that the place is empty before locking up?" Alice asked.

Len shook his head, "Unlikely. Everyone knows it's a Marshall's business so no-one is going to try anything, so they're pretty slack."

Colm nodded his agreement.

"Okay. I'll be in the lead car through the gates and Alice," Kate turned to the young woman, "good to have you back, by the way, you'll be in the second car with DC Coles."

"Who's going to be in the co-ordinating car?" Colm asked.

"Bart. He's going to be here," Kate pointed to the observation point she'd found the night before. "He will wait until the pickup is out of the lockup before giving the signal. Your job," she turned to Colm and Len, "is to stop them shutting the lockup once we spring our trap. If it's closed we're going to have a hard time getting permission to have a look inside. If it's open..." Kate smiled. They understood. The contents of the lockup could be far more than an ATM machine. Perhaps enough criminal stuff to put the Marshall Brothers out of business completely.

"Any questions?"

The teams shook their heads. "Right, back here for seven and a final briefing. Plans for today: we have some cage rattling to do," Kate grinned. "Colm you and I are going to visit Paul Marshall and ask him about his pickup truck."

"Won't he just claim it's in the lockup?" Len asked.

"He might, but I don't think he'll risk us going with him to look at it. He won't want us anywhere near his lockup, will he?"

"My bet is that he claims it's been stolen and that he hasn't had chance to report it," Colm offered.

Kate agreed. "In the meantime I want you two," pointing at Len and Alice to visit the storage reception and ask to see the register for the hire of their units."

"Well, they're not going to do that, are they?" Len frowned.

"No, but I bet the chap on the desk rings Paul or John to let them know that the police have been sniffing around."

Len grinned as understanding dawned upon him. "Another little pressure to make Paul think he needs to move his pickup and the ATM machine. Clever!"

"Right! See you back here at some point, but certainly by seven. If you need time off before tonight, take it and stock up on food and drink. We don't know how long our wait will be."

CHAPTER 75

Paul Marshall lived on a new build estate to the north of Westergate. Although not quite a gated community these houses were all executive builds. Detached houses with neat drives and enough garden for a pool or tennis court. Colm silently whistled as they drove through, "And they say crime doesn't pay!"

Marshall's home was a mock Georgian affair, complete with white columns guarding the front door. Kate noted the open double garage to one side, exhibiting a low-slung sports model of some description and a BMW saloon. Kate only knew this because she could see the logo. So where did Marshall normally keep his pickup?

The chime on the doorbell was suitably sonorous and they could hear its echo deep into the house. Several minutes passed before a forty something woman opened the door. Her face was lavishly made up and Kate thought Botox and fillers had added to the perpetual surprised look on her face. Despite her glamorous looks, her accent was pure Eashire.

"Yes?" Whatever was going to be said next was stopped with Kate and Colm's presentation of their ID cards, "Oh, for goodness sake! What do you want now?"

Kate assumed the slight indentation

between the woman's tattooed eyebrows was a frown, but the look was so fleeting she wasn't sure.

"Good morning, Mrs Marshall? Is your husband, Paul, in?"

The woman emitted a deep sigh, "Come in then." She held the door wider, and Kate and Colm stepped into the hallway. Kate suspected an interior designer had been employed. Everything was pale and shiny. Straight lines and sharp corners. Not a homely place. "Wait here. I'll go and find him." It was an instruction not a request. The woman's high heels clicked harshly on the marble, or marble effect floor. She disappeared through a door at the end of a short corridor.

"Welcoming!" Colm said sardonically.

Kate gazed round the small foyer. Or did you call it a vestibule? A glass topped table held a beautiful metal and blue enamel bowl which, Kate noticed, contained car keys. She wondered if the pickup truck's were in there but before she could cross the hall to look, the door that Mrs Marshall had exited through, re-opened.

Paul Marshall was a good-looking man. Age had defined his features and the grey at his temples was quite becoming. Unlike his wife he didn't look like he was working on keeping his looks, unless the trim physique was down to gym time. Marshall strode confidently across the gap between them, "Inspector Medlar?" he looked between Colm and Kate.

Kate stepped forward, "Mr Marshall? Paul Marshall?"

"Correct. My wife says you need to speak with me?"

"It's a matter pertaining to your pickup truck, Mr Marshall."

"My pickup truck?" Marshall's face remained bland but Kate was sure she saw calculation in his eyes.

"Yes, you see a pickup truck was seen in the vicinity of a crime," Kate knew she was stretching the truth.

"And you know it was my pickup truck because?"

"The vehicle passed a CCTV camera and the number plate was captured," Colm explained.

"And when did this supposed crime take place?"

"There's no supposed about the crime," Kate interjected, "we just need to know whether you were in the area at the time."

"If you could tell us if you used your vehicle the Saturday before last, sir," Colm stood with notebook and pen waiting.

"I'll need to check my diary," Marshall pulled out a small digital organiser and began to tap the screen, "Ah. Right. That Saturday I did use it. I drove to the Benford Riding Stables with my daughter at eight-thirty and spent a couple of hours using it to take poles and fences out to their show field, setting up for the gymkhana next week. And before you ask, yes you can confirm that with Alys Benford."

"What time did you leave the stables?" Kate asked.

Marshall looked thoughtful, "Middayish. I left my daughter there. She spends all her weekends at the stables. I went back to collect her about six and we came home."

"And did you go out after that, sir?" Colm asked.

"No. We had a quiet, family night in."

"And your wife will vouch for that, won't she sir?"

Marshall scowled at Colm's tone but nodded.

"Where is the vehicle now, sir?" Kate asked, "I notice it's not in the garages."

Marshall laughed, "Jolene would have my guts for garters if I parked it out front. Only the best cars are parked for the neighbours to see."

"So the pickup is where, sir?" Kate persisted. Now she was sure she could see calculations going on behind Marshall's eyes. Did he claim the lockup or the vehicles as stolen?

"It's parked in the back lane." Marshall turned to the enamel bowl and rummaged through for a set of keys, "Come on, I'll show you. You won't be satisfied until I do, will you?"

CHAPTER 76

Behind the executive homes was a service road. Not for these residents, the noise and inconvenience of a refuse lorry clanging and blocking the way. Each home had a parking bay alongside the back gate and Kate noted that several homes had cars parked in them. Not top-of-the- range ones, though. Like Mrs Marshall those were out the front. Marshall's bay was empty.

Kate had to admit that Marshall was a very good actor. If she hadn't been expecting to find an empty bay she could have been fooled by Marshall's apparent confusion and then anger, "The bastards. Somebody's stolen my car!" he looked up and down as though expecting to see the pickup in someone else's bay.

"When was the last time you used the vehicle, sir?" Colm kept up the pretence.

"That Saturday. I drove to the back so that my daughter could go straight to the utility room to take off her riding stuff. Jolene won't have it in the main house, she says she doesn't want the place smelling of horses all the time."

"And you haven't been out to this service road in the last ten days or so, sir? Not to take your daughter back to the stables this last weekend?"

Marshall shook his head. "No, Abigail has had a cold and Jolene said if she was too sick for school then she was too sick for the stables. I haven't used it at all."

"We'll report the theft as soon as we get back to the station," Kate offered.

"No, don't worry about it. Now I know it's stolen I'll get in touch."

"No problem, sir. One of us will ring you with the crime number."

With barely concealed ill grace Marshall accepted, "Thank you, Inspector. It's very kind of you."

"Do you have any CCTV on this road?" Colm asked.

Marshall shook his head. "Not on the road itself, no. CCTV coverage starts as soon as you enter through these gates." He turned and walked back through the said gates and pointed to a number of cameras that surveyed the house and gardens.

Walking back, Kate asked, "Is it likely that someone else has used the second set of keys and taken the pickup?"

Marshall kept walking, his face turned away from Kate, "Not without asking, no."

At that moment Marshall's phone rang out. He checked the screen and turned back to Kate and Colm, "If you would excuse me, I need to take this." He walked a few paces away and kept his back to them.

Kate listened hard. She was sure she heard, "What did they want?" and "You didn't let them." But the rest was lost to her. Finally closing his phone, Marshall turned back. Kate wondered if the call had been from the storage business. Marshall certainly seemed to be looking them over with a more appraising air.

"Sorry about that, business," Marshall said walking back to them.

"Not at all, sir. Thank you for seeing us and answering our questions."

"Not at all, Inspector." He opened the front door and ushered them out.

"I'll be in touch later," Colm called as they walked away.

Marshall looked puzzled and Colm clarified, "With the crime number for your stolen pickup."

Marshall gave a weak smile and a half-wave before closing the door on them.

"One cage well and truly rattled, I think!" said Colm gleefully, "and I think that was the storage unit guy on the phone, don't you?"

"I hope so." Kate smiled as they climbed back into their car, "All in all, a good morning's work."

CHAPTER 77

Len and Alice were already back in the office and a comparison of timings seemed to indicate that Marshall's call was indeed from the storage unit manager. Colm leaned across his desk to his phone saying, "I'll report Marshall's stolen pickup and then ring the crime number through to him."

Kate nodded and turned back to Alice and Len, "So what approach did you take with the manager, then?"

Len led the reply, "I said there had been rumours of posh cars being stolen to order and then being holed up in lockups and garages, had he heard anything?"

Alice took the role of the manager, "Nope!"

"Any chance we could take a look at your client list? Just to see if any names jump out."

"Nope!"

"You know we can come back with a search warrant."

"You do that then."

"Come on mate. My boss'll have my guts for garters."

"My boss'll bury me six foot under. You don't see nothing without a warrant."

"And we left it at that, but he was reaching for his phone before we'd even left the office,"

Len concluded.

"That sounds perfect. Let's hope it encourages Marshall to make a move tonight."

Colm came off his phone grinning, "I don't think Mr Marshall was that impressed with having a crime number!"

Their laughter was short-lived as Detective Chief Inspector Bartholomew strode into the office, closed the office door with care and then glared at the room. Addressing no-one in particular, he said, "They've only gone and lost them!"

It took Kate a minute to get his meaning, "You mean Collins and Harper?"

Bart nodded. Colm asked, "Before or after the deal?"

"Before," through gritted teeth.

"How the hell did they manage that?" Kate asked, more shocked than angry.

"Apparently, the tails picked them up leaving the theatre. Both were carrying, I quote, 'Heavily laden satchels'. The tails were acting in relays so that the couriers didn't get suspicious of the same two men behind them. They followed them to the market and there they've lost them. Wakeford and his team have spent all morning tracking down known associates of Phipps for a hope of catching up with the couriers. But nothing!" Bart threw his hands wide. "Not a sniff!"

Kate bit her lip to prevent the smile that

threatened at Bart's inappropriate metaphor. "Do they think they were rumbled?"

"Apparently, they were sauntering through the market when there was a commotion behind the stalls," Bart said. "They turned to look and when they turned back, the couriers were gone."

"What about the second set? Didn't they see them go?" Colm asked.

"They decided to hoof it round the stalls and wait at the far end. The couriers never materialised. Of course, they started searching the side roads but one side you have the Shamble Lanes; you could lose an elephant in there. And the other side is the new shopping centre."

"I assume they've checked the centre's CCTV?" Kate offered.

Bart nodded. "Nothing!"

Silence descended on the room as each of them considered the ramifications of the situation. "Phipps is not going to have the stuff close to him and I can't see him trusting many of his crew," Bart voiced out loud.

Kate agreed, "He's probably got a flat,"

"Or lockup," Colm offered.

"Or just a garage space," suggested Alice.

Bart nodded. "He's going to need somewhere to weigh and bag it. And if it's coke or heroin he's going to have to cut it."

"It sounds expensive. Does Phipps have that kind of money?" Kate asked.

"I doubt it. I think this is sale or return."

"Risky?" Colm asked.

"Not with these big boys. I think Phipps is clever enough to know not to piss these guys off," Bart offered. He then shook himself. "Right. Well, that's now Wakeford's headache. Are we all set for tonight? Hughes is organising extra bodies and they've been told to be back here for seven." With that he left with some of the fire having gone from his demeanour.

CHAPTER 78

With Bart's departure, Kate checked her watch. "Okay. Finish anything you're in the middle of and then clear off for a few hours."

"Boss, could I have a word?" Colm asked as Len and Alice returned to their computers.

Kate looked up, "Of course. What's on your mind?"

"Well, I've been thinking. If Len and I are found by the manager in the back of his car park it's going to be pretty obvious to him that something's going on and he's going to call Marshall."

Kate looked thoughtful and then nodded, "You're right. Have you got a solution in mind?"

"I did think about Alice but she's been seen today, so I wondered if there were any other female PCs on the list for tonight." Colm blushed but continued, "Then if we do get caught we can be a canoodling couple, trying to find some private time." He looked expectantly at Kate.

"Good plan! Let's see who Sergeant Hughes has on his list." She lifted her desk phone and punched in two numbers. In a short time it was answered, "Hello, Sergeant. Kate Medlar. Do you have a likely female to team up with DC Hunter. We want to give the impression of a lover's tryst." Kate listened and nodded and said, "Perfect. Is she in now? Good. Would you ask her to come up to the incident room? Thank you." Kate replaced the phone and looked at Colm, "PC Caroline Stone? Have you heard of her?"

Colm looked thoughtful. "I think she was in the new batch that started last May. I haven't heard anything about her, good or bad." Even as he said this, they could hear quick and light steps on the stairs. Seconds later a young woman, in her mid-twenties entered the room.

"Here was the tall, willowy brunette Kate always imagined herself to be before she passed a mirror! "PC Stone?"

"Yes ma'am, Caro Stone."

"Ok, Caro, let's gather round the middle table and I'll talk you through what we want. Unless Sergeant Hughes has already briefed you?"

"No, ma'am, he just asked me to come and see you."

Kate sat and Colm and Caro Stone joined her. Kate turned to Caro, "Right, first things first. I don't do 'ma'am'. It's Inspector or boss, okay?"

Caro blushed a little, "Yes, ma'... boss. Sorry, boss."

Kate waved a hand, "Nothing to apologise for. You didn't know." Kate turned back to the map of the storage unit and its environs and began to lead Caro through what they were planning to do on the stakeout.

Caro asked intelligent questions, "What about lighting in the compound m... boss?"

"No. There's one corner light to the left, where the caravans and stuff are parked but nothing to the right or round the back, where the lockups are."

"So, what is my task? It's obviously not part of the general briefing we're getting later with you and the DCI?"

"I'll let Colm explain." Kate looked to Colm to take over. Was it her imagination that he was blushing?

"I...er... The original plan was that PC Goodfellow and I would sneak in before the compound is locked for the night and conceal our vehicles between the two motorhomes and caravan parked behind the unit."

"What about if they do a sweep of the place before locking up?"

"Exactly! Two men, one a known copper, found sneaking in their car park, would tip off our known suspects. I thought that we needed another unknown person, preferably female, to pretend that..."

Kate was now sure Colm was blushing and intervened. "Equal ops and diversity apart, a heterosexual couple having a bit of a kiss and a cuddle."

Colm broke in, "Only if we're discovered, the kissing and cuddling bit."

Kate smiled, "Quite. Such a couple would be a more believable scenario and not alert our suspect. Are you up for that Caro?"

Caro grinned broadly, "Of course I am."

"Good. If you get off home now, and obviously civvies for tonight." Kate turned to Colm, "If you go down with Caro and let Sergeant Hughes know what we're doing and arrange with Caro what time to meet her."

"Sure boss." Colm grabbed his jacket and followed the already retreating figure of PC Caro Stone.

CHAPTER 79

Kate returned to her desk and checked through her emails. Mike had sent through the official report on the digger and concluded in his email,

> "...in short; if you can find me the ATM machine I can prove that the digger was used to extract it from the wall."

Kate fired off a quick response, with her tongue firmly in her cheek,

> "Your wish is my command! Hope to have said machine by tomorrow morning."

Rather than emailing back, Mike phoned. "Is tonight's stakeout your shout then?"

It never ceased to amaze Kate how all information seeped into the forensics suite. They always seemed to know what was going on. "It is. Have you a team on alert?"

"Of course. I might even hang around to see what comes in."

"No, don't do that Mike. I can't see this coming off until the early hours, if then. Go home, see your family and be bright and ready in the morning."

"Well, you have Merri on call, so you know she'll do it right."

"I do. So go home tonight. I'll be hassling you from early on tomorrow." Kate heard Mike laugh as he put the phone down. Kate was pleased Merri Probert was on the case. She was a small, wiry woman who wore enormous glasses that quite dwarfed her face and, disconcertingly for the viewer, enlarged her eyes, but she was a talented and perceptive forensic scientist. Kate often wondered why the likes of Mike and Merri, who were undoubtedly top of their field, chose to work in the quieter pond that was Eashire.

Having called Len and let him know the change of plan, Kate checked her watch. She still had time to go home before tonight's briefing but she knew she'd be like an ill-sitting hen. Perhaps she should go to the gym. She hadn't been for a week, or was it more? What with the cases she'd been tied up with. Perhaps a good work out would relax her aching shoulders and burn off some of the adrenalin that had been coursing through her veins since the Super gave the go ahead for tonight's action.

Kate was met by an affectionate smile as Jude ensured her client understood how to use the weights machine. Whilst she waited, Kate warmed up and was soon joined by Jude who asked, "Are you playing hooky? Who's out keeping the streets of Eashire safe?"

Kate grinned, "I've got an op on this evening

so I thought I'd spend my down time making up for my lax attendance. Are you free for a coffee in the next hour or so?"

"I've got my spin class now for forty-five minutes. Will that do? Is it long enough for you to exercise." This last was said with her tongue firmly in her cheek.

Kate poked her tongue out. "I'll make it long enough. Meet you in the café in fifty minutes.

Forty-five minutes later Jude exited the spin class mopping at her face, hair and arms. Kate was equally sweaty and more than a little breathless. "I must shower. Give me ten."

"No problem. I just need to check all the equipment's been wiped down."

Even with her task, Jude was first to the café and Kate arrived to find an egg and salad sandwich, a slice of carrot cake and a glass of apple juice waiting for her. "I thought you probably hadn't factored food into your schedule?"

Kate nodded, pleased that Jude was so thoughtful. And her happiness continued as Jude asked, "If you're going to be out late, do you want me to go across and feed Monster? I could stay and wait for you, if you wanted?"

Instinctively, Kate put her hand on one of Jude's. "That's really kind of you. Monster is used to me feeding him at all sorts of hours and I don't know when, or even if, I'll be home tonight." Kate saw the disappointment in Jude's face and she sighed, "I'm sorry, it's things like this that ruin a relationship. I really am sorry."

Jude smiled and placed her other hand over Kate's. "You have nothing to be sorry for. Of course I'm disappointed that I won't see you tonight but I do understand and," a pause, "I'm not Robyn."

"I know you're not Robyn."

"Good. Now, get that down you," pointing at the plates. "What time do you have to go?"

Kate checked her watch, "Half an hour."

CHAPTER 80

Kate had heard from Colm before the briefing. He had managed to conceal the car between a motorhome and a caravan and no-one had come to check out the car park before closing and locking up. It did mean that they were blind to the lockups and would be relying on the signal from Bart from his observation point. The briefing had been short and everyone was perfectly happy with their tasks. Kate was with a young PC, Gavin Culpepper. He seemed very nervous and Kate heard his audible gulp several times as they drew up to park outside a charity warehouse just fifty metres or so from the storage units' gate.

Alice was with DC Jan Coles, a more than competent officer and they were parked up on the other side of the road and the storage gates. Len was with another new officer, Reuben Homes. They were car one, back at the junction into the estate. Len knew the kind of car Paul Marshall might turn up in, especially if he got a lift with his brother. That just left DCI Bartholomew, who had opted to go solo as his task was purely observational and final signaller.

Everyone radioed in that they were in position and Kate ordered radio silence after reiterating that no-one was to move until the

DCI gave the signal. Then she settled down with the Joseph Mallory folder and a pen light. Somewhere in it Kate was sure that she'd come across something that had struck her as odd and that it might help DCI Wakeford track down the missing yobs.

Her partner tapped his fingers nervously on his knee. Kate was just at the point where the constant movement in her eye line was beyond bearing when she found what she was looking for. She knew it. This might be what the Drugs Squad needed. She couldn't let them know now but later she would let DC Gilbert know. A feather in his cap.

The time moved on and Kate tried to engage PC Culpepper in conversation. She'd tried where he was from, why he'd joined the force, what he'd liked and disliked so far but whether social inadequacy or nerves had got the better of him, his answers were monosyllabic and they lapsed into silence.

Kate hated the waiting, especially as they could not get out and move around to stay awake. She wound the window down slightly. The cool air was welcome and Kate was aware that the silence wasn't only inside her car. Consequently, her heart leapt when she heard an unearthly screech. What the hell was that? She must have said the thought out loud because PC Culpepper answered, "Female fox."

"Why the screech?"

"She's probably alerting her cubs. Most towns and even cities have been colonised by foxes. They are called 'urban foxes' because they've learnt to live in our environment, stay hidden and find food. Urban foxes have quite sophisticated food tastes."

In the stark white street light Kate could see a grin, which in itself looked somewhat unearthly as the light emphasised the shadows and contours of his face. "You into that sort of thing? Foxes?"

"That was going to be my other career choice, a ranger of some description. Sort of like policing but with animals being the protected species."

"And you opted for the police."

"Yes. Not really sure why. I could give all those platitudes about serving the community but it boils down to; it just seemed the right thing to do."

"Well, there are certainly worse reasons for joining!"

The radio crackled to life, "All cars. This is car one. Suspect vehicle, dark BMW saloon entering the estate."

Kate closed her window and gripped her steering wheel. This was it.

CHAPTER 81

The suspect vehicle turned into the road, the headlights briefly playing over the far pavement before coming to a halt in front of the compound's gates. The passenger door opened and Kate saw Paul Marshall get out and unlock them. She radioed her team, "Suspect vehicle is two up. Passenger positively identified as Paul Marshall. Suspect vehicle entering the compound now."

A minute or so passed and Bart took over the commentary. "Vehicle has stopped three doors from the left." A pause. "Passenger has opened the lockup and is now joined by driver. Both entering the building."

Kate waited, barely breathing. They needed at least one of them in the pickup. Five. Ten minutes passed. What were they doing? Bart came on air again, "A vehicle is backing out from the lockup. It looks like a cabbed pickup truck. Second figure is following out." And then, "Go! Go! Go!"

Kate sprang into action and was inside the compound before Bart's second "Go!" had finished. She drove with speed to the back of the storage building. In her rear view mirror, she could see DC Coles close behind. Tyres screeching, Kate swung the car across the nose of the pickup, which swerved to avoid her.

As if in slow motion, Kate became aware of a vehicle hurtling towards her. Headlights on full, forcing her to look away. Was one of the brothers trying to escape? Then she heard a heavy crash and saw that the vehicle had slammed to a halt in the lockup's entrance, preventing one of the suspects from closing it up. For a moment Kate thought he was going to make a run for it but a figure appeared from behind him and Kate watched as Paul Marshall was cuffed.

Even as she took note of all this she was out of her own car and running across the space to the driver's door of the pickup. She pulled it open and managed to grab the keys. The driver had managed to hit his head on his mirror when braking hard. "You should always wear a seatbelt, sir!" The driver turned to look at her. It was John Marshall.

Kate helped him out of the pickup and began to read him his rights, "Mr John Marshall you are under arrest on suspicion of driving a stolen vehicle."

Behind her she heard, "It's my own pickup. You know that." Paul Marshall was puce with rage.

Kate turned and feigned surprise, "Mr Marshall! You told us this morning that your truck had been stolen. We had a tip off that stolen vehicles were being moved tonight."

"Well, it's my truck so you can't arrest us."

"We certainly seem to have a bit of a mix up here, don't we, sir? We'll get back to the station and see if we can sort this all out. Do you know what's in your truck, sir?"

Paul Marshall tried to bluster, "There's nothing in it. I'd forgotten I'd left it here and was just coming to get it."

"Something is in it, sir. Look how low she is on her axles." Colm pointed out as they drew up closer to Kate.

"Let's take a look, shall we?"

John Marshall tried to intervene, "You can't do that. We've done nothing wrong."

"Well, sir. We do have some concern over a stolen truck and you are not the owner so it is a fair stop and we do have the right to check over your vehicle."

Using the back tail gate Kate opened the cabbed truck. There, gleaming in the weak internal light of the cab, was an ATM machine. Kate grinned, her ATM machine. She turned back to the Marshall brothers and schooled her face to look stern. "I think we need to discuss this matter back at the station, gentlemen."

Still shouting the odds, the brothers were led, one to Kate's car and the other to DC Coles'. Once they were safely installed, Kate turned back to Colm. "Great driving! We needed that lockup open."

"Not me, boss. PC Caro Stone. Apparently, she's hoping to join traffic!"

Len and his partner joined them and Kate gave out orders. "Len, you and PC..." Damn she'd forgotten his name.

"Homes, boss," Len supplied.

"Homes. Go back to the station with DC Coles and get those two booked in and book out a couple of interview rooms. Tell Alice to wait with a car and she can drive me back."

"Okay, boss." Len turned and walked back towards the cars and Kate turned to face the lockup. She noted that PC Stone had moved the car away from the entrance and was now standing there. Light from behind her threw her shadow long and thin.

"Come on then, Colm. Let's see what we have in there." If Kate was hoping for an Aladdin's Cave, she was sorely disappointed. Having donned protective gloves and footwear from the boot of Colm's car, they went in.

Kate surveyed the space. It was smaller than she had expected. It must have been a tight squeeze getting the pickup in, she thought.

A bench lay along the back wall and Colm was already looking it over. He turned back to Kate, "A few tools, probably trying to get into the ATM machine, but otherwise nothing." He too looked around the space, "I reckon they had to park on a slant to get that vehicle in."

Kate rotated slowly, taking in every aspect of the area. She'd hoped that more than the pickup had been stowed here, but there was nothing.

She was sure forensics would be able to match the tools to any marks on the ATM machine but that was all they were going to get on the brothers.

Kate sighed, "Okay, Colm. Can I leave you here, with PC Stone, until forensics arrive? I want the ATM dusted first and sent back to the station pretty damn quick, otherwise the brothers' smart legal bod will have them walking sooner than I want."

"Sure thing boss. I'll give Merri a ring and check they're on the way. No I won't." Colm looked over Kate's shoulder as a large transit van appeared around the corner. It was the forensic team.

"Okay. You come back to the station with me. Alice and PC Stone can wait here. You let Stone know and radio through to Alice. Quick as you can. I don't imagine the brothers' solicitor is going to be long in arriving. It will be interesting to see if one or two turn up."

CHAPTER 82

Back at the station, Colm peeled off to check that the booking was in progress and Kate returned to her office.

Len was at his desk. He looked as weary as Kate felt.

"Off you go. No need for us all to be here." Gratefully, Len put on his coat and left with a goodbye wave.

Kate checked through her emails in the vain hope that forensics had the fingerprints. Then she began to plan the interviews. The brothers were not going to roll over and confess their part in the robbery. It would be interesting to see what their reason was for having the ATM in the back of the pickup.

Colm entered, whistling tunelessly. He saw Kate and grinned.

"Everything okay down there?" she asked.

"Yes. The brothers have decided to go for the same solicitor, Jeremy Styne."

"What do we know about Styne?"

"Well, Styne senior, also Jeremy, set up the practice with his brother, Francis. Styne and Styne were very popular with the middle-income bracket, mainly business contracts, that sort of thing."

"Are the older Stynes still active?"

"Rumour has it that Francis, the uncle, took early retirement because he disagreed with the calibre of clients young Jeremy was bringing in. Styne senior backed his son."

"So, Styne & Styne has become Styne & Son?"

"Technically, yes but the signage still says Styne, Styne & Son."

"If the uncle objected to the clientele does that mean young Jeremy treads a tight line?"

"Most definitely. I have made sure that the custody sergeant knows that the brothers may not have joint interviews with their solicitor."

"Even so, he could set up a joint response?"

"Always that possibility."

"Surely he's going to have a conflict of interest?"

Colm rubbed his chin and Kate could hear the rasp of stubble, "Possibly. I think we're going to have to make that call when we start interviewing."

Kate's email alert on her computer pinged, she leaned forward, read it and smiled.

"Good news?"

"That's Merri, she's done an initial electronic analysis of the prints on the ATM and there are three distinct sets, the brothers and Terry Lennon's. She's sending the physical collections back for one of her crew to do a more thorough analysis but she's pretty confident about those three sets."

Colm punched the air. "So brother John

cannot say he had no idea what was in the back of the pickup he was driving."

"And it also ties Lennon to the brothers as well."

Further discussion was suspended by Kate's desk phone ringing, "Medlar. Okay. Thanks. No joint meetings. Yes. Let me know." Putting the phone down Kate said, "Jeremy Styne has arrived. Time we planned our interviews."

CHAPTER 83

Kate preceded Colm into interview room one. They had decided that Kate would be the cop from hell and Colm would try the *bloke dealing with a stroppy woman* role. Paul Marshall sat scowling alongside a thirty something, well-dressed man. Despite it being the early hours, he was impeccably dressed, in a suit and tie and had the relaxed air of a man in complete control. Before Kate had even placed her file on the table, Jeremy Styne launched in, "Detective Inspector Medlar I must protest the manner of the stop and search and subsequent arrest of my clients."

Kate held a hand up. "All in good time Mr…" She pretended not to know his name.

This tactic surprised him and Styne stopped mid- breath before automatically holding out his hand to shake Kate's, "Styne, Jeremy Styne."

"Thank you, Mr Styne. If we could save any discussion until the tape is running and then we know there will be no mis-steps in our actions."

Kate and Colm sat and Kate flicked the recording switch. She introduced herself and then waited as the other three each introduced themselves for the tape.

Opening her folder, Kate looked at Paul Marshall. "Mr Marshall, you were arrested on the charge of being in possession of a stolen ATM machine."

Before Marshall could answer, Styne began his truncated speech of earlier, "Inspector Medlar I have to protest the manner in which my client was stopped and his vehicle searched. It was an illegal stop and search."

Kate frowned and looked through her papers before looking up and answering Styne. "Your client and his brother were in the process of moving a stolen vehicle, that's why he was stopped and the vehicle searched."

As though explaining to a toddler, Styne said, "The vehicle belonged to my client, it was not stolen."

"Unfortunately, at the time of the stop and search the vehicle in question had been reported as stolen."

"Not by my client."

Colm lent forward and looked at Marshall, "Paul, you said your pick-up had been stolen when we visited you yesterday."

Again, Styne took up the comment, "But my client did not report it stolen."

Colm rubbed his chin, "No, I did that, on Mr Marshall's behalf and phoned him with the crime number. At no point did he say that the vehicle had not been stolen."

"So, at the time of Mr Marshall's stop and search, we were pursuing a stolen vehicle, Mr Styne." Kate stared the man in the eyes. She could see a glint of anger.

"Your actions were entrapment, Inspector Medlar. You forced my client into reporting his vehicle as stolen and then laid in wait for him."

"You are correct that we were waiting, but we had reason to believe that stolen vehicles were being moved from that location. Therefore, all our actions were within the law, as, I have already said, we believed the vehicle was stolen."

Styne looked at the recording device and said, "I wish it to be noted that I believe my client was the victim of an entrapment."

Kate nodded but did not respond, instead she turned to Marshall again, "Mr Marshall, can you explain why there was an ATM machine in the back of your vehicle when we stopped you?"

Marshall looked at Styne who gave a very subtle shake of the head before he said, "No comment."

Kate had thought this would be the approach the brothers would take but she continued with her questioning. "Mr Marshall, our forensic team have identified three distinct sets of prints on the ATM machine. One set belongs to a man found dead a few days ago, Terry Lennon."

At the word 'dead' Marshall's head shot up to look Kate in the eye and then turned to Styne who came to the rescue. "Are you accusing my client of being responsible for this man's death, Inspector?"

Kate shook her head. "No, we already have that person in custody."

That earned a raised eyebrow from Styne and Kate continued, "However, it does mean that we have had to look very closely at Mr Lennon's life and actions prior to his death and that has led us to your client."

Marshall returned to gazing at the marks scratched into the table's surface. "You did know Terry Lennon, didn't you?"

Another truculent shrug. Kate continued, "Terry was always on the lookout for a get rich quick scheme, but he had to include you, didn't he, if he was going to hit the ATM on Peace Way?"

Styne broke in again, "Inspector, my client has no idea what you are talking about. Why should Peace Way be of interest to my client?"

Kate allowed a little bit of temper to appear, "For goodness sake, Mr Styne we are well aware of your client's interest in Peace Way."

Marshall made no attempt to hide the smirk that briefly appeared.

Colm stepped in as though to ease things back, "Terry thought the ATM would be filled that afternoon and there would be thousands in it. You weren't to know that the courier got stuck and didn't make his final drop."

Kate came back in a little viciously, "You must have been furious! All that effort for a couple of grand! Hardly the heist of the year!"

Marshall bristled at her taunt, but Styne put a restraining hand on his client's arm. "Inspector, all this is pure speculation and my client will continue to respond with 'No comment'."

"Not entirely speculation, Mr Styne. We do have your client's fingerprints on the ATM machine so, at the very least, he will be charged with receiving stolen goods."

Kate decided that she didn't have the patience for the game playing Styne was invoking and called the interview to a close.

As she was leaving, Styne called after her. "I shall need half an hour with my other client, Detective Inspector."

Kate did no more that nod her head in acknowledgement that she had heard him.

CHAPTER 84

"Phew!" Colm breathed out heavily. "We're not going to get very far with them, are we?"

Kate sat down heavily. "No. I am sure CPS will allow us to charge with receiving but we've got nothing on them for planning or carrying out the actual job. Forensics is quite clear that it's only Lennon's fingerprints on the digger."

Colm shook his head, "A pity there wasn't more in the lockup. If it's just receiving, they're not going to get a custodial, are they?"

Kate ran her fingers through her hair. "No. We just don't have a strong enough case. A good prosecutor will flag up the idea of their further involvement in the theft but all we can be certain of is that they had the ATM and probably used the tools in the lockup to try and get into it."

"What's the plan with John Marshall?"

"I imagine it will be a re-run of Paul's. Styne will stop us playing them off each other. Although I might try the tactic that he may be seen as more guilty because he was driving the truck with it in." By now Kate's hair was a mass of spikes.

Colm leaned across her table and answered the desk phone. "Okay. We'll be down when we're ready."

"They're ready for us?" Kate asked.

"Apparently, Styne is keen to get it over with as soon as possible."

"Well, he's just going to have to wait a while. I have some information I need to send over to Terry Gilbert." Kate tapped her mouse and her screen came to life.

Colm raised a questioning eyebrow.

"I'll let you know if it pans out," Kate answered as she tapped away at her keyboard. She re-read what she had written and pressed send. "Right, let's get this over and done with."

As feared, the interview with John Marshall varied remarkably little from that Kate had had with Paul Marshall. Even down to Styne's opening complaint about the nature of the stop and search.

"You do understand, don't you Mr Marshall, that as the driver of the vehicle containing the ATM you will be seen as the instigator of the whole event?"

John Marshall's shrug was identical to his brother's. As was his reply, "No comment."

Having run through the basics, Kate terminated the interview. Before they could leave, Styne asked, "Will you be charging my clients, Inspector?"

Kate nodded. "We will be, Mr Styne. I am awaiting confirmation from CPS but I believe we will be charging them with receiving stolen goods as a preliminary charge."

"My clients will want bail."

"As soon as they have been charged, the custody sergeant will organise that, as you know, Mr Styne." Kate turned away.

"You could release them on police bail whilst you wait for a decision."

Kate turned back. "Mr Styne, I suggest you advise your clients to have some breakfast and get some sleep. The decision from the CPS will be through sometime this morning, I am sure. Then," Kate emphasised the word, "they will be released on bail." She disliked people like Styne. Defendants need legal representation, Kate had no dispute with that, but the likes of Styne treading such a fine legal line irritated her. As she turned she thought she heard Styne say, "Better luck next time." But when she turned back to him his face was entirely bland.

CHAPTER 85

Kate sat at her desk and washed her face with her hands before running her fingers through her hair, "Well, that was a waste!" She sat back and slumped a little.

"We've got them on possession, boss, if nothing else," Colm said, enthusiastically.

Kate shook her head slowly. "I'm not sure the CPS will say there's enough for a definite conviction. All we can do is say that they had the ATM. We can't find the money and we can't place them at the crime scene."

"Yes, but they had the ATM!"

"A slippery piece like Styne will suggest they found it, realised when we came calling that it was stupid to have it and they were trying to get rid of it when we stopped them. Styne will muddy the waters with his claims of entrapment." Kate nodded as she spoke, convincing herself that the CPS would not support a charge.

Colm sighed, "What you going to do now? Go home for a bit of a sleep?"

Kate shook her head. "No, I'll wait round here until the CPS come back to us and then sign off for the day. What about you?"

"I thought…"

Whatever Colm thought, Kate was not to

find out as her desk phone rang. She reached across and sat up straighter, "Medlar." A pause. "Hello Terry, it did?" Another pause. Colm could not hear the words but he thought Terry Gilbert sounded excited. "Yes, love to. Be with you in," Kate checked her watch, "fifteen minutes." Kate returned the receiver to its rest and grinned.

"Your idea paid off," Colm guessed, remembering Kate's cryptic response when she said she'd emailed Terry earlier that morning.

"May be. Do you fancy a trip to find a drugs lab?"

Colm was already reaching for his coat, "So what did you tell him?"

Kate talked over her shoulder as she skipped down the stairs, "I thought I'd remembered something in Terry's notes about his meetings with Mallory. At the time I read it, it seemed odd, which is why, I suppose, it snagged in my brain."

Kate had reached the door to the car park and held it back for Colm. "A few months ago, Phipps asked Mallory to rent a garage, supposedly so that some of his team had somewhere in the dry to mend their bikes and cars."

They climbed into their car with Colm taking the driving seat. "Does that sound like a Phipps kind of gesture?"

Colm shook his head. He was already calculating the purposes and smiled, "Perhaps this garage had another use? Like parcelling up drugs?"

"It would make sense, wouldn't it?" Kate agreed.

"So, that's where Terry is now? Have they found anything?"

"He's got the address and someone with a key but they've only got eyes on the garage at the moment to make sure they know what they might be up against. Terry said they'd wait until we arrive, unless anything goes down, of course."

"So, off to Mallory's?"

"Next road across. It's a block of garages in between two sets of flats. Do you know where I mean?"

Colm nodded, "I think so." And he put his foot to the accelerator.

CHAPTER 86

There was no mistaking the little group of cars and men as the police, Kate thought, as they drove up. Let's hope Phipps hasn't got the place under his own surveillance.

Terry Gilbert and his boss, DCI Wakeford approached their car as Colm drew to a stop. Wakeford called before they were out of the car, "A good lead, Kate, thanks for the heads-up."

"No problem. What have you got?"

"Number 53, the one with the swastika on it!"

"No activity," Terry supplied, "and the council haven't had any requests for a spare key so either Phipps has a key or it's not what we hope it is."

Walking towards a small group of plain clothes officer, a small woman in her fifties peeled off and addressed Wakeford, "DCI Wakeford, may we proceed?" She looked ostentatiously at her wrist watch."

Wakeford gave a little nod and everyone walked towards the garage. Standing either side of the door the group watched as Wakeford relieved the civilian of the key and directed her to wait at one side. The key fitted smoothly as did the overhead lift as Wakeford turned the handle and the door slid up into the roof space.

Everyone craned forward for their first glimpse of the inside and all were disappointed. In the gloom they could see a dismantled motor bike in the centre of the space, complete with oil stain and along the back wall a bench with an assortment of tools. Other than these and a tall cupboard in the back right hand corner, the garage was empty.

There was a collective sigh of disappointment. No drugs lab. No illicit goods of any sort. Kate and Colm followed Gilbert and Wakeford inside. Colm found a light switch but the electric lighting did little to improve the space. Wakeford said to no-one in particular, "Well, it was worth a shot."

Colm investigated the bench and Kate turned slowly round the area. It was unexpectedly small. She tried to measure it by eye and thought that anyone would be hard pressed to get a car parked here. She wandered over to Colm, who was lifting and examining the tools and parts on the bench. He held up parts in his hands. He was frowning as he turned back to Kate, "I don't know a lot about bikes, but I do know mechanical engines, from the farm, and I know that's a Kawasaki part," he lifted one hand slightly, "will not fit a Honda," he lifted the other hand, "and that," he pointed with one of the parts to the half-built bike, "is a Yamaha!"

Kate looked around the space again. Wakeford had one of his team get a crowbar on the lock of the tall cupboard.

She turned back to Colm, "Do you think this is a bit small for a garage? Could you get the car in here?"

Colm placed the engine parts back on the bench and looked around. He stepped outside and disappeared from view. Kate watched Wakeford's team whilst Colm was gone. The tall cupboard was empty as well. One shelf at waist height was the sum total of its contents. Kate heard steps behind her and Colm reappeared, breathing a little heavily. Starting at the entrance, he paced the depth of the space. He was grinning as he turned back to Kate. "It's too short! I'd say by about four feet." He pointed to the tools and parts, "Set dressing."

Colm and Kate were now side by side talking quietly, "So how do we access the back?"

"Must be from in here. I had a quick check and it's all blank brick walls at the back of these."

On the same wavelength, they turned and looked at the tall cupboard. They walked over to Gilbert and Wakeford and explained their findings.

"What do you mean, 'too short'?" barked Wakeford.

"I paced it out, sir," Colm explained.

"The entrance must be through that cupboard," Kate supported Colm.

Wakeford looked sceptical and as he turned to Gilbert, Kate heard him quietly say, "We're not in effing Narnia!" In a louder voice he said to Gilbert, "See if anything moves or whatever."

Gilbert went back to the cupboard. He tapped the sides and back and turned to face them, "The back does sound hollow, sir." He continued to tap. His muffled voice came through to them, "I'll take this shelf out before I knock meself out on it." With that there was a grating sound and Gilbert's shocked face reappeared. "It's a bloody door!"

Kate could just make out plastic strips swinging behind the opening in the cupboard. Gilbert's face was aglow with excitement, "We need the lab boys in here sir. We've found it!"

Wakeford turned back to Kate, "Marvellous out of the box thinking, Kate."

Kate smiled, "Team work, sir," stepping back. "We'll leave you to it, sir. Thank you for the invite."

Wakeford was already turning away and speaking into his mobile.

CHAPTER 87

Colm was mystified as he climbed back into the driving seat, "Don't you want to go and look and see what we've found?"

Kate didn't answer him directly, "What did you say about the Marshall's pickup truck in the lockup?"

Colm fought to remember, "Something about needing to park it at an angle?"

"Yes. Didn't you think that lockup was a little small?"

Colm was following her train of thought, "Another hidden space? Oh, come on, boss!"

"What did the lockup have in the back corner?"

Slowly Colm replied, "A tall cupboard. Are you seriously suggesting that someone offers their services at creating secret rooms?"

"In the circles that the Marshalls and Phipps move in, why not?"

Colm shook his head. "I don't know, boss. I think it sounds a bit far-fetched if I'm totally honest with you."

Unfazed by his doubts, Kate said, "Let's go and check, shall we?" Reaching for her mobile she put it on speaker phone and a few seconds later said, "Hi, Mike. Do you still have your team at the lockup?"

"On my way there now to check and then stand them down."

"Can you meet me there and wait before you do that?"

Mike sounded surprised, "Yeh, okay, I can do that."

"Thanks, Mike, be with you in twenty minutes."

Mike hung up and Kate frowned through the window taking little notice of the passing scenery. Her gut was telling her she was on the right track, but her common sense was siding with Colm's doubts.

◆ ◆ ◆

Mike was leaning nonchalantly on his car bonnet drinking from a takeaway coffee cup. He took a final drink and then placed it on the passenger seat, through the open window. Without preamble he asked, "What's on your mind, Kate? Apart from a few fingerprints my team found nothing of interest."

"Have they looked closely at the cupboard?" The three of them entered the lockup and Kate was struck again at how small it seemed to her expectations. One of the white clad officers came over, pulling back her hood. It was Zara Bakir. Kate knew her from a previous case.

"Hi DI Medlar. I'm afraid this has been a barren enterprise unless you're into umpteen different oil stains," she pointed to the dark marks on the floor. Some were thin and grey, others were darker and fresher, overlapping and spreading, creating continents of oil."

"Thanks Zara. What about the cupboard?" Mike pointed to the corner.

"Nothing, empty," Bakir stated. "Which was surprising because it had a padlock on it."

Kate's pulse quickened and she heard Colm take a deeper breath. "Have you tried taking the shelf out?" she asked.

Bakir frowned, "No, Inspector."

"Give it a try," Mike said.

Bakir wandered over to the closed cupboard, opened it to reveal a shelf at about shoulder height.

"Slight design variation?" Colm murmured.

They watched as Bakir shook and jolted the shelf and then suddenly her arms disappeared into the cupboard. A fraction of a second later she faced them, the amazement clear in her expression. "It's a secret doorway!"

Both Kate and Colm took a step forward, but Mike's voice restrained them. "Suited and booted first."

CHAPTER 88

The secret room was a long thin narrow space, lined with shelves. Here was the treasure house Kate had hoped for when they first arrested the Marshall brothers. The shelves were laden with a range of electrical gadgets: smart phones, laptops, tablets. Each still in its box and wrappers. Colm gave a low whistle. In the corner, opposite the entrance, a computer was set up at a tiny workstation.

"Bingo!" Kate breathed.

Mike stood in the doorway. "You two need to come out to let my team in."

Kate pointed to the computer. "Can you make that a priority, please? I need something substantial to nail the Marshall brothers."

Mike opened a large evidence bag. "I'll give this to Zara and send her back to the station with you. There's only room for two, maximum in there so Les and I will start cataloguing and call for evidence transport and some secretarial back up," handing the now sealed evidence bag back to Kate. "Zara's your best bet on that."

Back inside the garage, Mike gave his orders. Zara Bakir stripped off her white suit and came towards Kate and Colm. Kate was glad Zara was going to be working on the computer. She was a brilliant forensic IT officer. Kate handed the computer over and they headed for the car.

Travelling back to the station, Zara was fascinated to hear that the lockup had revealed the second secret space in a matter of hours. Kate sat silently. Would she get enough to put the Marshall brothers away? Staring sightlessly out of the window she realised that the adrenaline was draining away and that a thumping headache was taking its place. "Colm, just drop me and Zara back at the station and then go on home. We'll reconvene at seven tomorrow morning. Okay?"

"Sure, boss. But what about you?"

"I've a few bits and pieces to do and then I'm off home as well. Leave Zara and Mike to do their jobs without us peering over their shoulders!" She turned and smiled at Zara Bakir who grinned in response.

Kate was less than two paces inside the station when she was hi-jacked by Jeremy Styne. "Inspector! Where have you been? My clients want their bail organised."

Kate checked her watch before replying, "As it is not yet midday and your clients have been in custody for less than ten hours I'm not sure why we're having this conversation. But to answer your first question, I have been following up evidence in our case against your clients. As a result of which I will be seeking a continuation of their custody for the full thirty-six hours, and beyond if necessary."

Styne's colour changed from pink indignation to red fury, "Is this to give you time to cobble together some fantastical evidence?"

Kate pulled herself up to her full height and glared Styne down, "Are you questioning my professional integrity?"

Styne knew he had underestimated Kate's steel, "My apologies, Inspector. I let my emotions get the better of me."

Kate nodded, "Your clients will stay in custody so I would suggest you go home and to save you returning or contacting the station, shall we agree now that a second interview with each client will take place tomorrow from ten am?" Not waiting for a reply, she strode off and exited the corridor by the first door she came to.

Kate had to put a hand to her mouth to stifle the giggle that threatened to explode from her as she realised that she had entered the stores cupboard. Give it five minutes and she'd head for her office.

Kate's first port of call was Bart's office but he was out, so she sat at her desk and wrote a detailed email explaining the actions of the morning and her decisions with regard to the Marshall brothers. She also contacted the CPS and was put through to Elaine Murphy. They had never met but Kate was sure that Elaine was a fiery red headed Irish woman. She certainly brooked no dissension once the CPS decision was made.

"Pleased to hear from you, Kate. I'm not sure your possession case is worth the time and money."

Pretty much what Kate had feared but she explained the current position with new evidence. "That sounds more like it. Let me know as soon as you know what exactly your evidence is and I'll look again."

Putting the phone down, Kate saw an email from Terry Gilbert had appeared in her inbox. The space behind the garage had held the two satchels of drugs they'd lost when tailing. Most of it was cannabis, but a proportion was heroin. Terry was effusive with his thanks and signed off with the fact that his boss, DCI Wakeford kept muttering 'effing Narnia'!

Kate smiled to herself. Not a bad day's work; well a day-and-a-half, really. She knew she really should leave but the temptation to just rest her head on her arms was almost overwhelming. Breathing a deep sigh, she pushed herself out of her chair. At home, a comfy bed was calling.

CHAPTER 89

At home Kate was greeted, firstly by Monster and secondly by a note taped to the cupboard door where Kate kept Monster's food. She smiled as she read:

Hi Kate,
knew you'd feed Monster before sorting yourself out so this seemed a good place to leave you a note! There is a lasagne in the fridge but I thought you'd probably prefer the apple pie and custard in the microwave, 90 seconds.
I may pop in later but I will do it quietly if you are in bed.
Much love
Jude xx

Apple pie or lasagne, there really wasn't any question of her choice. Checking the dish was in the microwave, she set it and fed Monster whilst it whirled away and then pinged.

Tentatively she fed herself the first spoonful. Jude had judged it just right: hot enough to eat, cool enough to eat it straightaway. Even with the instantaneous nature of the food, Kate found her eyes drooping and decided she'd leave the rest of the pie for later. She went to the back door to let Monster out but he turned tail and stalked through into the living room. Kate shrugged and followed him. He preceded her up to the bedroom and jumped on the bed whilst Kate stripped off and then climbed in under the duvet. She was vaguely aware of Monster kneading the duvet behind her and then settling along her back and then she was gone.

Kate wasn't sure how long she'd been asleep. It was dark now but other than that she had no time reference. She was aware that Monster was no longer on the bed as she had turned in her sleep to face into the bed. Was that someone speaking downstairs? Was Jude here? If she was, it would be after seven. Resisting the urge to snuggle back down and drift off again, she turned and faced her alarm clock; 20:53. If she got up now she could spend a couple of hours with Jude and then come back to bed and sleep through.

Wrapping her fluffy dressing gown around herself she padded, bare footed across to the stairs. Definitely voices. Jude must have the telly on. She stepped down onto the living room carpet silently but Jude was aware of her presence and jumped up, guiltily switching the telly to mute. "Sorry! Was it too loud? Did I wake you?"

Kate smiled, "No to both questions. I wanted to spend some time with you before going back to bed."

"Do you want something to eat? The lasagne

this time?"

"Just a small portion and then I'll finish the pie and custard."

Jude grimaced, "Ah! Monster likes custard!"

It took a few moments for Kate to work out what Jude meant and then she whined, "He's eaten my pie and custard?"

Jude grinned, "Well, strictly speaking he has eaten the custard, but since the pie was clean, I thought he'd probably licked it too, so I binned it."

Kate pouted and "Humphed!" as she sat down on the sofa. She tucked her legs up under her and pulled her dressing gown to cover her knees. "I suppose it's just lasagne, then."

Jude disappeared to sort the food and Kate stared at the miming on the telly. The remote control was at the far end from where she sat and she was too lethargic to reach across for it. Much as she wanted to spend time with Jude, Kate thought she would eat and go back to bed.

CHAPTER 90

Despite Kate herself being early, Colm was at his desk when she arrived, carrying two takeaway coffee cups.

"Morning!"

Colm raised a hand in acknowledgement but continued to scroll through something on his screen.

"Stuff from the Marshall brothers?" Kate enquired as she slid off her jacket, sat at her desk and woke her computer into life.

"Yep. Zara must have been working on this all night," Colm said, pointing at his screen. "Basically the computer from the lockup wasn't connected to the internet. It was just used for record keeping."

By now Kate had her own copy of the document from Zara Bakir open and was reading through. "Sources and destinations are in code but she does have batch numbers and has found matches in our nationwide system."

"Bloody hell! Look at the amount of money involved."

Kate continued to read through her screen, "Some of these crime numbers are from as far away as Newcastle, Carlisle, Birmingham! This isn't small time Eashire crime, this is a national crime syndicate."

"Some of the codes for sources and destinations are the same, look! Halfway down page three. See? That's one of our crime numbers. Let me see what for."

Kate switched out of the document and called up the local crime numbers. A few seconds later, "Here it is, ten electric bikes stolen last May moved onto GT for six thousand pounds!"

Colm shook his head. "GT will still have made a good profit. I looked into getting an electric bike for my mum. A good one starts at a thousand, so even allowing for black market prices, he's making a killing!"

Kate sat back assimilating what they'd just read and began to summarise out loud. "Right! These two are involved in back of the lorry jobs in Eashire but send the stuff away so are never caught trying to get rid of the merchandise locally. In return other crime teams send their stuff to them. They keep the jobs small for ease of moving on and to hide under the radar in most areas. So how are the brothers off-loading the stuff in Eashire?"

Colm also sat back, daringly tilting his chair back on two legs and looked at the ceiling. "There's that electronics shop in Peace Way. What if that's a front and the brothers are selling their stuff through there?"

Kate nodded sagely. "Certainly a possibility. Do a search and find out who owns it and if he has a record. I'm going through to update Bart."

Kate left and Colm busied himself with finding out all he could about a shop called Electronic Deals. By the time Kate returned, Colm had amassed a sizeable folder for her to peruse. He passed it to her as she sat back at her desk. She thanked him as she took it but said, "Give me the highlights."

"Electronic Deals opened five years ago and is owned by Samuel Pennar. There is nothing on the system about Pennar as an adult but he does have a juvenile file from when he was in Manchester. Shoplifting, a bit of drug possession. Small time stuff but he turns up here six years ago and a year later is opening his own shop."

"Where did the money come from?"

Colm shook his head. "Can't find anything to show that."

"Okay," said Kate decisively, "whoever comes in first," nodding her head towards Alice and Len's desks, "take one of them with you and go and interview Mr Pennar. I need to work on the interviews I've arranged." She paused, "But first I'll check with Mike about what they got from the lockup's secret room other than electrical devices and serial numbers."

CHAPTER 91

On her way to Mike's desk, she passed PC Zara Bakir's. The normally elegant and tidy woman was showing signs of fraying at the edges. Smiling as she walked towards her, Kate said, "Thanks for the stuff on the computer but don't you have a home to go to?"

Bakir lifted her arms and arched her back as she stretched and yawned, "I was on my way about three hours ago but your computer turned up something interesting."

"Really!? I thought the brothers were just using it for record keeping."

Bakir nodded, "Yes, so did I, until I clicked on this icon." Bakir pointed to her screen and Kate walked round to look over her shoulder. Kate saw a symbol she recognised.

"That's Powerpoint, isn't it? I use it to make cards and things."

Bakir nodded. "Yes. That's what I thought, which is why I left it until last. I wasn't expecting to find anything on it as the only programme in constant use is Excel. However," Bakir clicked on the icon and an unfamiliar page set up appeared, "it's taken me a bit of time but I think I have worked out what this does."

Bakir clicked on the toolbar and a police timesheet proforma came up and she explained,

"This programme was empty, or more accurately all work done with it had been deleted," she grinned, "but as you know deleted doesn't mean gone completely. I found a number of invoices for a range of electronic goods. Some had been scanned and some had been amended. Look I'll show you."

Kate grabbed a nearby chair and sat alongside Bakir as she began to show the programme's properties. "This is the original scan of the timesheet. However, if I copy it," a few clicks of the mouse, "and place it in this programme," her fingers did what she was explaining, "it maintains the original template but all the additions can be changed." With that, she changed the date on the timesheet and the numbers worked, even the name on the document.

Kate sat back, "So the brothers could take an original invoice, scan, copy and change to produce whatever they need?"

"Pretty much." Bakir also sat back.

"I got the impression from your first report that the brothers weren't much in the IT department but this shows a bit of skill."

"Agreed, but I think they were given it. The lazy way they deleted the original documents makes me think someone gave them this," tapping the screen, "and showed them how to use it, which they did without much understanding."

Kate grinned to herself. Every step was getting them closer to nailing the Marshall brothers. As she got up, she said, "Zara, you are amazing! Thank you, you have just made my case a lot easier."

Bakir smiled and looked bashfully down at her keyboard, "It's what they pay me for."

Kate waved goodbye and went to find Mike. As usual he was bent over a machine. Without lifting his head, he said, "Hang on a moment Kate." And continued to gently turn the dial under his right hand. Then there was a click and a slight flash and he stood up. "Thank you. Just needed to secure that. Right, secret room number two." He grinned. "Never had a concealed room before and then we get two on the same night!"

Kate held her hands out, "What can I say? I was a CS Lewis fan!"

"Yes, I understand DCI Wakeford is a little obsessed with Narnia at the moment!" he winked as he turned away. "Right, not a lot to give you really from your little room. Electronic devices: I've already emailed you the inventory with serial numbers. Fingerprints: numerous on the boxes and shelf supports but many smudged and overlaid. We're still trying to isolate prints and then put them through the system. The computer, and the desk it was on, just shows the Marshall brothers prints. John's especially on the computer itself."

"Thanks, Mike. You and Zara have given me plenty of ammunition for my next interview with the Marshall brothers and I think Colm may be bringing in even more."

CHAPTER 92

They were just pulling up outside Electronic Deals as Colm finished his conversation with Kate. Alice pulled up the handbrake and waited. The shop was still in darkness, but checking his watch, Colm saw that it was still a few minutes before nine.

"That was a further update from the boss. Zara has found a programme on the computer we seized last night that can produce authentic looking invoices, so we're going to need to get a couple of copies of any Pennar has and some serial numbers of his stock. I don't want to alert him that we might be on to him so you may need to distract him at some point."

"Okay, sir. What's our story for checking on him now?"

"Rumour machine says there are a few knock off mobile phones in the area. Has he been offered any? Heard anything? Can we check his stock? We'll try to match the serial numbers to his invoices and then, back at the station, see if they match any documents that Zara has found."

Alice nodded her head towards the shop, "Opening time." A slight, youngish man with modern glasses and a straggly beard was unlocking the door and turning the sign in the window next to it.

Colm opened his car door and hauled himself upright, "Come on then. Show time!"

An electronic buzzer sounded as Colm stepped onto the mat inside the door. For a moment the counter was empty and then Pennar appeared from behind a swinging bead curtain. Colm already had his ID ready and introduced himself, "Mr Samuel Pennar? I am DC Hunter and my colleague PC Giles." He held out his warrant card but Pennar merely glanced at it. "We'd like to ask you a few questions in relation to some mobile phones." Was it his imagination that Pennar looked a little sweaty?

"Of course, how can I help you Detective Hunter?"

Colm smiled engagingly, "A rumour has reached the police station that someone is trying to flog some knock off phones. Has anyone approached you?"

Pennar pulled himself up to his full five foot six, "Certainly not. This is a respectable business. All my stock comes in with proper invoices or bills of sale."

Colm continued smiling, "I thought that would probably be the case, sir, but we will need to look at your phone stock and any paperwork you have."

"Don't you need a warrant for that, Detective?"

Colm replaced his smile with a puzzled frown, "We could get a warrant, sir, but this is merely by way of excluding you from our investigations. But if you prefer," Colm turned to walk back out, raising his eyebrows as he did so. Alice moved to follow, also giving Pennar a puzzled look.

Pennar looked undecided but just as Colm opened the door, he said, "No, it's okay. You can have a look. I've got nothing to hide. As I said, I have paperwork for all my stock."

Colm turned back, all smiles again. "Thank you, sir. That's very good of you. Look, to get out of your hair quickly may PC Giles look at the stock in here against a copy of your invoice and you show me any stock out back and your invoices? Just for the mobiles." With a nod Alice Colm followed Pennar behind the counter and through the bead curtain.

Pennar walked ahead into a narrow, gloomy space. He spoke over his shoulder. "There's not a lot of space back here so I don't hold a lot of excess stock. He indicated a few shelves on the wall backing the shop. "The phones are on your right. There should be twenty."

Colm turned, looked and counted. "Yep. Can I see the paperwork that goes with them, please?"

Pennar walked through to a small office and disappeared from sight. Colm took that opportunity to photograph a few serial numbers. He heard the sound of a printer and then Pennar moving behind him. He slipped his phone into his pocket and turned, holding one of the boxes.

"Just took one at random. Can we match the serial number?"

Pennar nodded and handed over the invoice.

"Could we also see the paperwork for the stock in the shop, sir?"

Pennar sighed but handed over another invoice.

"I'll just give this to PC Giles and then I'll be back to check a few more numbers, if that's okay?"

Pennar merely nodded. He didn't look too happy about all this but he wasn't stopping them. Perhaps they'd got it wrong, Colm thought. Perhaps Pennar was a legitimate businessman.

They walked back into the shop. Colm called out, "PC Giles would you select a phone and read off its serial number, please?"

Alice did so and Colm, with Pennar peering round his arm, checked it off. Colm smiled, "Thank you for your co-operation, sir. As I thought, everything matches." As they left the shop, Colm was waiting for Pennar to ask for the invoices back, but he didn't. Colm grinned as they sat back in the car.

Pennar smiled weakly and watched the two officers leave his shop before wiping his sweating hands on his trousers.

CHAPTER 93

Colm and Alice were still grinning when they returned to the office. Kate looked up and raised an enquiring eyebrow. "Success?"

Colm nodded. "We focused on the mobiles and have two invoices and some serial numbers."

"So, now we see if they match to anything either with a crime number or the invoices produced by the brothers."

Kate's desk phone rang. "Quick as you can. That will be Stynes arriving for the Marshall brothers' interviews." Kate picked up the phone as Colm and Alice hastened to their desks.

Leaving her desk, Kate called out, "I'm going to ask Bart to apply for an extension on the Marshall brothers' custody and then go and talk to Styne."

"Have you got your flak jacket for Styne?" Colm grinned.

Kate returned it. "He's going to be even less happy when I tell him I want to delay the interviews. I'm not talking to the brothers again until we have everything we can possibly get on them."

❖ ❖ ❖

By the time Kate returned from her

conversations with Bart and Styne, Colm and Alice were collected around Colm's computer and Kate heard, "And there's another one."

They both looked up as Kate walked in. "What have you got?" she asked, sensing a tingle of excitement in the air.

Alice turned and leant back against Colm's desk whilst he swivelled his chair round. "Clearly something," she said returning their grins.

"Oh yes!" Colm crowed. "We have a genuine invoice and a Marshall invoice."

"And the Marshall invoice has a copy on their laptop," Alice interrupted.

"And that invoice has crime numbers attached to every item on it!" Colm concluded, punching the air.

"Oh, well done. And you're sure the other invoice is genuine?"

Colm nodded. "The way I see it is that every so often he has a legitimate order delivered. Perhaps he's worried that neighbours may notice he never has deliveries."

Kate nodded as she thought that idea through. "And the brothers deliver out of hours when there are no witnesses."

"Or, if there are, they won't say anything," Colm suggested, remembering how deaf and blind the residents of Peace Way were when the ATM was hoisted away.

"What were Pennar's prices like?"

Alice answered that, "The ones on display

were a little cheaper than you'd get in some of the chains but not by much.

"I expect he offers the buyers a 'little deal'," Colm's fingers framed the quotation marks. "So he gets a reputation for good prices, perhaps even a bit of bartering."

Kate looked thoughtful. "Bring Pennar in." Kate decided, "Try to get him to come voluntarily, helping us with our enquiries, but if not, arrest him for handling stolen goods."

"Come on, Alice," Colm said as he put his jacket on. "We're going to have a repeat visit."

Kate listened to their fading footsteps. Could they get Pennar to come clean? With the electronic evidence and this they could nail the brothers once and for all. In the meantime, she thought, she'd better bone up on the life and times of Samuel Pennar.

CHAPTER 94

Kate watched Pennar through the one-way mirror. He looked innocuous enough. He was clearly agitated about where he was. He kept looking at the mirror, the duty officer and the door. Colm joined her.

"Did he put up a fight?"

Colm shook his head. "I let him make a call at the shop but there was no reply."

Kate raised a questioning eyebrow.

"I thought keep it low key since he was almost at the point of agreeing to come with us," Colm said, "anyway, he phoned John Marshall. I checked the Marshalls' mobile log."

"Wanting advice about what he should do, no doubt."

"That's what I thought."

"How did he respond to you? When you asked him to come in and on the journey?"

"I kept it quite light." Colm blushed a little, "I made out that you were a bit of a slave driver and my life wouldn't be worth living if he didn't come in."

"So, what, quite pally?"

"Yes. Ganged up a bit on Alice. All boys together."

"Good. I want you to keep up that side. Let's see if Mr Pennar will roll over."

♦ ♦ ♦

Kate introduced herself for the tape and invited Pennar and Colm to do the same. Pennar had sat up a little straighter when Kate entered and smiled nervously at Colm while she was setting up the recorder.

"Thank you for coming in, Mr Pennar. I believe DC Hunter has explained that we need a little more information. You are at liberty to leave at any point."

Pennar looked towards the door once again, before looking at Colm, who smiled encouragingly. Pennar nodded.

"Now, Mr Pennar, just some background information. I understand you came to Eashire about six years ago. What brought you here?"

Pennar shuffled in his seat, "I expect you've seen my record, so you know I was running with the wrong crowd in Manchester. A friend of a friend said he could get me work here, so I moved."

"Just like that?" Kate allowed a note of scepticism to drop through.

Pennar's right leg was doing a jig under the table and a sweaty sheen clung to his forehead. "No, not just like that."

Colm interceded, "It must have been bad in Manchester to make you want to leave? That must have taken some nerve."

Pennar smiled weakly. "I'd got in with some very hardnosed drug dealers. I saw what happened to one of their gang and..." He tailed off, paused and resumed, "I knew that could be me in a few years. So I left."

Conversationally, Colm asked, "So what kind of work was it?"

"Driving, mainly. Delivering stuff."

"In Eashire?"

"Not always. Sometimes I'd go out of county. All over in fact."

Kate cut back in, "Was it a well-paid job?"

"It was okay," Pennar said. "Gave me enough to live on and enjoy myself."

"So where did the money for the shop come from? Because you are the owner, aren't you?"

Pennar was deliberately using his right hand to still his leg. The moisture on his forehead was dripping and his top lip beaded with sweat. He seemed stuck for an answer.

Colm asked, "Do you have silent partners. Money men who leave you to get on with it?"

Pennar's eyes were now wide and the smell of fear was palpable. "I think I'd like to leave now. You said I could go whenever I wished."

"It would be really helpful if you could stay," Colm said reassuringly.

Pennar shook his head. "No, I'm going." He made to rise but his legs wouldn't hold him.

Kate nodded to Colm. She would make the arrest. She might still need Pennar to see Colm as an ally. "Samuel Pennar I am arresting you..." Kate intoned the Miranda rights whilst Pennar sat there open mouthed and spluttered when Kate said, "...on suspicion of handling of stolen goods."

CHAPTER 95

Once again Kate was observing Pennar through the two-way mirror. He had requested a solicitor. For a moment she had feared he was going to ask for Styne but he hadn't. Either the brothers hadn't thought he would be taken in or they reserved the skills of Styne for themselves. Kate watched as the duty solicitor was shown in. It was Sandra Colbridge. Kate had dealt with her before and always found her very fair. Leaving the observation post so Pennar could meet with his solicitor in private, Kate headed back to her office.

Colm and Alice were still checking the invoices. Colm turned as she walked in. "Well, we have crime numbers from all over the country, but the bulk are the West Midlands and the Home Counties. Not London, but areas around it."

"Good. Tidy it all up and add it to our case file. I want as much as we can get to send to the CPS for the Marshalls." Kate reached for the phone as she sat at her desk. She rang the custody sergeant and asked that Styne be informed that she would be ready to interview his clients by early afternoon. She then sat back and began to muse out loud. "They must be running some kind of courier service." No-one replied. She continued, "I hope Pennar can give us a handle on the inside workings."

These thoughts were interrupted by her phone. As she replaced the receiver, she said, "Come on, Colm. We're on."

Pennar sat, head bowed, as Kate entered the room. He raised it momentarily for the tape and then resumed his intimate study of the table's surface.

Sandra Colbridge began, "Inspector, my client would like to aid your investigations in any way he can but he does have some concern about his personal safety should knowledge of his statement become public."

Kate looked at Pennar, "Mr Pennar, Sam," he looked up. "I believe I know who you are worried about but I need you to tell me."

Pennar looked at Colbridge who gave a nod. He licked his lips, "John and Paul Marshall."

Kate nodded, "I believe that your information could make water tight the case we are making against John and Paul Marshall. They are already in custody awaiting charging."

Pennar continued to look at the table. Colbridge tapped his arm and he looked at her. There was a whispered conversation. Then Pennar looked up. "Okay."

Kate shuffled her papers and then sat forward with her forearms on the table. "Let's start from the beginning. Why did you come to Eashire?"

Pennar gave a half-smile. "I really did think it

was going to be a fresh start. A friend of a friend got me a job. Sort of courier type driving."

Kate's ears pricked up.

"It was for John Marshall," Pennar continued. "It didn't take long for me to twig that it wasn't on the level. Exchanging boxes in out of the way lay-bys and the chap, Andy, who was always with me, he had wads of cash."

"So how come you ended up managing the shop?"

"Well, not sure but I think I passed a test." He settled back in his chair and looked unseeing, past Kate. "One day, Andy asks if I want a new phone. Now I knew by then that we were moving knocked off electronics. So, I knew he meant nick one from the van. I tell him, I'm not stupid as he'd get caught, and he did. I never saw Andy again." Pennar refocused on Kate. "But the rumour mill said he'd had a near fatal accident."

Kate nodded her understanding and Pennar continued. "Anyway a few days later John Marshall, I hadn't met Paul yet - he asks me if I fancy running a shop for him. Well, I thought it's got to be better than eating the miles up every day, so I said yes."

"What was the arrangement with the stock?" Kate asked.

Pennar's look was almost sardonic. "You have the invoices. I imagine you've already worked that one out."

Kate removed the two invoices from her file.

She turned the fraudulent one to Pennar. "We have found crime numbers for all the serial numbers on this invoice." Then she turned the genuine article, "But these are all legitimate?"

Pennar nodded, "We had some proper orders otherwise some nosey neighbour might have noticed that I didn't get deliveries. This way," he tapped the genuine invoice, "I got some."

"How was the money worked out?"

"The Marshalls decided on a minimum price for the merchandise. I would have it in the shop at a slightly cheaper rate than other retailers and, if necessary 'do a deal', if I needed to, as long as it was with what the brothers wanted."

"What was your cut?"

Pennar shook his head. "They gave me a monthly wage and they took the money. They paid for everything the shop needed, like the rent."

"Did you know the stock they were giving you was stolen?"

Pennar sighed deeply, "Of course I did. Once I'd agreed to be the manager they told me the rough outline of their business. Mind you, it doesn't really take a brain surgeon to work out what was going on, does it?"

Kate and Colm spent a further twenty or so minutes clarifying points and then Kate said, "Thank you, Sam. We'll bring your statement in to read and sign. You'll then be charged with receiving stolen goods."

Pennar looked crest fallen and Kate continued, "You will be released on police bail and your help with this matter will be a positive factor in your defence."

"What about my client's safety?" asked Colbridge.

"I will arrange for Sam to be taken to a safe house and, if my superior thinks it is necessary, we will contact our witness protection team."

Colbridge and Sam Pennar nodded their agreement.

CHAPTER 96

Having treated Colm and Alice to lunch at a local café, Kate was set for her interview with the Marshall brothers and Styne. She and Colm had discussed tactics and agreed that playing hard ball wouldn't work with the likes of the Marshalls. Kate's tactic was to be conciliatory. With that in mind, as she walked into the interview room she began, "Apologies Mr Marshall, Mr Styne, for the delay in this interview."

That seemed to take the wind out of Styne's sail if not John Marshall's as he looked deadpan at Kate. Styne recovered sufficiently that once they had introduced themselves for the tape, he launched in, "Both my clients are very unhappy with your conduct, Inspector Medlar and we will be considering a complaint. However, my clients wish to be as helpful as possible with the police."

Kate did not respond to Styne but looked at John Marshall, "Thank you, Mr Marshall."

John Marshall nodded his head as if in acknowledgement.

Kate began, "Mr Marshall, for the benefit of the tape, would you mind if I addressed you as John, so that it is clear which Mr Marshall I am interviewing?"

As though fearing a trap, Marshall looked

at his solicitor, who gave a negligent shrug. Turning back, Marshall nodded his acceptance at the informality.

"Thank you, John. Very much appreciated." Kate then opened her file and shuffled a few papers. She wanted Marshall to think that she didn't have the case at her finger tips. Stopping at a page, Kate leant forward. "Do you and your brother have equal shares in the storage units?"

Marshall frowned and Kate continued, "Do you have fifty-fifty shares? Neither one of you has a controlling share or makes the ultimate decisions?"

Marshall shook his head, "No, we own it together. We decide things together."

Kate nodded and seemed to refer back to the paper in front of her. "There is no record on the storage units system to indicate who was using the lockup you drove the pickup truck out of."

"My brother's pickup!" Marshall growled.

"Agreed, but we'll come to that in a while. Was it you or your brother that mainly used the lockup?"

"We just thought it would be handy to have somewhere to store stuff," Marshall said.

"What kind of stuff would that be, John? Because it was virtually empty when we checked it."

Kate was sure she saw a smirk before Marshall lowered his face. It was gone when he next looked up. "Depends, really. We had some car parts a while back and we stored them there until we moved them on."

Kate was sure that the car parts would have been legitimate. Marshall wouldn't be offering the information otherwise. "So, it's somewhere you both use?"

Marshall nodded and Kate continued, "Were you expecting to see an ATM machine in the back of your brother's pickup?"

Styne stepped in. "That stop and search was unlawful."

Sighing, Kate addressed Styne directly. "I believe my colleagues furnished you with a copy of the crime number and details reporting Mr Paul Marshall's pickup as stolen. We were within our legal rights to both stop and search the pickup. We believed it had been stolen and we had information that stolen vehicles were being moved from the storage units. If you wish to challenge that with my superiors, then please do, but not now!"

Kate launched her attack, "Was it you or Paul who organised for the secret room to be built in the lockup?"

Both the men opposite her sat up straighter.

Styne was the first to say anything, "Would you like to explain your comment, Inspector?"

Kate continued to look at Marshall. His eyes had narrowed, and a slight frown line had appeared between his eyebrows. Finally, he responded, "No comment."

Kate sat back and let her fingertips ruffle the edges of the papers in her file, "You do understand, don't you, John, that you will do jail time for this? We have fraudulent invoices, stolen goods and your fingerprints all over them."

It was clear from his expression that Styne did not have a clue what was going on and his client just sat impassively and said, "No Comment."

As though she hadn't heard, Kate continued, "You could help yourself out here. Clearly you and your brother are involved in a countrywide network. Help us with that and you know it will have an impact on your sentence."

"No comment."

Kate turned to Styne, "We will conclude the interview here but I would recommend that you talk with both your clients about their likely jail terms, both with and without their co-operation."

With that Kate closed the tape down and she and Colm left. Kate gave instructions to the officer outside to take John Marshall back to his cell and give him time with his solicitor, if he asked for it.

CHAPTER 97

"Well done, boss. You got both him and that smarmy solicitor on the back foot."

Kate smiled. "I have to confess to having a little spurt of joy when Styne was floundering!"

"Do you think they'll go for a deal, really?" Colm asked as Kate sat at her desk and ran her fingers through her hair, making it look as if she suffered an electric shock.

After a moment or two, Kate answered, "No. No, I don't think either of them will."

"What, honour amongst thieves, type of thing?"

"No, more personal safety. If it got out that they'd helped us, their lives would be very uncomfortable, if not downright dangerous inside. We know these villains have long arms."

Colm nodded thoughtfully. "Well, at least we have enough to charge them. Do you think they'll get bail?"

"I'll talk to the CPS and suggest they are a flight risk or an intimidation risk. I haven't let on what Pennar has told us but they'll find out and we can both guess what could happen."

Colm nodded again as Kate reached for her desk phone. Minutes later she was talking with Elaine Murphy. Colm could only hear Kate's side of the conversation, but it looked like it was going well for them. Yes, to charging both Marshalls. She'd have a chat to someone about not giving bail. Kate replaced the receiver and Colm gave her the thumbs up sign with raised, questioning eyebrows.

Kate smiled and returned the thumbs up. "Yes, we can charge and she'll do everything she can to prevent a bail application." Kate's phone rang. It was the custody sergeant. Mr Styne and Mr Paul Marshall were in interview room two.

"Come on then, Colm. We'll use the same tactics but I'm not expecting a great deal from him either."

Kate was right in her assessment. Paul Marshall replied, "No comment," to every question, even the one asking if Kate could call him Paul. Having gone through the motions, Kate terminated the interview with, "Mr Styne both your clients will be charged with possession of stolen goods and fraud, as a start. My colleagues in the tax office have shown an interest in this case, so they may also press charges and the Serious Crime Unit will want to talk to them in relation to the criminal network your clients are part of."

Styne knew this was coming and merely nodded. Kate tried one last attempt with Paul Marshall. "You know that you can do yourself a favour if you help the police with these additional enquiries."

For the first time, Marshall looked her

directly in the eye, "Sod off, bitch."

◆ ◆ ◆

"Well, that told me," Kate laughed as they returned to the office. "Okay, Colm. We are going to work until five getting our case together and then I am taking you, Alice and Len, if he's around, out for a drink and a meal. Would you mind if I asked Jude to come along, if she's free?"

"That'll be lovely boss."

"What about Jenna? Could she get away to join us?" Kate asked as she fumbled her way through a text message to Jude.

"I'll ask," Colm said already tapping on his mobile. A few minutes later all was arranged with Jude and Jenna. It was the first time Kate had openly identified Jude as her significant other to Colm. He'd met Jude once before but Kate hadn't made their relationship clear. But it didn't seem to faze Colm one bit. Settling down at her desk and reaching for her computer mouse, Kate reflected that she had a pretty amazing team.

EPILOGUE

Kate turned up the news headlines as she drove through Eashire on her way to work. The news presenter sounded a bit excitable as he began, "Drugs worth millions of pounds were stopped at Dover last night by Customs Officers. Working from a tip off, it is believed the officials stopped and searched a travelling theatre company. Officials found many stage props stuffed with heroin and cocaine. No further details have been given at this time."

Kate smiled. That case was definitely a long game.

ALSO FROM TIM SAUNDERS
PUBLICATIONS

Now hair's a story by Garry Davidson
Three of a kind by Marion Desmond
The Light Will Always Return
by Frank McMahon
Hong Kong by Mary Levycky
A Lesson in Murder by Lin Bird
Love and Death by Iain Curr
The Fourth Rising Trilogy
by Tom Beardsell
The Price of Reputation by Lin Bird
Letters from Chapel Farm
by Mary Buchan
That was now, this is then
by Philip Dawson-Hammond
Shadows and Daisies by Sharon Webster
Lomax at War by Dan Boylan
A Life Worth Living by Mary Cochrane
Dreams Can Come True by
Rebecca Mansell
The Office Diaries by Garry Davidson

tsaunderspubs.weebly.com

Unsolicited manuscripts accepted

Printed in Great Britain
by Amazon